THE RED LAMP

THE RED LAMP

MARY ROBERTS RINEHART

THORNDIKE PRESS • THORNDIKE, MAINE

Library of Congress Cataloging in Publication Data:

Rinehart, Mary Roberts, 1876-1958.
 The red lamp.

 Large print.
 1. Large type books. I. Title.
[PS3535.I73R4 1984]   813'.52   83-18074
ISBN 0-89621-504-0

Large Print edition available through arrangement with
Holt, Rinehart & Winston, a Division of CBS Educational
and Professional Publishing.

Cover design by Armen Kojoyian.

THE RED LAMP

Introduction to the Journal of William A. Porter, A. B., M. A., Ph. D., Litt. D., etc.

June 30, 1924.

A few weeks ago, at a dinner, a discussion arose as to the unfinished dramas recorded in the daily press. The argument was, if I remember correctly, that they give us the beginning of many stories, and the endings of as many more. But that what followed those beginnings, or preceded those endings, was seldom or never told.

It was Pettingill, of all persons, who turned the attention of the table to me.

"Take that curious case of yours, Porter," he said. "Not yours, of course, but near your summer place two years ago. What ever happened there? Grace and I used to sit up all night to see who would get the morning paper first; then − it quit on us. That's all. Quit on us." He surveyed the table with an aggrieved air.

Helena Lear glanced across at me maliciously.

"Do tell us, Willie," she said. She is the only

7

person in the world who calls me Willie. "And give us all the horrible details. You know, I have always had a sneaking belief that you did the things yourself!"

Under cover of the laugh that went up, I glanced at my wife. She was sitting erect and unsmiling, her face drained of all its color, staring across the flowers and candles into the semi-darkness above the buffet. As though she saw something.

I do not know, I never shall know, probably. I saw little Pettingill watching her unobtrusively, and following her eyes to the space over the buffet behind me, but I did not turn around. Possibly it was only the memories aroused by that frivolous conversation which made me feel, for a moment, that there was a cold wind eddying behind my back...

It occurred to me then that many people throughout the country had been intensely interested in our Oakville drama, and had been left with that same irritating sense of non-completion. But not only that. At least three of the women had heard me make that absurd statement of mine, relative to the circle enclosing a triangle. There were more than Helena Lear, undoubtedly, who had remembered it when, early in July, the newspapers had announced the finding of that diabolical symbol along with the bodies of the slain sheep.

It seemed to me that it might be a duty I owed to myself as well as to the University, to clarify the matter; to complete the incomplete; to present to them the entire story with its amazing climax, and in effect to say to them and to the world at large:

"This is what happened. As you see, the problem is solved, and here is your answer. But do not blame me if here and there is found an unknown factor in the equation; an X we do not know what to do with, but without which there would have been no solution. I can show you the X. I have used it. But I cannot explain it." . . .

As will be seen, I have taken that portion of my Journal extending from June 16th, 1922, to September 10th of the same year. Before that period, and after it, it is merely the day by day record of an uneventful life. Rather fully detailed, since like Pepys I have used it as a reservoir into which to pour much of that residue which remains in a man's mind over and above the little he gives out each day. Rather more fully detailed, too, since I keep it in shorthand, an accomplishment acquired in my student days, and used not to insure the privacy of the diary itself, although I think my dear wife so believes, but to enable me, frankly, to exercise that taste for writing which exists in all of us whose business is English literature.

Show me any man who teaches literature, and I will show you a man thwarted. For it is our universal, hidden conviction that we too could write, were it not for the necessity of earning our daily bread. We start in as writers, only temporarily side-tracked. "Some day———" we say to ourselves, and go to our daily task of Milton or Dryden or Pope as those who, seeking the beauties of the country, must travel through a business thoroughfare to get there.

But time goes by, and still we do not write. We find, as life goes on, that all the great thoughts have already been recorded; that there is not much to say that has not been already said. And, because we are always staring at the stars, we learn the shortness of our arms.

We find a vicarious consolation in turning out, now and then, a man who is not daunted by tradition, and who puts his old wine into new bottles. We read papers before small and critical societies. And we sometimes keep Journals.

And so — this Journal. Much the same as when, under stress of violent excitement or in the peaceful interludes, I went to it as one goes to a friend, secure against betrayal. Here and there I have detailed more fully conversations which have seemed to bear on the mystery; now and again I have rounded a sentence. But in the main it remains as it was, the daily history of that strange series of events which culminated so dramatically on the night of September 10th in the panelled room of the main house at Twin Hollows. . . .

Of this house itself, since it figures so largely in the narrative, a few words should be said. The main portion of it, the hall which extended from the terrace toward the sea through to the rear and the drive, the panelled den and the large library in front of it are very old. To this portion, in the seventies, had been added across the hall by some long forgotten builder a dining room opposite the library and facing the sea, pantries, kitchen, laundry, and beyond the laundry a nondescript room originally built as a gun room and still containing the gun cases on the walls.

In later years the gun room, still so called, had fallen from its previous dignity and served divers purposes. In my Uncle Horace's time old Thomas, the gardener, used it on occasion as a potting room. And on wet days washing was hung up in it to dry. But it remained the "gun room," and so figures in this narrative.

In the re-building considerable judgment had been shown, and the broad white structure, with its colonial columns to the roof, makes a handsome appearance from the bay. It stands on a slight rise, facing the water, and its lawn extends to the edge of the salt marsh which divides it from the sea.

This is Twin Hollows. A place restful and beautiful to the eye; a gentleman's home, with its larkspurs and zinnias, its roses and its sundial, its broad terrace, its great sheltered porch and its old panelling. Some lovely woman should sweep down its wide polished staircase, or armed with basket and shears, should cut roses in the garden with its sun-dial — that sundial where I stood the night the bell clanged. But it stands idle. It will, so long as I live, always stand idle.

Of my Uncle Horace, who also figures largely in the Journal, a few words are necessary. He was born in 1848, and graduated from this University with the class of '70. He had died suddenly in June of the year before the Journal takes up the narrative, presumably of cardiac asthma, from which he had long suffered. A gentleman and a scholar, an essential solitary, there had been no real intimacy between us. Once in awhile I passed a week-end in the country with him, and until the summer of the narrative, my chief memory of him had been of a rather small and truculent elderly gentleman, with the dry sharp cough of the heart sufferer, pacing the terrace beneath my window at night in the endless search of the asthmatic for air, and smoking for relief some particularly obnoxious brand of herbal cigarette.

Until the summer of the narrative – ...

Ever since I have been considering the making public of the Journal, I have been asking myself this question, as one which will undoubtedly be asked when the book is published: What effect have the events of that summer had on my previous convictions?

Have I changed? Do I now believe that death is but a veil, and that through that veil we may now and then, as through a glass, see darkly?

I can only answer that as time has gone on I find they have exerted no permanent effect whatever. I am still profoundly agnostic. My wife and I have emerged from it, I imagine, as one emerges from a seance room where the phenomena have been particularly puzzling; that is, bewildered and half convinced for the moment, but without any change in our fundamental incredulity.

The truth is that if these things be, they are too great for our human comprehension; the revolution demanded in our ideas of the universe is too basic. And, as the Journal will show, too dangerous. ...

"All houses in which men have lived and suffered and died are haunted houses," I have written somewhere in the Journal. And if thoughts are entities, which may impress themselves on their surroundings, perhaps this is true.

But dare I go further? Re-state my conviction at the time that the solution of our crimes had been facilitated by assistance from some unseen source? And that, having achieved its purpose, this force forthwith departed from us? I do not know.

The X remains unsolved.

But I admit that more than once, during the recent editing of this Journal for publication, I have awakened at night covered with a cold sweat, from a dream in which I am once more standing in the den of the house at Twin Hollows, the red lamp lighted behind me, and am looking out into the hall at a dim figure standing at the foot of the staircase.

A figure which could not possibly be there. But was there.

(Signed)
WILLIAM A. PORTER.

June 16th.

Commencement Week is over at last, thank

heaven, and with no more than the usual casualties. Defeated at the ball game, 9 — 6. Lear down with ptomaine, result of bad ice-cream somewhere or other. Usual reunions of old boys, with porters staggering under the suitcases, which seem to grow heavier each year.

Nevertheless, the very old 'uns always give me a lump in the throat, and I fancy there was a considerable amount of *globus hystericus* as the class of '70 marched onto the Field on Class Day. Only eight of them this year, Uncle Horace being missing. Poor old boy!

Which reminds me that Jane thought she saw him with the others as they marched in. Wonderful woman, Jane! No imagination ordinarily, meticulous mind and only a faint sense of humor. Yet she drags poor old Horace out of his year-old grave and marches him onto the Field, and then becomes slightly sulky with me when I laugh!

"I told you to bring your glasses, my dear," I said.

"How many men are in that group?" she demanded tensely.

"Eight. And for heaven's sake lower your voice."

"I see nine, William," she said quietly. And when she stood up to take her usual snap-shots

15

of the Alumni procession she was trembling.

A curious woman, Jane. . . .

So another year is over, and what have I to show for it? A small addition to my account in the savings bank, a volume or two of this uneventful diary, some hundreds of men who perhaps know the Cavalier Poets and perhaps not, and some few who have now an inkling that English literature did not begin with Shakespeare.

What have I to look forward to? Three months of uneventful summering, perhaps at Twin Hollows — if Larkin ever gets the estate settled — and then the old round again. Milton and Dryden and Pope. Addison and Swift.

"Mr. Sims, have you any idea who wrote the Ancient Mariner? Or have you by chance ever heard of the Ancient Mariner?"

"Wordsworth, I believe, sir."

Yet I am not so much discontented as afraid of sinking into a lethargy of smug iconoclasm. It is bad for the soul to cease to expect grapes of a thistle, for the next stage is to be "old and a cynic; a carrion crow," like the old man in Prince Otto, with rotten eggs the burthen of my song.

Yet what is it that I want? My little rut is comfortable; so long have I lain in it that now my very body has conformed. I fit my easy

16

chair beside my reading lamp; my thumbs are broadened with much holding of books. *I depend on my tea.*

Yesterday, calling on Lear, I must have voiced my uneasiness, for he at once suggested a hobby. His bed was littered with mutilated envelopes.

"Nothing like it," he said. "It's the safety valve of middle life, and the solace of age."

"I'm not quite sure I want a safety valve," I said, and I fancied he looked at me suspiciously.

A hobby! Shall I gather postage stamps, and inquire of a letter not from whom it comes, but from where? Or adopt Jane's camera, and take little pictures of unimportant folk doing uninteresting things? Or go, as Lear finally suggested, a-fishing? Is it to be my greatest adventure to pull a fish out of the water and watch it drown with wide-opened mouth, in the air? Ah me!

"Greatest rest in the world for the brain," Lear said. "Fishing."

"I'm not sure I want a rest for my brain," I protested. "I dare say what I need is a complete change."

"Well, try ptomaine," he said drily, and with that I went away.

But I dare say Lear is right. The prospect of my three months' vacation has gone to my head somewhat. And I dare say too that I am much like the solitary water-beetle Jock found on the kitchen floor last night. That is, willing enough to leave my snug spot behind the warm pipes of life until danger threatens, or discomfort, and then all for scurrying back, a-tremble, into unexciting security again.

June 17th.

After all, security has its points.

I am the object of a certain amount of suspicion to-day on the part of my household! There is no place in the world, I imagine, for a philosopher with a sense of humor, a new leisure, and an inquiring turn of mind! In fact, I sometimes wonder whether any philosopher belongs in the present day and generation. These are times of action. Men think and then act; sometimes, indeed, they simply act.

But a philosopher, of course, should only think. . . .

And all this because last night I set Jane's clock forward one hour. Because, forsooth, I had determined to cease casting my eyes out on the world, and to study intensively that small domain of my own which lies behind the drain pipe!

During some nine months of the year I bring

home to Jane from the lecture room the mere husk of a man; exhausted with the endeavor to implant one single thought into a brain where it will germinate, I sink into my easy chair and accept the life of my household. Tea. Dinner. A book. Bed. And this is my life. My existence, rather.

But with the close of the spring term I find a faint life stirring within me.

"Isn't this a new tea?" I will say.

"You have been drinking it all winter," Jane will reply, rather shortly.

Yesterday was my first free day, and last night I wandered about the house, looking over my possessions and re-discovering them.

"You've had the sofa done over, my dear."

"Before Christmas," Jane replied, and glanced at me. In return I glanced at Jane.

It dawns on a man now and then that he knows very little about his wife. He knows, of course, the surface attributes of her mind, her sense of order, — Jane is orderly — her thrift, and Jane is thrifty. She has had to be! But it came to me suddenly that I knew very little of Jane, after all.

She is making one of those endless bits of tapestry, which some day she will put on the seat of a chair, and thereafter I shall not be expected to sit in that chair. But it is not a work which requires profound attention. She was working at it at the moment, her head bent, her face impassive.

"What are you thinking about, Jane?" I asked her.

"I really wasn't thinking at all."

I dare say from that I fell to speculating on Jane's mind, and that does not imply a criticism. Rather on the contrary, for Jane has an excellent mental equipment. But I am sometimes aware that she possesses certain qualities I do not possess. For example, it would be impossible for me to imagine, as Jane did on Class Day, that I saw Uncle Horace. Although, like all men with defective vision, I have occasional optical illusions. But it is equally impossible for me to deny that she did see Uncle Horace, and there has been a certain subtle change in her since which convinces me of her sincerity.

What then, I considered, is the difference between Jane's mind and my own? She has some curious ability, which she hides like one of the seven deadly sins, and which makes her at times a difficult person with whom to live.

I have already recorded in this Journal that one occasion in my life when at the reunion of my class, (1896), some wag proposed mixing all that was left of the various liquors in the punch bowl and drinking a stirrup cup out of it, and the fact that I was extremely dizzy on my way home.

But I did not record, I think, the fact that after I had quietly entered the house and got myself to bed, Jane came into my room.

"Oh! So you are back!" she said.

"Certainly I am back, my dear."

It seemed unnecessary to state that neither she nor the doorway in which she stood seemed entirely steady at the moment, nor did I so state. But perhaps it was not necessary, for after eyeing me coldly for a moment, she said:

"Were you supporting the chapel half an hour ago, William, or was it supporting you?"

"I don't know what you are talking about!"

"Don't you?" she observed, and retired quietly, after removing my shoes from the top of my book case.

But the humiliating fact remains that I *had* stopped for a moment's rest beside the chapel, and that somehow Jane knew it.

Or take again that incident already recorded in this Journal, under the date of June 28th of last year, when she wakened me at seven o'clock and said she had seen Uncle Horace lying dead on the floor of the library at Twin Hollows.

"Dreams," I said drowsily, "are simply wish

21

fulfillments. Go on back to bed, my dear. The old boy's all right."

"I wasn't asleep," she said quietly. "And you will have a telephone message soon telling you I was not."

And so true was this that she had hardly ceased speaking before Annie Cochran called up to tell us she had found him, at seven o'clock, dead on the library floor.

(Note: In preparing these notes for publication one thing occurs to me very strongly, and that is this: it is curious that my wife's vision, or whatever it may be called, did not occur until some hours after the death. If there came some mental call to her, why not when he was *in extremis?* Not only would it have helped us greatly in the mystery which was so soon to develop, but it would have been more true to the usual type of such phenomena.

In this case, if we are to admit anything but coincidence, it is easier to accept the fact that we are dealing with mental telepathy. In other words, that the servant Annie Cochran who actually found the body at seven in the morning, at once thought of Jane and so flashed the scene to her.

But I admit that this is merely explaining one mystery with another.)

So I was reflecting, as Jane pushed her needle

through her tapestry, slow, infinitely plodding and absolutely composed. What portion of Jane, then, wandered out at night, and saw me with a death-grip on the chapel wall? Or, with a fine contempt of distance and a house she loathed, went to Twin Hollows and found Uncle Horace on the floor?

It was an interesting thought, and I played with it out of sheer joy in idleness. The Jane then, whom I could reach out and touch at night, might only be the shell of Jane, while the real Jane might be off on some spirit adventure of her own! I considered this. It has, one must admit, its possibilities. And just then she glanced up at me.

"What are you thinking about?" she asked.

"My dear," I said gravely, "I am worrying."

"What about?"

"About you."

"I'm all right," she said. "Although of course I'd like to get away somewhere."

"That's precisely what I'm worrying about!" I observed, and she looked puzzled but said nothing.

I went back to Jane's mind, with a volume of von Humboldt unnoticed on my knee. Had she true clairvoyance, whatever that may mean? Or was telepathy the answer? She is Scotch, and the Scots sometimes claim what is called "second sight." I know that in her heart she believes she has this curious gift. She was, they say, a queer child, seeing and hearing things unseen and unheard by others. And I know she fears and hates it; it is somehow irreligious to her.

But — has she?

No immediate answer being forthcoming, I went back to my book, and very soon I happened on the following paragraph: "A presumptuous scepticism which rejects facts without examining them to see if they are real, is more blameworthy than an irrational credulity."

It was, in a way, a challenge, but there were no facts to examine. I could believe that Jane is merely a fine recording instrument on which telepathic impressions are recorded, or I could accept that she is able to leave that still lovely but slightly matronly body of hers on occasion and travel on the wings of space. But, because my interest was aroused, I consulted the dictionary on clairvoyance, and found that it was the faculty of being able to perceive objects without the customary use of the senses.

It was "vision without eyes."

Even then — on so small a base does one's comfort behind the pipe sometimes depend — all would have been well had not Clara entered with the dish of fruit which is my method of telling the seasons; the winter orange and banana gradually giving way to the early berries which mark the spring, and so on. And with that Jane looked at the clock.

That glance was at once my downfall and my triumph. For it occurred to me then to make a simple experiment, and to "examine the facts."

"Jane," I argued, "rises by her bedroom clock every morning, and punctually to the minute. But Jane does not look at her clock. Then, if I set it forward one hour———?"

And set it forward one hour I did, after Jane was asleep. And at the moment its hands indicated seven-thirty, although it was but half past six, did Jane open her eyes, rise from her bed without so much as a glance toward the clock, and call her household.

So Jane saw her clock without eyes, Clara has been sulky all day, and I am in extreme disfavor.

"Really, William," Jane said with a sigh this afternoon, "you are very difficult in the holidays."

"Difficult?"

"You know perfectly well you turned my clock on."

"Why in the world should I turn your clock on?"

"It is your idea of being funny, I dare say."

"It isn't funny to be wakened an hour too soon, my dear."

But she is suspicious of me, and cold toward me. Thus I suffer the usual lot of the seeker after truth. And Jane, my dear Jane, can see without her eyes. But she cannot understand why I turned her clock on for all her curious ability. Nor, after eating the burned biscuits Clara served to-night, can I.

But if Jane can see without her eyes, if she can perceive objects not visible to those of us who depend on the usual senses, then is one to admit that she saw Uncle Horace, as she said she did, marching at the head of his class procession last Tuesday?

June 18th.

I feel to-night rather like the man who had caught a bull by the tail and daren't let go. And yet I am certain there is a perfectly natural explanation.

The difficulty is that I cannot very well go to Jane about it. If it is what it appears to be, and not a double exposure, it will frighten her. If *is* a double exposure, she will wonder at my inquiry, and think I am watching her. She has not, even to-day, quite forgotten the clock.

26

But certain things are very curious; she thought she saw Uncle Horace marching onto the Field with his class. So much did this upset her that, when she stood up to take her picture, the camera shook in her hands. Then she takes the picture, and instead of the eight old men of the class of '70 there are nine.

And she knows it. Why else would she hide the print, and pretend that she had mislaid it? It was that fact which made me suspicious.

"I'll look them up for you later, William," she said. "You aren't in a hurry, are you?"

"In the bright lexicon of vacation there is no such word as hurry," I observed, brightly. And she who usually smiles at my feeblest effort turned abruptly away.

So Jane had lost her picture. Jane, whose closets are marvels of mathematical exactness, who keeps my clothing so exactly that I can find it in the dark, save for that one incident, duly noted in this journal, when I unfolded a washcloth at the President's dinner, having taken it from my handkerchief box.

And shortly after Jane went out for a walk, Jane who never exercises save about her household. Poor Jane, I feel to-night, face to face with the inexplicable and hiding it like one of the seven deadly sins.

There are nine men in the picture; there is no

getting away from it. And there is no denying, either, a faint difference in the ninth figure, a sort of shadowiness, a lack of definition. Under Jane's reading glass it gains nothing. The features, owing to the distance, are indistinct, but if one could imagine the ghost of old Horace, in his brocaded dressing gown and slightly stooped to cough, in that blare of noise, shouting and sunshine, it is there.

Later: I have shown the picture to Lear, and he says it is undoubtedly a case of double exposure.

"What else could it be?" he said, with that peculiar irritation induced in some people by any suggestion of the supernatural.

"I don't think she ever took a picture of him in her life."

"Well, somebody has," he said, and handed the print back to me. "If you don't believe me, show it to Cameron. He's a shark on that sort of thing."

(Note: Cameron, Exchange Professor of Physics, at our University. A member of the Society for Psychical Research, and known, I understand, among the students as "Spooks" Cameron.)

But I have not shown it to Cameron, and I do not intend to. I hardly know the man, for one thing. And for another, Lear is right. The

University looks with suspicion on the few among the faculty who have on occasion dabbled with such matters.

"Personally," he said, "I think it's a double exposure. But whether it is or not I'm damned certain of one thing, the less said about it the better."

June 19th.

Curious, when one begins to think on a subject, how it sometimes comes up in most unexpected places.

I dropped into the dining room for tea this afternoon after Jane's bridge party, to find Jane looking uncomfortable and an animated conversation on spiritualism going on, with Helena Lear leading it.

"Ah!" she said when she saw me, "here comes our cynic. I suppose you don't believe in automatic writing either?"

"I should," I replied gravely. "I have seen as many as fifty men taking notes while in a trance in my lecture room."

"Nor in spirits?"

"Certainly I do. And in the Smoke of Prophecy, and the Powder of Death."

She looked rather blank, and Jane flushed a trifle.

"What is more," I said, a trifle carried away by the tenseness of the room, perhaps, "I know that if I take a piece of chalk — have you any chalk, Jane? — and draw on the floor here the magic circle, and a triangle within it, no evil spirits can approach me. Get the chalk, dear; I promise I shall not be disturbed by so much as one demon."

In the laughter which followed the subject was dropped. But Helena Lear, when she gave me my tea, eyed me with amusement.

"You and your circle!" she said. "Don't you know that half these women more than half believe you?"

"And don't you?"

"You don't believe yourself."

"Still," I said, remembering von Humboldt, "I am not an out and out sceptic. I will admit that Jock there, who is acting as a vacuum cleaner under the table, can hear and see and smell things that I cannot. But I do not therefore believe he communicates with the spirit world."

"But he sees things you don't see. You admit that."

"Certainly. He may see further into the spectrum than I do."

"Then *what* does he see?" she said triumphantly.

30

A fortunate digression enabled me to escape with a whole skin, but I think there was something rather quizzical in her smiling farewell. After all, if Jock does see things I do not, what does he see? I'm blessed if I know.

Jane knows that I have seen the picture, and that I know it lies behind her refusal to go to Twin Hollows for the summer. When I came back from Larkin's office to-day, the final papers having been signed, I could see her almost physically bracing herself.

"So it's all set, my dear," I said. "And if we can get Annie Cochran to clean the place a bit———"

"Would you mind so very much," she asked, almost wistfully, "if we don't go there?"

"But it's all settled. Edith is coming back on purpose."

(Note: The "Edith" of the Journal is my niece, who makes her home with us. At this time she was absent on a round of house-parties. A very lovely and popular girl, of whom more hereafter.)

"It's too large for us," said Jane. "I need a rest in the summer, not a big house to care for."

And there was a certain definiteness in her

31

statement which ended the conversation. As a result, and following our usual course when there is a difference between us, we have taken refuge in a polite silence all day, the familiar armed neutrality of marriage. An uncomfortable state of affairs, and aggravated by Edith's absence. When she is here her bright alk fills the gaps and in the end she forces a *rapprochement*. . . .

Lear has told Cameron about the picture. I met Cameron while taking Jock for his evening walk to-night, and he re-introduced himself to me. After to-day's repression I fear I was a bit talkative, but he was a good listener.

Evidently he has a certain understanding of Jane's refusal to go to Twin Hollows, although he said very little.

"Houses are curious, sometimes," was his comment.

But on the matter of the picture he was frankly interested.

"There is," he said, "a certain weight in the evidence for psychic photography, Mr. Porter. Of course it is absurd to claim that all the curious photographs — and thousands of them come to me — are produced by discarnate intelligences. But there is something; I don't know just what."

Jane has gone to bed, still politely silent, and

32

I am left alone to wrestle with my two problems; where to spend the summer, and why Jane finds the house at Twin Hollows what Cameron describes as curious.

A mild term, that, for Jane's feeling about the house. Actually, she hates it. Has always hated it. She has had no pride in our acquisition of it; she has even steadfastly refused to bring away from it any of that early American furniture with which old Horace had filled it.

Yet she collects early American furniture. I write to-night at an utterly inadequate early American desk, because of this taste of hers: Jock has at this moment curled his long length on the hard seat of a Windsor chair, because of it! And yet she will have none of Uncle Horace's really fine collection.

Nor is she of the type to listen to Annie Cochran's story that the old portion of the house is haunted by the man killed there.

(Note: An old story and not authenticated, of the shooting of a man many years ago as he hid to escape the Excise. As a matter of fact, none of our later experiences in the house bore out this particular tradition at all.)

If she has a distaste for it, it may possibly relate to the occupancy of the house by the Riggs woman before Uncle Horace bought it. But even here I am doubtful, for Mrs. Riggs was caught in most unblushing fraud and entirely discredited as a medium.

Edith is back. She came in this morning, kissed Jock, Jane and myself, Jock first, demanded an enormous breakfast and all the hot water in the house, and descended gaily a half hour later to the table, in her usual aura of bath salts, bath powder and sunshine.

"Well," she said, attacking her melon, " and when do we go to the haunted house?"

"Ask your Aunt."

She glanced at me and then shrewdly at Jane.

"Good heavens!" she said. "Don't tell me there's any question about it?"

"It isn't decided yet," Jane said uneasily. "It's a big house, Edith, and————"

"All the more reason for taking it," said Edith, and having finished her melon flung out her pretty arms. "Grass," she said, *"and* flowers, *and* the sea. I shall swim" she went on. "And old Father William shall fish, and Jane shall sew a fine seam. And at night the ghosts shall walk. And everything will be lovely."

She turned to me.

"You do believe in ghosts, don't you, Father William?"

34

And somehow even Jane caught some of the infection of her gaiety. "Ask him about the triangle in a circle," she said.

"What's that?" Edith inquired.

"The triangle in a circle, drawn around you, will keep off demons," I explained gravely. "Surely you know that?"

"How — convenient!"

"And that the skins of four frogs, killed on a moonless night, will make one invisible if worn as a cap? And that the spirits obey solomon's seal — not the plant, of course! And that if you eat a stew of the eyes of a vulture, and the ear-tufts of an owl, you will be wise beyond all dreams of wisdom?"

"Who wants to be wise?" said Edith. "But go on. I love to hear you."

"Very well," I agreed, with an eye on Jane, "now take the figure five. Five is the magic number, not seven. We have five fingers, five toes, five senses. There are five points to a star. Perhaps you noticed my wild excitement when my automobile license this year was 555."

Jane got up, and I saw that my nonsense had had its effect. She was smiling, for the first time in days.

"If you care to go out and look at the house tomorrow, William," she said, "I will go."

And perhaps Edith had sensed a situation she

did not understand, for she kissed her, and as I left the room I heard her requesting Jane to bring back with her marketing some frog skins and the ear-tufts of an owl. . . .

So this afternoon things are looking brighter. And thus does man deceive himself! Only three days ago I was filled with vague yearnings and aspirations; I recorded here that my little rut was comfortable, but that I feared it. I wrote: "Was my greatest adventure to be to drag a fish out of the water, and watch it drown, open-mouthed, in the air?"

And yet, at the mere thought of not going to Twin Hollows, of being thrown on the mercies of some Mountain House, or set on a horse in the far west, I have been frightened almost into a panic.

The water-beetle indeed. . . .

The town is very quiet to-night. The annual student exodus is almost over, although still an occasional truck goes by, piled high with trunks. The Lears intend to stay. Sulzer and Mackintyre are off for the Scottish Lakes, and Cameron, I hear, is going soon to the Adirondacks, where he spends his summer in a boat, and minus ghosts, I dare say.

I have mailed him the picture to-day, and can only hope Jane does not miss it.

One wonders about men like Cameron.

Slight, almost negligible, as is my acquaintance with him – I would not know him in a crowd, even now – there is something of Scottish dourness in him. He neither smokes nor drinks; he lives austerely and alone. He has a reputation as a relentless investigator; it was he who exposed the hauntings at the house on Sabbathday Lake, in Massachusetts.

But he is a believer. That is, he believes in conscious survival after death, and I suspect that he has his own small group here. Among them little Pettingill. It would be a humiliating thought, for me, to feel that after I passed over, as they say, little Pettingill might hale me to him, in the light of a red lamp, and request me to lift a table! . . .

Warren Halliday is on the verandah with Edith. I can hear her bubbling laughter, and his quiet, deep voice. After all, I dare say we must make up our minds to lose her sometime, but it hurts.

And it will not be soon. He has not a penny to bless himself with, nor has she. I think, if I were very rich, I would provide an endowment fund for lovers.

But something is wrong with our university system. It takes too long to put a man on a wife-supporting basis. Halliday is twenty-six; he lost two years in the war, and he has another year of law. Truly, Edith will need the eyes of a vulture and the ear-tufts of an owl.

June 22nd.
"All houses in which men have lived and suffered and died are haunted houses." But then, all houses are haunted. Why, then, did Jock refuse to enter the house at Twin Hollows to-day, but crawled under the automobile and remained there, a picture of craven terror, until our departure?

This old house where I am writing to-night, undoubtedly it has seen the passing of more than one human soul. Yet Jock moves through it unconcernedly, his stump of a tail proudly upraised, his head unbowed. His attitude to-night, too, is even slightly more flamboyant than usual, as though to testify that although he may have given the impression of terror during the day, we are laboring under a misapprehension. He but sought the shelter of the car for coolness.

"He may see further into the spectrum than I do," I said to Helena Lear the other day, and she countered:

"Yes. But *what* does he see?"

Old Thomas met us in Oakville with the keys, and we drove out to the house. I sensed in

38

Jane a reluctance to enter, but she fought it back bravely, and we examined it with a view to our own occupancy. It is in excellent condition and repair, although the white covers over the library furniture and in the den behind gave those rooms a rather ghostly appearance. Jane, I saw, gave only a cursory glance into those rooms, and soon after, pleading the chill inside, moved out into the sunlight.

Edith, however, was enchanted with it all, and said so. She danced through the house, shamelessly courting old Thomas, selecting bedrooms for us all, and peering into closets, and I caught up with her at last on the second floor, looking at the boat-house on the beach beyond the marsh.

"What's above it?" she asked. "Rooms?"

"When the old sloop was in commission, the captain slept there," I told her.

"How many rooms?"

"Two, I think, and a sort of kitchenette."

"Are they furnished?"

Old Thomas, being appealed to, said they were, and Edith's face assumed that air of mysterious calculation which I have learned to associate with what she calls "an idea. "Whatever it was, however, she kept it to herself, and I left her selecting a bedroom for herself, and putting into it sufficient thought to have served a better purpose.

Her surroundings and belongings are very important to her; and yet I believe she is in love with young Halliday, who can, so far as I see, give her neither.

It is a curious thing, to go into a house left, as Twin Hollows has been, without change since old Horace died, and not to find him there; his big arm chair near the fireplace in the library, his very pens still on the flat-topped desk which is the only modern piece in the room, the books he was reading still in the desk rack. I had a curious feeling to-day that if I raised my voice, I would hear the little cough which was so often his preliminary to speech, from the den beyond.

The den too is unchanged. (Note: From an ugly room, the original kitchen of the old house, he had made it a sort of treasure house of early American old pewter, brought over perhaps in ships which had anchored in the very bay outside; of early framed charters and deeds of land, signed by English kings and hung on the walls above the old panelling, which he himself had found somewhere and installed; of quaint chairs, a settle and an old chest, hooked rugs on the floor, and old glass candlesticks.)

I threw back the covering which protected

the desk top, and sat down at it. Just there, in all probability, he had been sitting when the fatal attack took place. He may have felt it coming on, but there was no one to call, poor old chap. We had not been overly close, but the thought of him, writing perhaps, or reading, the sudden consciousness that all was not well, an instant of comprehension, and then the end — it got me, rather.

I think he had been reading. Among the other books on the desk was the one with a scrap of paper thrust in it to mark the place, and a pencil line drawn on the margin of the page to mark a paragraph. But it gives me rather a new line on him. I had always thought that his purchase of a house locally reputed to be haunted, a reputation considerably enhanced by the Riggs woman's tenancy, was a rather magnificent gesture of pure Calvinism.

But to-night I am wondering. The marked paragraph is in a book entitled "Eugenia Riggs and the Oakville Phenomena," and I have brought it home with me. It is a creepy sort of thing, and I find myself looking back over my shoulder as I copy it into this record.

"It is to be borne in mind that the room was always subjected to the most careful preliminary examination. Its walls were plastered, and no doors or windows (see photograph) were near the cabinet. As an additional precaution strings of small bells were placed across all possible entrances and exits, which were also closed and locked.

"It is also to be remembered that the medium herself was always willing to be searched, and this was frequently done by Madame B———. This had been done on the night when the hand was distinctly seen by all present, reaching out and touching those nearest on the shoulder, and later making the impression in the pan of soft putty left in the cabinet.

"It is to be borne in mind too that, except when the controls rapped for no light, there was always sufficient illumination for us to see the medium clearly. A small red lamp was found to offer least disturbance and was customarily used.

"There was occasional fraud, but *there were also genuine phenomena.*"

The last few words are italicized.

So to-night I am wondering. Does one find, as life goes on, that the lonely human spirit revolts at the thought of eternal peace, and craves a relief in action in the life beyond? Would I not myself, for instance, prefer even coming back and lifting little Pettingill's table to the unadulterated society of the saints?

There is a division in my family. Edith has come out with her plan, which is to "spread out," as she puts it, in the main house at Twin Hollows, and to let Warren Halliday spend his vacation at the boat-house!

"*Renting* it to him, I suppose?" I inquired over my breakfast bacon.

"Renting it?" she said indignantly. "You wouldn't have the nerve to ask money for that tumble-down place, would you? And anyhow, you can't get blood out of a stone."

There is a terrible frankness about Edith at times.

But Jane is as equally determined not to occupy the house at any cost. It was written all over her yesterday, and there is still an ominous set look about her mouth. Between them I am more or less trimming skiff.

If Jane would be more open it would be easier; if she would only come to me and say that she is afraid of the house I think I could reassure her. It may be that that silly photograph is still in her mind. But why would she not even stay in the house yesterday? She went out into the garden and picked some of its neglected flowers instead.

"It's a pity not to use them," she said, and then looked at me with such a white and pitiful face that I put my arm around her.

"I must have been a very bad husband," I said, "if you think I am going to force you to live here. Who am I," I added, "against you and Jock?"

But she did not smile.

"If you want to come here," she said, making what I felt was a painful concession, "why couldn't we live at the Lodge? It is really quite sweet. And we could rent this."

"Would that be quite normal, under the circumstances? I'm not asking the circumstances," I added hastily. "I'm simply putting the question."

"We could ask a lower rent."

There is, I sometimes think, a fundamental difference in the ethical views of men and women. To Jane it is quite proper to let a house with what she believes is a most undesirable quality, if she lowers the price. She does not suggest advertising: "One house, furnished, reputed to be haunted." On the contrary, she proposes to entice tenants with a lower rent, and once having got them there, to be able to say, in effect: "What would you? The house is cheap. True, it has certain disadvantages; I am sorry you have been bothered. But you have saved money."

Aside from this viewpoint, however, the idea

is sound enough. We can be comfortable at the Lodge. And — let me always be frank in this Journal — I may have my occasional yearnings for adventure, but they have their limitations, and the talk Edith has reported as taking place between old Thomas and herself yesterday after I left them has revealed them to myself.

Edith, on the contrary, finds the situation "really thrilling."

"It's a good house, yes'm," said Thomas. For them as likes it. I wouldn't be caught dead in it at night myself."

"I hope you never will be," said Edith.

"It ain't nothing you can put your finger on," said Thomas. "It's just knocks and raps, and doors opening and closing. But I say that's enough."

"It souns like plenty," said Edith. "Of course it may be rats."

"It's a right husky rat that'll open a closed door, and I ain't yet seen a rat that could move a chair. Besides, I ain't ever heard that rats are partial to a red light."

"Now see here, Thomas" Edith reports herself as saying, "either you've said too much or you've said too little. What about a red light? Nothing scandalous, I hope!"

Stripped of further trimming, it appears that some two years ago a small red lamp was installed in the den at Twin Hollows, and is now still there, Thomas having declined to destroy it for fear of some dire and mysterious vengeance.

"Not for light, as far as I could see, miss," he said. "I never seen him read by it. But put in it was, and the night it first came Annie Cochran said something came into her room and pulled the covers off her bed."

"How — shameless!" said Edith.

"More than that," he went on stolidly, "the furniture was moving through the house all night, and the next morning she found the tea-kettle sitting in the pantry, and tea had been made in the tea-pot."

"But surely she did not begrudge the poor things their tea, Thomas? It must be thirsty work, moving furniture and chasing about rapping on things."

"She'd left the kettle on the stove, and there it was," he said, doggedly.

Like the lady of color who said to the judge that she had "just sort of lost her taste" for her husband, I begin to lose my taste for this lamp. But one wonders whether its evil reputation is not a survival from the days of Mrs. Riggs, when "a small red lamp was found to offer least disturbance, and was customarily used."

Edith has lost and Jane has won. We shall spend the summer at the Lodge.

But I feel that Jane's victory brings her no particular pleasure, that even to go to the Lodge is a concession she is making against some hidden apprehension. Yet to show just how baseless are most of these things, this morning Clara has been in a low mood, and I heard Jane inquire the reason.

"I dreamed last night that I'd lost a tooth," said Clara. "That's a sign of death, sure, Mrs. Porter."

Edith, however, has won in one way. Warren Halliday is to have the boat-house.

We motored out together to-day, I to look over the Lodge more carefully, and Halliday to inspect his prospective quarters. He is thoroughly likeable, a nice clean-cut young fellow, not too handsome but manly and with a good war record, and badly cut up at his failure to find a job for the summer.

"I'd do anythying," he said. "Sell neckties if necessary! But I can't even land that. Although —" he forced a grin "— I have a nice taste in neckties!"

On the way out I told him something of the history of the house, and a little — very little — of Jane's nervousness concerning it.

"Of course," he said, "it's all nonsense. But a surprising number of people are going bugs on it."

"Darned uncomfortable nonsense, too."

"It's not only that, sir. It's dangerous. Imagine what a general conviction of this sort would do. Think of the fellows who find things getting a bit thick for them here, and how quickly they'd hop out of it! Think of the crimes it would cause. And take wars. Nobody would care whether he lived or not. Talk about civilization going! Why, the whole darned populace would go!"

In view of that conversation, it was interesting later that day, at the Lodge, to have old Thomas intimate that Uncle Horace had not died a natural death, but had "seen something" which had caused it.

As a matter of fact, he brought out certain rather curious facts, which appear to have been somehow overlooked, or at least considered unimportant, at the inquest.

For instance, he had been writing at his desk when the attack came on. His pen was found on the floor. But there was no sign of what he had been writing, save for a mark on the fresh blotter, as if he had blotted something there. The most curious thing, however, according to old Thomas, was the matter of lights.

When Annie Cochran found him the following morning, on the floor beside his desk, all the lights were out, including his desk lamp.

"But the red lamp was going in the den," said old Thomas. "It didn't make much light, so nobody noticed it until the doctor came. He saw it right off. I leave it to you, what shut off that desk lamp?"

I rather gather from Thomas that the ill-repute of the red lamp has spread over the country-side. The house had a bad reputation to start with, which Mrs. Riggs' tenancy did nothing to redeem, and now comes Annie Cochran and her red lamp, and a fairly poor outlook so far as renting the property is concerned.

There has been, according to Thomas, considerable interest as to whether we will inhabit the house or not, and if ever I saw relief in a man's face it was in his when I announced the decision. As Halliday observes, it would be interesting to know if either Annie Cochran or Thomas has ever heard that red is the best light for so-called psychic phenomena.

The Lodge proves to be weatherproof and in good condition, and the boat-house quite liveable, with the addition of a few things from the main house.

It will need thorough screening, however, on

account of the mosquitos.

(Note: It is necessary, for the sake of the narrative, to describe the boat-house. It is built up on piles which raise it above tide level, and the dory and canoe belonging to the house are stored in the lower portion of it in winter. The old sloop, however, not in commission for several years, was at this time anchored to a buoy about a hundred yards out in the bay, and showed the buffeting of wind and tide.

Across the salt marsh, from the foot of the lawn, extended a raised wooden run-way which led to the boat-house and the beach. This walk also prolongs itself into a sort of ramshackel pier, from which a run-way extends to a wooden float. At the time of our visit examination showed the float badly in need of repair, a number of the barrels which supported it having more or less gone to pieces.

It was, as will be seen, during Halliday's repair of this float that he made that discovery which was later to see the commencement of my troubles.)

All in all, Jane's scheme is practical, although Edith is frankly disappointed.

"I would have looked so sweet on that terrace!" she says, and makes a dreadful face at me.

I have asked her to say nothing to Jane about

old Thomas's ravings, as she calls them. She has agreed, but accuses me of extreme terror, and maintains that I am merely putting the responsibility on Jane.

"You know perfectly well," she says, "that you believe in ghosts. And if you rent that house old Horace *ought* to come back and haunt you."

But she is secretly pleased. She sees herself in the cottage, in a bungalow apron, presenting a picture of lovely but humble domesticity to young Halliday, and thus forcing his hand. For if I know anything of Edith, she is going to marry him. And if I know anything of Halliday, he is going to marry nobody he cannot support.

It may be an interesting summer. . . .

Curious about that lamp on the desk, the night the poor old chap passed out. Of course, he might have turned it out and risen to go upstairs when he felt the attack coming on. But wouldn't he have laid the pen down first? One would do that automatically.

It's a pity the blotting pad has been destroyed.

June 25th.

The last, or almost the last, word Uncle Horace

wrote the night of his death was "danger."

But how much significance am I to attach to that? We speak of the danger of taking cold, of levity in the lecture room, of combining lobster and ice-cream. To poor old Horace there would have been danger in over-exertion; in that sense of the word he was always in danger. But it was not a word he was apt to use lightly.

Yet what conceivable danger could have threatened him? . . .

This morning, clearing my desk preparatory to our exodus, I resorted to an old trick of mine. I turned over my large desk blotter and presented a fresh and unblemished side to the world. It came to me then that thus probably since the invention of blotters had neatness been established with a minimum of effort, and that it might have been resorted to by Annie Cochran.

After luncheon I started to Twin Hollows with the back of the car piled high with a varied assortment of breakable toilet articles, a lamp or two, and a certain number of dishes. The Lodge was open, and Annie Cochran vigorously cleaning it, and having deposited my fragile load there, I wandered up to the house.

Thomas was cutting the lawn, with a mare borrowed for the purpose pulling the old horse mower, and the Oakville constable, Starr, who is also the local carpenter, was replacing old boards with new on the raised wall to the beach. What with the sunlight, the put-put of a two-cycle engine in a passing motor boat, a flock of knock-abouts and sloops poised on the water like great butterflies, and the human activities about, the absurdity of abandoning the old house to some unappreciative tenant grew on me.

"Hear you're going to live in the Lodge," said Starr, spitting over the rail.

"Mrs. Porter feels the main house is too large for us."

He eyed me sharply.

"Yes," he said. "Pretty big house. Well, I'm in a dollar on it."

"A dollar?"

"I bet you'd never live in it," he said, and there was a furtive gleam of amusement in his eye as he marked a board preparatory to sawing it.

"It's my opinion, Starr," I said, "that you people around here have talked this place into disrepute."

"Maybe we have," he said, non-committally.

"Mr. Horace Porter lived here for twenty years."

"And *died* there," he reminded me.

"Of chronic heart trouble."

"So the doctor says."

"But you don't think so?"

"I know he had got a right forcible knock on the head, too."

"I thought that came from his fall."

"Well, it may have," he said, and signified the end of the conversation by falling to work with his saw. I waited, but he evidently felt he had said enough, and his further speech was guarded in the extreme. He didn't know whether Mr. Porter had been writing or not when it happened. No, he'd been the first to get there, and he had seen no paper.

Asked if he had had any reason, any experience of his own, to make him wager we would not live in the house, he only shook his head. But as I started back he called after me.

"I don't know as there's any truth in it," he said. "But they do say, on still nights, that he's been heard coughing around the place. I ain't ever heard it myself."

So Thomas thinks that Uncle Horace was frightened to death, and Starr intimates that he was murdered, and all this was seething in the minds of these country people a year ago, without it reaching me at all. There had been no inquest; simply, as I recall, Doctor Hayward notifying the Coroner by telephone, and giving organic heart disease as the cause.

I was, I admit, startled this morning as I turned back to the main house. But I knew the tendency of small inbred communities to feed on themselves, for lack of outside nutriment, and by the time I had reached the terrace I was putting Starr's statement about a blow in the same class with the cough heard at night. I stood looking out over the sweep of lawn, and the words occurred to me of that other ancient Horace, confirmed city-dweller that he was.

"There was ever among the number of my wishes, a portion of ground, not over large, in which was a garden and a fountain, with a continual stream close to my house, and a little woodland besides. The gods have done more abundantly, and better for me, than this."

So I felt that the gods had done even better for me than I had thought. My little woodland, to my left as I faced the sea, covered thirty acres, extending beyond Robinson's Point; true, I had no fountain, but I had a garden of sorts. And I had a ship, which apparently the old Roman had never dreamed of. The old sloop bobbed and swung in the wash of a passing tug.

I turned and went into the house to find that Annie Cochran had turned the blotter and that the last word the poor old boy had written had been "danger."

Women are curious creatures. Throughout the winter it is of vital importance to Jane that her tea cups are old Chelsea, and that the mirror over the hall table is pure early colonial, even if it does raise my right eye an inch or so. The Queen Anne chairs in her bedroom, the Adam sideboard in the dining room, apparently divide her affection with me, and she has been known to make considerably more fuss over a scratch on the Sheraton cabinet than over a similar injury to myself.

We are settled to-night in the Lodge, and whatever Edith may say as to its romantic outside appearance, within it is frankly hideous. It is all a cottage should not be. From the old parlor organ downstairs to beds that dip in the center above, it is atrocious. Yet to-night Jane is a happy woman.

Can it be that women require rest from their possessions, as for instance I do from my dinner clothes? That it gives them the same sense of freedom to don, speaking figuratively, a parlor organ and the cheapest of other furnishings, as it does me to put on my ancient fishing garments?

Or is Jane simply relieved?

I confess that to-night with Larkin's advertisement for the other house before me, I feel not only in the position of a man attempting to sell a gold brick, but that I have a secret hankering for the gold brick myself.

"For rent for the season, large handsomely furnished house on bay three miles from Oakville. Beautiful location. Thirty-two acres, landscaped. Flower and kitchen gardens. Low rental."

Yet I dare say we shall do well enough. After all, there comes a time when ambition ceases to burn, or romance to stir, and the highest cry of the human heart is for peace. Here, I feel, is peace.

I have brought with me those books which all the year I have promised myself to read, so that my small room overflows with them; a spare note-book or two for this Journal, to be filled probably with the weights of fish and the readings of the barometer; Jane for solid affection, Edith for the joy of life, and Jock for companionship.

But the latter I am questioning to-night. Jock has deserted me. He will not occupy the window seat of my room, although his comforter is neatly spread upon it. When I showed it to him he leaped up obediently, then glanced out the window toward the main house, emitted a long and melancholy howl, and with an air of firmness not to be gainsaid, retired under the bed in Jane's room, which faces toward the highroad. Nor could I later coax him past the main house for a moonlight stroll upon the beach.

He joined me there later, having reached it by some devious route of his own through the marsh, but without enthusiasm.

Later: There has been wild excitement here, and only now have we quieted down. It is clear that already Clara has heard some of the local talk.

At eleven o'clock we heard wild screams from Clara's attic bedroom, and all three of us arrived there in varying stages of undress. Clara was outside her door, which was closed, and was hysterically shrieking that there was a blue light under her bed.

I opened the door, entered the room, which was dark and stooped down. There *was* a blue light there, luminous and spectral, and my very scalp prickled. I think, had it not been for the women outside, I would have howled like a dog. And the worst of it was that it had an eye, a large staring eye that gazed at me with all the concentrated malevolence in the world.

It was a moment before I could say in an unshaken voice:

"Turn on the lights, somebody."

There was a delay until the switch was

found, and for that moment the blue light stared at me and I at it. I heard Edith flop down on the floor beside me and give a little yelp, and Clara snivelling outside and saying she would never go into that room again. Never.

Then Jane turned on the lights, and I saw under the bed the large phosphorescent head of a dead fish, brought by Jock from the beach and carefully *cached* there!

June 27th.

I have found Uncle Horace's letter, and in a manner so curious that there can be, it seems to me, but two interpretations of it. One is that, somehow, I have had all along a subconscious knowledge of its presence behind the drawer. But I hesitate to accept that. I am orderly by instinct, and when I went over the desk after his death, the merest indication of a paper caught behind the drawer would have sent me after it.

The other explanation is that I received a telepathic message. It came, as I fancy such messages must come, not from outside but from within. I heard nothing; it welled up, above the incoherent and vague wanderings of a mind not definitely in action, in a clear cut and definite form. "Take out the bottom drawer on the right."

But if I am to accept telepathy, I am to believe that I am not alone in my knowledge of this letter. Yet considering the tone of it, the awful possibility it indicates, who could have such a knowledge and yet keep it to himself? . . .

How did it get behind the drawer? If the brownish smudge on the corner turns out to be blood, and I think it is, then it was placed in the drawer after he died. Annie Cochran and Thomas both deny having seen any paper about. The doctor, perhaps? But would he not have read it first?

It had been crumpled into a ball and thrown into the drawer, and the subsequent opening of the drawer had pushed it back, out of sight. So much is clear.

But — after he fell!

Suppose — and in the privacy of this Journal I may surely let my imagination wander — suppose then, that some other hand picked up this paper, ignorant of its contents, and in a hurried attempt to put the room in order, flung it into the drawer? Or toward the waste basket beside it, and it fell short? Suppose, in a word, that he was not alone when he died? Suppose that some other hand, again, turned out the desk light and the others, and somehow overlooked the dim red lamp in the next room, or left it to see the way to escape?

I must not let my nerves run away with me. Murder is an ugly word, and after all we have Hayward's verdict of death by heart failure. But a sufficient shock, or a blow, might have brought that on. Fright, even, for the poor old chap was frightened when he wrote that letter. Trembling but uncompromising. That was like him.

"I realize fully the unpleasantness of my own situation; even, if you are consistent, its danger. But———"

But what? But in spite of this I shall do as I have threatened, probably.

I am profoundly moved to-night. We did not love one another, but he was old and alone, and menaced by some monstrous wickedness. Just what that wickedness was no one can say, but I fully believe to-night that he died of it. . . .

This morning I went with Edith to the main house, she to select some odds and ends for the boat-house, against Halliday's coming, and I to clear out the library desk, to have it moved to the Lodge.

Edith was in high spirits as I unlocked the front door, and was gravely telling Thomas, who accompanied us, that we had seen a blue light under Clara's bed the night before. But he expressed no surprise.

61

"Plenty of them, folks tell me," he said. "First time I've heard of them in the Lodge, though."

"Oh!" said Edith slightly daunted. "So there are lights, too."

"Yes'm," he replied. "Annie Cochran, she had one here, used to hang around the shower-bath off the gun room. And there used to be plenty outside. Fellows setting trawl out in the bay used to see them over the swamp."

"Marsh gas," I suggested.

"Maybe," he said, with his take-it or leave-it attitude, and we went into the house.

There Edith and Thomas left me, and I opened the shutters of the library and sat down at the desk. I could hear Edith insisting on seeing the shower-bath off the gun room. Then their voices died away, and I began to go through the desk once more. All important papers had been taken away after the death, and the drawers contained the usual riff-raff of such depositories, old keys, ancient check books, their stubs filled in Uncle Horace's neat hand.

Naturally, I was thinking of him. More or less, I was concentrated on him, if this is any comfort to my spiritualistic friends. He had, indeed, fallen out of the very chair in which I sat when he was stricken, and had apparently cut his head badly on the corner of the desk. All this was in my mind, as I closed the last drawer and surveyed the heap of rubbish on the desk.

I suppose I was subconsciously reconstructing the night of his death, when he had penned that word "danger" which now lay, clearly outlined in reverse, on the blotter. And that when I wandered into the den, looking for a place to store what Lear calls the detritus piled up on the desk, I was still thinking of it. But I cannot feel that my entrance into the room, or my idly switching on the red lamp which stood there, had the slightest connection with the message I seemed at that moment to receive: "Take out the bottom drawer on the right."

I have heard people who believe in this sort of thing emphasize the peculiar insistence of the messages, and this was true in this case. I do not recall that there was any question in my mind, either, as to which bottom drawer on the right I was to remove. But I must record here a rather curious incident which my spiritualistic friends would add to the picture as proof positive of its other-earth origin.

Edith came back. I could hear her in the library.

"I've found Annie Cochran's blue light," she called. "A piece of phosphorescent wood. No wonder this neighborhood's haunted!" Then she came into the doorway, with Thomas behind her, and suddenly stopped.

"Why!" she said, "what funny shadows!"

"Shadows?"

Then she laughed and ran her fingers across her eyes.

"My error," she said. "When I came in I seemed to see a sort of cloud under the ceiling. It's gone now."

Old Thomas stood by, quietly.

"Lots of folks have seen them shadows," he said. "Some say they're red and some brown. I ain't ever seen them myself, so I can't say." He turned to go. "Maybe it's phosphorescence!" he said, and went away with a sort of hideous silent mirth shaking him.

Behind the drawer I found the letter.

(Note: I made no copy of the letter in the original Journal, so I give it here.)

Unfinished letter of Mr. Horace Porter, addressed to some one unknown, and dated the day of his death, June 27th of the preceding year:

"I am writing this in great distress of mind, and in what I feel is a righteous anger. It is incredible to me that you cannot see the wickedness of the course you have proposed.

64

"In all earnestness I appeal to you to consider the enormity of the idea. Your failure to comprehend my own attitude to it, however, makes me believe that you may be tempted to go on with it. In that case I shall feel it my duty, not only to go to the police but to warn society in general.

"I realize fully the unpleasantness of my own situation; even, if you are consistent, its danger. But———"

The letter had not been finished.

June 28th.

I slept very little last night, and this morning made an excuse to go up to town with the letter. Larkin had telephoned me that he had an inquiry on the house through Cameron, and this gave me a pretext. Jane at first wished to go with me, but Edith coaxed her into helping with the rooms over the boat-house, and I finally got away.

Larkin is impressed with the letter, but does not necessarily see its connection with Uncle Horace's death.

"After all," he said, "you've got your medical man's statement that he died of heart failure. Suppose he *was* scared to death? That isn't a crime in law. And you've got to remember the old gentleman was pretty much of a pepper pot. He attacked me almost as violently as that once for my politics!"

"He didn't threaten you with the police, did he?"

"No; he recommended a Sanitarium, I think. You haven't an idea who it's meant for, you say?"

"Not the slightest. He hadn't any friends, intimates, so far as I know. The Livingstones, very decent people with a big place about six miles from him, his doctor, and myself — that's about all."

" 'Enormity of the idea,' " he read again. "Of course that might be a new poison gas, or this thing the press is always scaring up, the death ray. Some fellow with a bee in his bonnet, you may be sure."

"That wouldn't imply danger to himself."

"Any fellow with a bee in his bonnet is dangerous," he said, and gave me back the letter.

"Of course," he went on, "you've made a nice point about the stain on the corner. If it's blood, it's hardly likely he got up again and put it where you found it. But I think you'll find the servant there, what's her name, picked it up in her excitement and threw it into the drawer.

66

People don't always know what they do at such times. However, if you like, I'll have that stain tested and see what it is."

I tore off the corner, and left him putting it carefully into an envelope. He glanced up as I prepared to go.

"What's this I hear about your keeping off demons by drawing some sort of a cabalistic design around yourself?" he asked. "You'd better let me in on it; I need a refuge now and then."

Which proves that a man may shout the eternal virtues and be unheard forever, but if he babble nonsense in a wilderness it will travel around the world.

Nevertheless, I am the better for the talk with him. I have been too closely consorting with my womenkind, probably; the most virile man can become effeminized in time. And Larkin's attitude as to renting the house is an eminently sane one.

"Rent it without saying anything," he said, "and ten to one whoever takes it will have a peaceable summer. But do as you suggest, tell the tenant the place has the reputation of being haunted, and ghosts will be as thick as mosquitos from the start."

He has asked for some photographs of the property, and I have promised them for the day after tomorrow. . . .

We have settled down into our routine here very comfortably. Our eggs and milk are brought each morning by a buxom farmer's daughter, one Maggie Morrison, a sturdy red-cheeked girl who drives in a small truck, and backs and turns before the Lodge rather than circle around the main house.

"Surely," I said to her yesterday, "you aren't afraid of the place in daylight?"

"Not afraid," she said, "but it gives me the shivers." And weakened that somewhat by her statement that she never liked a place where there had been a death. Yet she handles callously the cold corpses of her chickens, pulling up their poor rigid wings to show the tenderness of the dead skin beneath, and bending their stilled breast-bones to prove that they have died young!

With the lawns cut and the shrubbery trimmed, the place grows increasingly lovely. At low tide the beach is covered with odds and ends from the mysterious life of the sea, red and white starfish, sea urchins, and disintegrated jelly fish. Sea-gulls pick up mussels, hover over a flat-topped rock, drop them onto its surface and then swoop down upon the broken shell, with a warning cry to other gulls to keep away.

So clear was the water this afternoon that, rowing to the old sloop, I could see the barnacles encrusting it, and the long strings of kelp which hang fromit like green and matted hair. Edith, bare-armed and slim in the canoe, paddled around it appraisingly.

"Needs a shave and a hair cut," she decided.

The boat-house is ready for young Halliday. She has put in it a great deal of love and one or two of my most treasured personal possessions.

"That isn't by any chance my smoking stand?"

"But you aren't going to smoke much this summer, Father William," she says, and tucks a hand into my arm. "I heard you say so yourself."

It has a sitting room, bedroom and kitchenette, but no bath.

"He can use the sea," says Edith, easily. "And take a cake of soap in with him."

"And wash himself ashore," I suggest, and am frowned down, probably as too old for such ribaldry.

Jane is very serene. Now and then, as she sits on our small verandah with her tapestry, I see her raise her eyes and glance toward the other house, but she does not mention it, nor do I. I notice that, like Maggie Morrison, she does not go very near to it, but she appears to have adopted an attitude of *laissez faire.*

But she absolutely refused to take the pictures of the house Larkin asks for. Not that she put it like that.

"I haven't had any luck with the camera lately, she said. "You take them, or let Edith do it."

The result of the collaboration, which followed early this afternoon is still in doubt. Jane intends to develop and print them this evening.

And so our life goes on. We retire early, I generally slightly scented from the cold cream of Edith's good night kiss. Clara, too, goes up early, probably looking under her bed before retiring into it. And Jane sits and sews while I make my nightly entry in this Journal; she is, I think, both jealous and faintly suspicious of it!

At ten o'clock or so we let Jock out, and he looks toward the main house and then turns out the gates and into the highroad, where for a half hour or so he chases rabbits and possibly looks for a bear. At ten-thirty he scratches at the door, and we admit him and go up to bed. Behind the drain pipe!

Later: I have just had a surprise amounting to shock. Jane finds she has forgotten the black japanned lantern with a red slide which she uses in the mysterious rites of developing pictures, and suggests that we go to the other house and use the red lamp there.

"But I can bring it here."

"I am through being silly about the other house, William," she says with an air of resolution. "Anyhow, the pantry there is better, and you can sit in the kitchen. Bring a book or something."

She has, poor Jane, very much the air of Helena Lear's kitten the day Jock cornered it and it came out resolutely and looked him in the eye. In effect, Jane is going out to meet her bugaboo and stare it down.

June 29th.

Jane is in bed to-day, and I am not all I might be, although I managed to get an indifferent print or two to Larkin this morning.

It is well enough for cold-blooded and nerveless individuals to speak of fear as a survival of that time when, in our savage state, we were surrounded by enemies, dangers, and a thousand portents in skies we could not comprehend, and to insist that when knowledge comes in at the door, fear and superstition fly out of the window.

It is only in his head that man is heroic; in the pit of his stomach he is always a coward.

Yet, stripped of its trimmings, — the empty, echoing house, its reputation, and my own private thoughts about its possible tragedy, the incident loses much of its terror; is capable, indeed, of a quite normal explanation.

That is, that Jane either saw someone outside the pantry window, or was the victim of a subjective image of her own producing. . . .

To put the affair in consecutive shape.

At eleven o'clock I had moved the red lamp from the den in the other house to the pantry and there connected it. I also lighted the kitchen, and established myself there with "The Life and Times of Cavour," a book which I considered safe and sufficiently unexciting under the circumstances.

Jane seemed to be going very well beyond the pantry door, and after a time I ceased the reassuring whistling with which I had been affirming my continued presence within call, and grew absorbed in my book.

It must have been 11:15 when she called out to me sharply to know where a cold wind was coming from, and although I felt no such air I closed the kitchen door. It was within a couple of minutes that, or thereabouts, that I suddenly heard her give a low moan, and the next instant there was the crash of a falling body.

When I opened the pantry door I found her in a dead faint, underneath the window. When she revived, she maintained that she had seen Uncle Horace.

Her statement runs about as follows: She had not felt particularly uneasy on entering the house, "although I had expected to," she admits. Nor at the beginning of operations in the pantry. The cold air, however, had had a peculiar quality to it; it "froze" her, she says; she felt rigid with it.

And it continued after she heard me close the kitchen door.

This wind, she says, was not only so cold that she called to me, but she had an impression that it was coming from somewhere near at hand, and she seemed to see the curtains blowing out at the window. The lower sash was down, as she could tell by the reflection of the red lamp in it, but she went to the window to see if the upper sash had been lowered.

With the darkness outside, the glass had become a sort of mirror, and she said her own figure in it startled her for a moment. She stood staring at it, when she realized that she was not alone in the room. Clearly reflected, behind and over her right shoulder, was a face.

It disappeared almost immediately, and I have my own private doubts about her recognition of it as Uncle Horace, which I believe is *post facto*. But I am obliged to admit that Jane saw something, either outside the window and looking in, or the creation of her own excited fancy.

As soon as I could leave her I went outside, but I could find no one there, and this morning I find that my own foot prints under the window have entirely obliterated anything else that may have been there.

Jane herself believes it was Uncle Horace, but I cannot find that she received anything more than an indistinct impression of a face. She rather startled me this morning, however, by asking me if I had ever thought that Uncle Horace had not died a natural death.

"Why in the world should I think such a thing?"

But pressed for an explanation she merely said she had heard that the spirits of those who have died violent deaths are more likely to appear than of others who have passed peaceably away; that the desire to acquaint the world with the circumstances of the tragedy is overwhelming!

What seems much more likely is that she had caught from me, with that queer gift of hers, some inkling of my own anxiety. . . .

Larkin's report from the laboratory shows that the stain on the corner of the letter is blood. One lives and learns. Not only does the report state that it is blood, but that it is human blood. Moreover, that it is about a year old, and that it is the imprint of a human finger, but is too badly blurred for identification, as it was made while the blood was fresh.

So does science come to the aid of the police to-day. Truly one lives and learns.

Larkin watched me while I read the report.

"You see?" I said. "It is human blood."

"What else did you expect it to be?"

"Still, it shows something."

"Certainly it does," he agreed easily. "It may even show a crime, for all I know. But where do you go from there? That finger-print is valueless. Say there was a crime, — where's your criminal? You can't go through the world rounding up all the individuals society ought to be warned against."

"No," I said, rather feebly. "No, I dare say not."

He went with me to the door of his office, and put his hand on my shoulder.

"Go on out to the country and forget about it," he advised. "You're looking rather shot, Porter. Draw your magic circle or whatever it is about your cottage, and retire inside it! Whatever happened there last year, it's too late to do anything about it now."

He is right. I shall get out my fishing gear to-morrow and perhaps Edith will spare me young Halliday now and then. He is, she said the other day in the inelegant vernacular of present day youth, "about as psychic as a door knob."

June 30th.

I have been brought to-day, for the first time, into active contact with the feeling of the country people against my house, and especially against the red lamp. It is an amazing situation.

Thomas came to the doorway this morning while I was at breakfast, followed by Starr the constable, who remained somewhat uneasily behind him. It developed that half a dozen sheep, in a meadow beyond Robinson's Point, were found the night before last with their throats cut. The farmer who owned them heard them milling about and ran out, and he declares he saw a dark figure dart out of the field and run into my woods at the head of Robinson's Point.

It appears that the farmer, whose name is Nylie, abandoned the pursuit as soon as he saw where the fugitive was headed, and went back to his dead sheep. They were neatly laid out in a row.

"At what time was all this?" I asked.

"Eleven o'clock, or thereabouts."

"How about a dog?" I asked. "They kill sheep, don't they? Catch them by the throat or something?"

"They don't stab them with a knife. Not

76

around here, anyhow," said Starr.

The ostensible object of the visit was to ask if we had been disturbed that night, and for some reason or other I did not at once connect the situation with Jane's curious experience.

"No," I said. You'll probably find that Nylie has an enemy somewhere, some hand he has discharged, perhaps."

Starr took himself away very soon after that, but before he left he exchanged a glance with Thomas, and I had a feeling that something lay behind this morning visit. It was not long before Thomas brought it out. It appears that Nylie ran after the figure to the edge of the wood, and there stood hesitating. The woods, I gather, share in the ill-repute of the house. And as he stood there, although everyone knew the house was empty, he distinctly saw the evil glow of the red lamp from it!

I dare say Jane is right, and my sense of humor is perverted, but I could not resist the opportunity of baiting Thomas. In which I realize now I made a tactical error.

"Really?" I said. "Nylie was certain of that, was he?"

"Saw it as plain as I see you," said Thomas. "I know you don't believe me———"

"But I do believe you. What about the red lamp?"

"Well," he said, "it's pretty well known about these parts that that lamp ain't healthy. Some say one thing and some say another, but most folks is agreed on that."

"Still, I don't see how it could kill sheep, do you?"

And even now I do not distinctly see the connection. I imagine the local belief is that the lamp exerts some malign influence, possibly even that it liberates some sinister spirit. Not, I imagine, that this is ever put into words. The nearest they come to that is the statement that the lamp is not "healthy," and that "George" has come back.

At least that is all that I can make out of that strange mixture of hysteria, superstitious fears and local mishaps to which Thomas gave birth in the next ten minutes or so. It began with Annie Cochran in the house after the lamp came, and gradually extended into the country-side; cows had mysteriously and prematurely calved; a meteorite had dropped into a field nearby; a fisherman's boat had been found empty in the bay on a quiet day and its owner never seen again; blight, pestilence and death had visited the community, equalled only in its history by the last few months of Mrs. Riggs' occupancy of the house. And the tradition was that Mrs. Riggs had used a red lamp to call her particular spirit.

" 'George' was his name," said Thomas, "and by and large he gave us a lot of trouble."

"Let me get this, Thomas," I said. "You mean that you think this 'George' has come back?"

"I'm not saying that," he said with his usual caution. "But there's some talk of it."

"And killed those sheep?"

"I'm not saying that either. But there's not a man, woman or child around these parts would have gone into those woods night before last, heading for the big house."

I felt that I had gone far enough, and I proceeded to explain the lighting of the lamp that night. But, although I saw that he believed me readily enough, it did not for a moment alter his attitude toward the red lamp.

"And, as a matter of fact," I concluded, "I think Mrs. Porter actually saw the man Nylie chased, looking in through the pantry window."

"That'll have been 'George' all right," said Thomas, and creaked heavily out of the room....

To leaven the gloom of the morning, Halliday arrived to-day, in boisterous high spirits, broken with a sort of husky emotion when he saw his quarters.

"It's so darned good of you all," he said, and

although the words were to Jane the look was for Edith.

We all escorted him down, Thomas carrying his kit bag, I his overcoat, Jock the newspaper and Warren himself staggering under a box of groceries and the canned goods on which he apparently intends to subsist. He has definitely refused Jane's offer to take his meals at our table.

"I'm the world's best cook with a can opener," he said boastfully. "And when bacon and beans begin to pall on me, I'll come up for a hand-out."

We stood around, Edith with entire shamelessness, while he unpacked and settled them. She herself insisted on arranging the top of the chest of drawers, and I saw her there, handling his hairbrushes caressingly. Poor little Edith, so frankly in love, so ready to believe that love is enough, and that such things as she has always taken for granted, food and shelter, will automatically follow in its train.

Afterwards we had tea on the narrow verandah over the water, and Halliday examined the old sloop with a professional eye.

"Pretty well out of condition, I'm afraid."

"Any boat's a good boat, sir," he said with his quick smile. "You shall be the skipper, and I'll be the mid-shipmite, the bo'sun tight and the crew of the — what's its name, anyhow?"

There followed a prolonged dispute between Edith and the new crew as to a name for the sloop, which was compromised by the announcing that it was to be called "The Cheese."

"Why? It has no holes in it," I protested.

"Because it's to have a skipper in it," said Edith conclusively.

After the women left we sat on the small verandah which surrounds the boat-house on three sides, and smoked. He told me his circumstances; he has exactly enough money to finish his course which will take another year. At the end of that time he is to have a junior partnership in a law firm in Boston.

"But you know what that means, at first," he said. "A sort of sublimated clerical job. It will be a long time before I am independent."

Before he could marry, was what he meant. And again I thought of my endowment fund for lovers. There are so many funds for preserving human life, and so few to make it worth the preserving. But I must talk to Edith. It is no use making the boy more unhappy than he is, or breaking down the restraints he is clearly putting on himself.

"I lost two years in the war," he said. "That threw me back, you see."

"I dare say it was not lost."

"No," he agreed. "I suppose a man must gain something by a thing like that, if he survives."

From that to the stories about the main house, and to Thomas's recital this morning, was not a long step, nor from that to the history of the house itself and to Mrs. Riggs.

"Curious," he said, "how these people rise, prosper, and then are found fraudulent, without discrediting the next generation of their kind. Eventually they are all caught between bases, and it begins all over again."

But the red lamp interested him.

"Some night, sir," he suggested, "you and I might go up there and try rubbing the thing; see if we can evoke the *genii.* . . .

About 8:30 to-night I took Jock and walked to Nylie's farm, where the sheep had been killed. I found the field, and wandered idly in. To my surprise, a man with a shot-gun rose from a fence corner and confronted me, and Jock's hair rose as he prepared to spring.

"What do you want here?" he demanded, suspiciously.

"Go easy with that gun," I said. "My name's Porter, and I'm out for a stroll. That's all."

He apologized gruffly, while I held Jock by the collar, and even condescended to point out where the dead sheep had been found, but there was certainly no cordiality in his manner, and even a trace of hostility.

More sheep were killed last night. The Livingstones have lost a dozen of their blooded stock, and several farmers have suffered.

In each case the method is the same; the sheep are neatly stabbed in the jugular vein and then as neatly laid out in a row.

We are buying no mutton from the local butcher!

I assured Thomas this morning that I had not lighted the red lamp again, but he did not smile. He is quite capable of believing, I dare say, that I have summoned a demon I cannot control.

But he tells me that a county detective from town, sent by the sheriff, is coming out to look into the matter. And there is a certain relief in this. It seems to me that we have to do with some form of religous mania, symbolistic in its manifestation. The sheep is the ancient sacrifice of many faiths.

This belief is strengthened by Thomas's statement that in each case save the first one there has been left on a nearby rock or, in one instance, on a fence, a small cabalistic design roughly drawn in chalk. . . .

8:00 P.M. I feel like a man who has dreamed of some horrible or grotesque figure, and wakes to find it perched on his bed-post.

The detective sent by Benchley, the Sheriff, has just been here, a man named Greenough, a heavy-set individual with a pleasant enough manner and a damnable smile, behind which he conceals a considerable amount of shrewdness.

He had, of course, gathered together the local superstitions, and he was inclined to be facetious concerning my ownership of the red lamp. But he was serious enough about the business that had brought him.

"It's probably psychopathic," he said, "and the psychopath is a poor individual to let loose in any community, especially when he's got a knife."

My own suggestion of religious mania seemed to interest him.

"It's possible," he said. "It's a queer time in the world, Mr. Porter. People seem ready to do anything, think anything, to escape reality. And from that to delusional insanity isn't very far."

I suppose I looked surprised at that, for he smiled.

"I read a good bit," he said, "and my kind of work is about nine-tenths psychology, anyhow.

You've got to know what your criminal was thinking, and then try to think like him. The third degree is nothing but applied psychology." He smiled again. "But that's a long way from sheep-killing. Now I'll ask you something. Did you ever hear of a circle, with a triangle inside it?"

I suppose I started, and I had a quick impression that his eyes were on me, shrewdly speculative behind his glasses. But the next moment he had reached into his pocket and drawn out a pencil and an envelope. "Like this," he said, and drawing the infernal symbol slowly and painstakingly, held it out to me.

To save my life I could not keep my hand steady; the envelope visibly quivered, and I saw his eyes on it.

"What do you mean, hear of it?" I asked. And then it came to me suddenly that that ridiculous statement of mine had somehow got to the fellow's ears, and that he was quietly hoaxing me. "Good Lord!" I said, and groaned. "So you've happened on that too!"

"So you know something about it?" he said quietly, and leaned forward. "Now, do you mind telling me what you know?"

He had not been hoaxing me. There was a curious significance in his manner, in the way he was looking at me, and it persisted while I told my absurd story. Told it badly, I realize, and haltingly; that I had picked up a book on Black Magic somewhere or other, and had as promptly forgotten it, save for one or two catch phrases and that infernal symbol of a triangle in a circle; how I had foolishly repeated them to a group of women, and now seemed likely never to hear the last of it.

"As I gather, the Lear woman has spread it all over town," I said. "She dabbles in spiritualism, or something, and it seems to have appealed to her imagination."

"It has certainly appealed to somebody's imagination," he said. "That's the mark our friend the sheep-killer has been leaving."

He was very cordial as he picked up his hat and prepared to depart. He was sorry to have had to trouble me; nice little place I had there. He understood I was fighting shy of the other house. He would do the same thing; he didn't believe in ghosts, but he was afraid of them.

And so out onto the drive, leaving me with a full and firm conviction that he suspects me of killing some forty odd sheep in the last few nights, probably in the celebration of some Black Mass of my own psychopathic devising.

Larkin thinks he has rented the house. I made a telephone message from him the excuse to go to town this morning. Mr. Bethel was not present, but his secretary was, a thin boy with a bad skin and with his hair pomaded until it looks as though it is painted on his head. He smoked one cigarette after another as we talked.

If to-morrow is fair, Mr. Bethel will motor out and look over the property. It appears that he is in feeble health. If it is not, Gordon, the secretary, will come alone. It develops that, although the boy is a local product, and not one to be particularly proud of, Mr. Bethel comes from the west; Cameron's note to Larkin merely introduced him, but assumed no responsibility. As, however, he offers the rent in advance, the matter of references becomes, as Larkin says, an unimportant detail.

I get the impression from the secretary that the old man is writing a book, and wishes to be undisturbed, and if his choice of a secretary fairly represents him, he will be.

From Larkin I learned that he had heard of the circle in a triangle from Helena Lear herself, at a dinner table, and that he has no idea that it is at all wide-spread. He regards the use of it by the sheep-killer as purely coincidence, which greatly cheers me.

Nevertheless, I went to the Lears and lunched there. Helena has agreed to spread the thing no further, and I came away with a great sense of relief. Into the bargain, Lear tells me that Cameron, after studying the photograph I sent him, is inclined to think it is the result of a double exposure.

"Double exposure or a thought image," Lear says. "He has had some success himself in getting curious forms on a sensitized plate. Got the number five once, after concentrating on it for an hour! I asked him about Doyle's fairies, but he only laughed."

All in all, I feel to-day that I was unduly apprehensive last night. The weather is magnificent; Edith, in knickerbockers and a sweater, has been holding nails for young Halliday to-day while he repairs the float. Jane has taken over from Thomas the care of the flower beds around the cottage, and has been busy there all afternoon with a weed-puller and a hoe, and I have found the sails for the sloop, mildewed but usable, in the attic of the Lodge.

No more sheep were killed last night. I understand Greenough has put guards on all the nearby flocks, and advised outlying farms to do the same thing. Maggie Morrison told us this morning that they were doing it, but in, I gathered, a half-hearted manner. Most of them believe that, by his very nature, the marauder is impervious to shot and shell.

"Joe Willing," she says, "saw something moving around his cow barn a night or so ago, and he fired right into it. But when he ran up there was nothing there."

One curious thing, however, has been brought in by Starr, who stopped on his way past to-day. In a meadow not far from the Livingstone place two large stones, which had lain there for years, have been moved together and stood on their edges, and a flat slab of rock laid across them. On top of this, when it was found, there lay a small heap of fine sand.

One can figure, of course, that here is an altar, erected by the same unbalanced mind which has been killing the sheep. But no offering has yet been laid on it.

Later: Halliday spent the evening here, and I walked back with him. He tells me that on his first night in the boat-house, he saw a light moving over the salt marsh, about three hundred feet away.

He was sitting on the small balcony of the boat-house, which surrounds it on three sides, and glancing toward the marsh, saw a light there. It seemed to float above the marsh at a distance of three or four feet, and was intermittent.

At first he thought it was someone on the way to the beach, with a flash light or a lantern, and he watched with some curiosity. Earlier in the evening he had himself walked along the edge of the swamp and decided it was not passable. But half way through the marsh the light stopped and then disappeared.

"I decided the chap, whoever it was, was in trouble," he said, "so I called to him. But there was no answer, and the light didn't appear again."

"Marsh gas," probably," I explained. "Methane, C.H., of course."

"Marsh gas burns with a thin blue flame, doesn't it? This was a small light, rather white. I waited an hour or so, but it didn't show again."

I have, since my return, looked up the book on the Oakville phenomena which I discovered on the desk of the main house. It is not significant, but it is interesting, to find that Mrs. Riggs produced fleeting lights, sometimes of a bluish-green, from the cabinet, again a sparkling point which generally localized itself near her head. But I cannot find any record of a light persisting for any length of time, or following a definite course.

July 3rd.

The house is rented. As it rained this

morning, the secretary came alone, and seemed very well satisfied.

But at the last moment my conscience began to worry me, and perhaps too, for none of our motives are unmixed, I was afraid he suspected something. He made some observation about the rent being low for a property of that size, and glanced at me as he said it, so I plunged.

"I think I'd better be honest with you, even if it costs me money," I said. "The house is cheap because it — well, it isn't an easy house to rent."

"Too lonely, eh?"

"Partly that, and partly because — a portion of the house is very old, and there have been some stories about it circulating in the neighborhood for years."

"Ghost stories?"

"You can call them that."

He seemed to be amused, rather than alarmed. He grinned broadly and took out a cigarette.

"Ghosts won't bother me any," he said rather boastfully. "What kind of a ghost?"

"I don't believe anyone claims to have seen anything. The reports are mostly of raps and various noises."

He seemed to take a peculiar, almost a furtive, enjoyment out of my statement, my confession, rather.

"Hot dog!" he said. "Well, raps won't bother me, and Mr. Bethel's got a deaf ear; he can turn that up at night if they worry him."

So the house is rented, unless something unexpected turns up, and I have done my part. But I confess to an extreme distaste for the secretary and Edith may find herself with a small problem on her hands. For just before we left he spied her on the float, and gave her a careful inspection.

"That looks pretty good to me," he said. And although his gesture embraced the water front his eyes were on her.

I have arranged with Annie Cochran, following Gordon's query about a servant, to resume her old position at the main house. She refuses to remain after dark, but I presume this will be satisfactory. She will also commence to-morrow to get the house in readiness.

With that strange swiftness with which news travels in the country, already the word has gone out that the place is rented, and I lay to that our sudden popularity this afternoon. The first to arrive was Doctor Hayward, as nervous and jerky as ever, fiddling with his collar, and when for a moment excluded from the talk, gnawing abstractedly at his finger ends. Nothing escapes the man; I sometimes feel that he goes about on his rounds, collecting gossip as assiduously as he disperses the medicines he puts up in his small dispensary, and that his mind is similarly stocked with it, put up neatly on shelves and in order, so that he can conveniently put his hand on it.

He addressed himself mostly to Jane — there is a certain type of medical man who wins his way into families by the favor of women, and is more at his ease with them than with its menfolk — and only beat a circuitous route to the subject uppermost in his mind, which clearly was that an elderly invalid had taken Twin Hollows and would probably require a physician.

In the course of this roundabout talk, however, I came finally to the conclusion that, like the detective, he was watching me. And, as had happened with Greenough, I became absurdly self-conscious. The very knowledge that, the moment I looked away, his eyes slid to me and there remained, made me awkward. As a result I upset my tea-cup, and while Jane was hurrying for a cloth to repair the damage, he said:

"Pretty nervous, aren't you?"

"Not particularly. But I happen to specialize in upsetting tea-cups."

"How are you sleeping?"

"Like a top," I assured him with a certain

truculence, I dare say. But he is fairly thick-skinned. He passed it over by giving his collar a twitch.

"Dream any?" he inquired.

By heaven! The fellow was not only watching me; he was analyzing me. And with that peculiar perverse humor which, I feel to-night, may get me into trouble yet, I answered. I who seldom dream, and then the benign dreams of an uneventful life and an easy conscience, I answered:

"Horribly!"

He leaned back and took to biting a finger, staring at me over it. "What do you mean by 'horribly'?" he inquired. But some gleam of reason came to me then, and I laughed.

"Sorry, Hayward," I said, "I couldn't resist it. I never dream, at least nothing I can remember. But you were being so professional———"

Jane's return prevented the apology which was on his lips, and he went back to the local gossip. Once I mentioned the matter of the sheep, but he rather dexterously side-stepped it, and finally brought the talk around to the renting of the house. But I am confident that Greenough has been to him about me, and has asked him to give him an opinion on my mental balance.

I was on guard after that; determined to exhibit myself in my most rational manner. But there is something upsetting in the mere thought that one's sanity is being brought into question. One's usually automatic acts become self-conscious ones. And to-night I could laugh, if I were not somewhat disturbed by it, at the care with which I placed my cigarette on the saucer of my tea-cup and flung the silver spoon into the grate; at the sudden comprehension of what I had done, and my wild leap to recover the spoon; and at Hayward's intent expression as I turned from the fireplace with the spoon in my hand, and muttered something about being the original man who put his umbrella to bed and stood himself in the corner. He was too absorbed to smile.

He left finally, when the Livingstones arrived.

"You must take good care of this fine husband of yours, Mrs. Porter," he said, holding her hand in the paternal fashion of his type. "He's probably been overdoing it a bit." The result of which is that Jane herself has taken to watching me quietly, over her tapestry, and that she suggested this evening that I take a course of bromide for my nerves.

Irritated at Hayward as I was, and annoyed at myself, I saw him to his car, and asked him the question which has been in the back of my mind ever since I found the letter in the library desk.

"By the way," I said, "you knew my Uncle Horace pretty well. Better than I did, in recent years. Did he have many friends — I mean, locally?"

He straightened his tie with a jerk.

"He had no intimates at all, so far as I know. I knew him as well as anybody. He rather liked Mrs. Livingstone, but he had no use for Livingstone himself."

"Well, I'll change the question. Do you know of any quarrel he had had, shortly before he died?"

"That's easier. He quarreled with a good many people. I imagine you know that as well as I do."

"He never mentioned to you that he had had a definite difference of opinion with anyone?"

Looking back to-night over that conversation, I am inclined to think that he had an answer for that question, and that he almost gave it. But he changed his mind. The purpose of his visit must have come to him, Greenough's story about the idiotic circle and my own lame explanation of it, and all the outrageous mess in which I had involved myself.

"I'd like to know why you ask me that," he said instead.

"He had never talked to you about calling

on the police, in some emergency?"

"Never. I see what you're driving at, Porter," he added. "I admit, I had some thought of that myself at the time. But the autopsy showed the cause of death all right. He wasn't murdered."

"The blow on the head had nothing to do with it, then?"

He glanced at me quickly.

"If it *was* a blow," he said, "it didn't help matters any, of course. But I prefer to think that the head injury was received as he fell." He hesitated. "Don't you?"

"Naturally," I agreed.

But there was a significance in that pause of his, followed by "don't you" which has stayed with me ever since. It was almost as though, in view of Greenough's visit to him and my own questions, I had been somehow responsible for the poor old boy's death, and was seeking reassurance. . . .

1:00 A.M. I am not able to sleep, and so, recipient of all my repressions, I come to you. I have repeated my little formula over and over, as some people count sheep. "Milton and Dryden and Pope." "Milton and Dryden and Pope," but without result. Yet I have seen whole class-rooms succumb to the soporific effect of that or some similar phrase in the early hours of a bright morning.

I have even been out, in dressing gown and slippers, and wandered a way down the main road, where I was surprised by a countryman with a truck load of produce and probably recognized. If any more sheep are killed to-night!

What am I to think about this red lamp business?

Into every situation it insistently intrudes itself. It was burning when old Horace died; I had turned it on in the closed and shuttered den the day I received that curious message about the letter; Jane lights it todevelop the pictures of the house for Larkin, and Nylie's sheep are killed. What is more, Jane sees a face, either outside the window or behind her in the pantry. From the moment of its entrance into the house, after eighteen years of quiet, the old stories of hauntings are revived, raps are heard, footsteps wander about, and furniture appears to move.

Is Greenough right, and am I ready for the psychopathic ward of some hospital? Is this accumulation of evidence actual, or have I imagined it? And yet I am sane enough, apparently. I listen, and I hear the familiar sounds of night-time here, Jock moving about uneasily in Jane's bedroom next to mine; the rhythmic creaking of the run-way to the float, as the wash of the tide swings it to and fro on its rollers. I hear no voices whispering. . . .

Yet Mrs. Livingstone was most explicit this afternoon. She clearly has no nerves, being complacent with the complacence of fat rapidly gained in middle age, and no imagination, or she would have taken lemon in her tea, and no sugar. But she sat there, ignoring little Livingstone's attempts to change the subject, and soberly warned me against renting the house.

Jane's face was a study. So far I had been able to keep from her much of the local gossip about the house, and all of the talk about the red lamp. But now she heard it all, garnished and embellished, and I caught her eyes fixed on me piteously.

"Is it too late, William?" she asked. "Must we rent it now?"

"It's all signed, sealed and delivered, my dear," I said. "But all is not lost. To-morrow morning I shall take my little hatchet and smash that lamp to kingdom come."

Mrs. Livingstone took a slice of cake.

"I'm sure you have my permission," she said, "and as I gave it to your Uncle Horace, I dare say I have a right to say so."

"Perhaps you would like to have it back?"

"God forbid!" she said quickly.

"Oh, for heaven's sake," Livingstone put in

irritably, "let's talk about something else. Mrs. Porter, will you show me your garden?"

I had a feeling that his wife had wanted just this, perhaps had given him some secret signal, for she settled back the moment they had gone and, so to speak, opened fire.

"You're not a spiritist, Mr. Porter?"

" 'I am a cynic; I am a carrion crow,' " I quoted. But I saw the words had no meaning for her. She may have felt some underlying amusement in them, however, for she stiffened somewhat, and rather abruptly changed her point of attack.

"I have often wondered," she said slowly, "whether you have ever considered your uncle's death as − unusual."

"You mean that you do?"

"Personally," she said, looking directly at me, "I think he was frightened to death." She hesitated. She gave me the impression of venturing on ground which was unpleasant to her. "Either that or −" She abandoned that, and began again, hurriedly.

"My husband dislikes the subject," she said. "But I will tell you why I believe what I do, and you can see what you can make of it. You remember that Mrs. Porter was not well when you both came out, the day he was found dead, and toward evening you took her home? Well,

100

Annie Cochran would not stay alone that night, and I stayed with her. It was very — curious."

"Just what do you mean by curious?"

"That there was somebody in the house that night, or something."

"And you don't believe it was somebody?"

"I don't know what I believe," she said, rather breathlessly. "I suppose, since you claim to be a cynic you will laugh, but I have to tell you just the same."

Stripping her narrative to the skeleton, she had been sceptical before, but that night the house had been strangely uncanny. They had sat in the kitchen with all the lights on, and at two o'clock in the morning she distinctly heard somebody walking in the hall overhead, on the second floor. Doors seemed to open and shut, and finally, on a crash from somewhere in the dining room, "like a doubled fist striking the table," Annie Cochran had bolted outside and stayed there. At dawn she came back, and said she had distinctly seen a ball of light floating in the room over the den, shortly after she went out.

"And was the red lamp lighted, while all this was going on?"

"That's one of the most curious things about it. It was not, when I made a round of that floor early in the evening. But it was going at dawn."

There is, of course, one thing I can do. I can meet Mr. Bethel when he arrives and lay my cards on the table. It will take all my courage; I know how I should feel if I had taken a house, and at the moment of my arrival a wild-eyed owner came to turn me away, on the ground that his house is haunted. Or, we will say, subject to inexplicable nocturnal visits. . . .

Shall I take Halliday into my confidence? I need a fresh brain on the matter, certainly. Someone who will see that the local connection of the murdered sheep with the red lamp, and so with old Horace's death, is the absurdity it must be.

July 4th.

A quiet Fourth, but in spite of all precautions, more sheep were killed last night, and in fear of my life I have been expecting a visit from Greenough this morning. But perhaps old Morrison — it looked like the Morrison truck — did not recognize me last night.

But to make things more unpleasant all around, the fellow this time did not leave his infernal chalk mark! One can imagine Greenough straightening from his investigation and deciding that his recent talk with me has put me on my guard. Heigh ho!

The neighborhood is in a wild state of alarm. The failure of the detective from town to stop the killings has probably added to the superstitious fears which seem mixed up in it. But the more intelligent farmers have got out their rifles and duck guns, and there will be short shrift for the fellow if he is seen at work.

Public opinion appears to be divided between a demon and a dangerous lunatic at large. . . .

Otherwise, I have recovered from last night's hysteria. The cleaning of the house for Mr. Bethel begins to-day, and I have decided to let it go on. If on hearing my story he decides not to stay no harm will be done; if he remains, it is in order for him.

Jane said at breakfast: "Are you letting him come, William?"

"I shall tell him all I know, my dear. After that it is up to him."

"But is it? Suppose something happens to him?"

"What on earth could happen?" I inquired irritably. "He doesn't need to light that silly lamp. Anyhow, I'm going to destroy it. And as for the other matter, the sheep, the fellow is sticking to sheep, thank God."

But I am not so certain, just now, as to destroying the lamp. This is the result of a conversation with Annie Cochran, as I admitted her, armed with broom and pail, to the house this morning.

She represents, I imagine, the lowest grade of local intelligence, and I daresay she is responsible for much of the superstitious fear of the lamp. But after all, her attitude represents that of a part of the community, and if I destroy the lamp I shall undoubtedly be held responsible for any local tragedies for the next lifetime or two.

In a word, Annie Cochran not only believes that the lamp houses a demon; she believes that to smash the lamp will liberate that demon in perpetuity.

Incredible? Yet who am I to laugh at this, who went a-running to Lear with a double-exposure photograph, and have been secretly annoyed that little Pettingill has never asked me to one of his table-tipping seances? Or who have, in deference to Annie Cochran and her kind, most carefully locked away the red lamp in an attic closet of the other house, there to contain its devil unreleased. Or who am, at this moment, somewhat oppressed by a so-called spirit message I have just received, forwarded to me by Cameron's secretary.

It is a difference of degree, not of kind.

This is my first letter from the spirit world, and it comes via Salem, Ohio! I have had a curious message or two, witness the unknown correspondent who for several years at intervals sent me a playing card in an envelope, so that it was nothing unusual for me to receive the deuce of spades with my bacon and eggs, or the knave of diamonds for tea. But this one stands in a class by itself.

It has, in Mr. Cameron's absence, been forwarded to me by his secretary.

"My dear Mr. Porter:

"In Mr. Cameron's absence on his vacation I am forwarding the enclosed message at the request of the writer, who appears to have considerable faith in our ability to locate the person for whom it is intended!

"We have had no previous correspondence with the young lady. At least I can find none in our files. But I know you will not mind my saying, in Mr. Cameron's absence, that he has always regarded these ouija board communications as purely subconscious in origin; in other words, as unconscious fraud."

The enclosed note is very long, and fully detailed. Even the arrangement of the furniture in the room is described, and the lighting of it.

How she came to omit a red lamp I cannot tell; I have somehow grown to expect one! But no amount of light handling of the matter on my part can alter the fact that I am not as comfortable about the thing as I might be. The damnable accuracy of it is in itself disconcerting. The name is right, even to my initial; I am living in a lodge, which even my own subconscious mind could hardly have anticipated a few days ago. And I am warned of danger, on a morning when I feel that danger is, as Edith would say, my middle name.

According to the writer, she and the other sitter, who she naively explains was her *fiancé*, received twice the name, William A. Porter. Assured then that they had it accurately, the "control" spelled out as follows:

"Advise you and Jane to go elsewhere. Lodge dangerous."

It sounds, I admit, like a telegraphic message, with one word to spare. One rather looks for the word "love," so often added to get full value for one's money. But it is a definite warning for all that.

So the Lodge is dangerous, and Jane and I advised to go elsewhere. Heaven knows I'd like nothing better. . . .

Our love story goes on, and I am as helpless there as in other directions; Edith proffering herself simply and sweetly, in a thousand small coquetries and as many unstudied allurements, and young Halliday gravely adoring her, and holding back.

To-day, along with the rest of the summer colony, they made a pilgrimage in the car to the scenes of the various meadow tragedies, ending up with the stone altar, and I suspect matters came very nearly to a head between them, for Edith was very talkative on their return, and Halliday very quiet and a trifle pale.

And to-night, sitting on the verandah of the boat-house, while the boy set off Roman candles and sky-rockets over the water, Edith asked me how I thought she could earn some money.

"Earn money?" I said. "What on earth for? I've never known you to think about money before."

"Well, I'm thinking about it now," she said briefly, and relapsed into silence, from which she roused in a moment or so to state that money was a pest, and if she were making a world she'd have none in it.

I found my position slightly delicate, but I ventured to suggest that no man worth his salt would care to have his wife support him. She ignored that completely, however, and said she was thinking of writing a book. A book, she said, would bring in a great deal of money, and "nobody would need to worry about anything."

"And you could get it published, Father William," she said. "Everybody knows who you are. And you could correct the spelling, couldn't you? That's the only thing that's really worrying me."

And I honestly believe the child is trying it. Her light is still going to-night as I can see under the door.

July 5th.

The Sheriff has offered a thousand dollars reward for the apprehension and conviction of the sheepkiller. A notice to that effect is neatly tacked on a post outside our gates, and must rather appeal to Greenough's sense of humor, if he has any. I understand Livingstone is privately offering another five hundred.

Mr. Bethel and his secretary arrive to-morrow, and the house is about ready for them, in spite of the fact that Annie Cochran moves about it, unoccupied as it is, like a scared rabbit. I shall see him at once on his arrival.

Halliday will finish the float to-day, and I understand intends then to start on the sloop. He has found a way to address me, instead of the formal "sir" of the first day or two, and now calls me skipper.

He is visibly more cheerful since yesterday. However hopeless the future looks, he must, during that "show-down" yesterday, as Edith would undoubtedly call it, have been fairly assured of her love for him. To-day I overheard a conversation between him and Clara.

"Well, I must be getting on," he said. "It's my wash day."

"Wash day, is it?" she commented sceptically. "I'd like to see your clothes after *you* wash them."

"Who said anything about clothes?" he demanded. "It's my dish-washing day. I always do them every Monday morning."

I watched him go down the drive, his head virtuously erect and Jock, who adores him, bidding him a reluctant good-bye. He will not follow him in that direction.

The boy wheedles Clara out of food, too, while Jane stands by and smiles. Passing the pantry window yesterday I saw him stop abruptly, and stare at the table inside.

"I beg your pardon, Clara," he said, "but are those *custard* pies?"

"They are. And you needn't be thinking——"

"Real, honest-to-goodness custard pies?"

"That's what the cook-book calls them."

"Would you mind if I came a little closer, Clara?" he inquired. "I have heard of them, but

109

it is so long since I have seen one, let alone tasted it———!"

"They're too fresh to cut," said Clara, weakening, one could see, by inches.

"But I could come back," he said gently. "I could go and sit in my lonely boat-house, surrounded by the cans I live out of, and think about them. And later I could come back, you know."

And although he did not come back, a half hour later I saw Clara carrying one down to him, neatly covered with a napkin.

To-day, for the first time, I have taken him fully into my confidence. I had been half way debating it, but the matter of the dressing gown decided it.

(Note: I find that in the original Journal I made no note of this incident. The facts are as follows):

At Jane's suggestion I proceeded to the main house, to remove such of Uncle Horace's clothing as remained in the closets and so on, to a trunk in the attic. Since the night of her experience in the pantry she had not entered the house. Armed with a package of moth-preventive, I was on my way when I met Halliday, and he returned with me.

We worked quietly, for there is something depressing in the emptiness of such garments, and in their mute reminder that sooner or later we must all shed the clothing that we call the flesh.

I said something of this and the boy gave me rather a twisted smile.

"It can't be so bad," he said. "Not worse than things are here sometimes, anyhow. And as Burroughs said — wasn't it Burroughs? — 'the dead do not lie in the grave, lamenting there is no immortality.' "

"Then you don't believe in immortality?"

"I don't know what I believe," he replied. "I know it isn't any use telling us we're going to be happy in the next world, to make up for our being darned miserable in this."

It was shortly after this that I located the dressing gown which poor old Horace was wearing when he was found, and discovered that there were blood-stains on it near the hem.

"I'm going to ask you something," I said to Halliday. "A man dies of heart failure, and as he falls strikes his head, so that it bleeds. He lies there, from some time in the evening until seven o'clock in the morning. There wouldn't be much blood, would there?"

"Hardly any, I should say."

"And none in this location, I imagine."

I showed it to him, and he looked at me curiously.

"I'm afraid I don't get it, Skipper," he said. "You mean, he moved, afterwards?"

"If you want to know exactly what I mean, I believe the poor old chap was knocked down, that he got up and managed to dispose of something he had in his hand, something he didn't want seen, and that *after that* his heart failed."

He picked up the dressing gown and carried it to the window.

"Tell me about it," he said quietly.

As neither one of us knows anything about the heart, or what occurs when a fatal seizure attacks it, it is possible Halliday is right. That is, that feeling ill he got up, crumpled the letter in his hand, turned out the desk light, and then fell. But that he recovered himself and managed to drag himself to his feet again, when the full force of the seizure came, and he fell once more, not to rise.

"There is no real reason to believe that he was not alone," he said. "Nor even that he 'saw something,' as Mrs. Livingstone intimates."

But the letter I found in the drawer interests him. He has made a copy of it, and taken it home to study.

"I appeal to you to consider the enormity of the idea. Your failure to comprehend my own attitude to it, however, makes me believe that you may be tempted to go on with it. In that case I shall feel it my duty, not only to go to the police but to warn society in general.

"I realize fully the unpleasantness of my own situation; even, if you are consistent, its danger. But————"

"But – what?" said Halliday. " 'But I shall do what I have threatened, if *you go on with it.*' " He glanced up at me. "It doesn't sound like sheep-killing, does it?"

"No," I was obliged to admit. "It does not."

July 6th.

I am in a fair way to go to jail if things keep on as they have been going! And not only for sheep-killing. If we have not had a tragedy here, certainly to-day there is every indication of it. And with the fatality which has attended me for the past week or so, I have managed to get myself involved in it.

Last night a youth named Carroway, sworn in by Starr a few days ago as deputy constable, was assigned the highroad behind our property as his beat. He was armed against the sheep-killer with a 30-30 Winchester, which was found this morning in the hedge not far from our gates.

Nothing is known of his movements from

nine o'clock, when he went on duty, until a few minutes after midnight, when he appeared breathless on the town slip, minus his rifle, and jumping into a motor launch moored at the float, started off into the bay.

Peter Geiss, an old fisherman, was smoking his pipe on the slip at the time, but Peter is deaf, and although Carroway shouted something the old man did not hear it. There is, however, an intermediate clue here, for on his way Carroway had run into the Bennett House, and told the night clerk there to awaken Greenough and get him to our float; that the sheep-killer had taken a boat there and was somewhere out on the water.

The deputy's idea was probably to drive the fugitive back to the shore, and as there are, due to the marshes, but few landing places there, he seems so far as I can make out to have figured that the unknown would be forced back to our slip.

Greenough appears to have lost no time. He threw an overcoat over his pajamas, took his revolver, and commandeering a car in the street, was on our pier before Carroway had been on the water ten minutes. And here, with that fatality which has recently pursued me, he found me returning from the float!

There are times when misfortune apparently

picks up some hapless individual as her victim and, perhaps for the good of his soul, hammers him on this side and on that until he himself begins to think he has deserved it. He is guilty of something; he knows not what.

I was a guilty man as I faced Greenough! And yet the scene must have had its elements of humor. I, rather shaken already with the night air, my teeth rattling, and this ghostly figure suddenly appearing on the run-way above me and turning my knees towater; a terror which only changed in quality when this ghost instructed me to put up my hands.

But I knew the voice, and I managed as debonair a manner as was possible under the circumstances.

"Nothing in them but a flash-light," I said. "However, if you insist——"

He seemed to hesitate. Then he laughed a little, not too pleasantly, and came down the run-way to me.

"Out rather late, aren't you, Mr. Porter?" he asked.

It was my turn to hesitate.

"I came down to pull the canoe up onto the float," I said finally. "Mrs. Porter thought the sea was rising."

"Sounds quiet enough to me," he retorted and turning on his flash, he ran it over the surface of the water, which was as still as a mill-pond, and onto the canoe, which lay bottom-up and still dripping, on the float.

It is indicative of the whole situation, I think, that he lighted the flash. He was no longer lurking in the dark, waiting for the motor boat to drive the marauder ashore. That marauder, in the shape of a shivering professor of English literature, slightly unbalanced mentally, was before him.

Then he seemed to be listening, and knowing the story this morning, I daresay he was listening, for the beat of the motor engine. There was no sound, and this I imagine puzzled him, as it is puzzling the entire community to-day. I am myself not particularly observant, and any testimony I might give would, under the circumstances, he discredited in advance. But my own impression is that there was the sound of an engine from somewhere on the bay as I crossed the lawn, and that it had ceased before I reached the water's edge.

Greenough was frankly puzzled. He had, one perceives, a problem on his hands. He wanted Carroway to come in and identify me, for without that identification he was helpless. And somewhere out on the water was Carroway, possibly with a stalled engine. He put his hands to his mouth and called:

"Hi! Bob!" he yelled. *"Bob."*

But there was no answer, except that Halliday came running out and asked what the trouble was. Greenough was thoroughly irritated; he lapsed into a sulky, watchful silence, and offered no objection when I shiveringly suggested that I go back to my bed. I left them both there, Halliday preparing to row out and locate the launch if possible, and came back to the Lodge.

This morning I learn that Carroway's boat was found by Greenough who had a fast launch with a searchlight, at one o'clock this morning, drifting out with the tide and about two miles from land. It was empty, and no sign of young Carroway was found. As it trailed no dory, our mystery has apparently become a tragedy.

And I am under suspicion. I have put that down, and sitting back have stared at it. It is true. And suppose what I am expecting at any moment takes place, and Greenough comes into the drive, to confront me with the damnable mass of evidence he has put together, the circle enclosing the triangle; the fact that the sheep-killing did not commence until after our arrival at the Lodge; the night Morrison, driving his truck-load of produce, saw me on the road; and most of all, with last night!

Suppose I tell him the actual fact? That my

wife has some curious power, and that in obedience to it she last night roused me from a virtuous sleep, to tell me she had clairvoyantly seen a man taking a boat from our float, and that I must immediately go down; that there was, she felt, something terribly wrong? Suppose I told him that, which is exactly the fact? And also that, once there, I found that Edith had left the canoe in the water, and that I had, like the careful individual I am, drawn it up out of harm's way? Will he believe that? I wonder———

Quite aside from my unwillingness to drag Jane into this, particularly as the possessor of a faculty which she herself only reluctantly reveals even to me, is my conviction that such a story, soberly told, would only increase Greenough's suspicion of my sanity.

And as if to add to the precariousness of the situation, Halliday himself in all innocence has added another damning factor; gave it, indeed, to the detective last night.

Yesterday, it appears, in repairing the float, he found a new and razor-sharp knife between the top of one of the barrels and the planks which made the flooring.

"I didn't tell you, Skipper," he says, "because I was afraid of alarming you. And, of course, there might have been some simple explanation. Starr might have dropped it, during his carpentering."

He was first amused and then infuriated by the web which seems to be closing around me.

"Of course they can't do anything," he says, "unless they catch you in the act."

But the unconscious humor of that statement set me laughing, and after a moment he saw it and grinned sheepishly. "You know what I mean," he said. "And in one way, if you can stand it, it's not a bad thing."

Pressed for an explanation, it appears that he had been thinking of going after the reward himself, and that this matter of Carroway has decided him.

"Reward or no reward," he said, quietly, "I've had a bit of training; they put me in the Intelligence in Germany, during the occupation. And of course the way to catch a criminal is to keep him from knowing who's after him. Then again, if he learns the police are watching you — and he may — he's watching *them*, you know — it may make him a bit reckless. You never can tell."

But he has a third reason, although he has not mentioned it. He is chivalrously determined to protect me, and through me, Edith.

July 7th.

Another day has gone by, and I am still at large.

119

Free, I suppose in order that I may eventually again sally forth, some dark night, with my piece of chalk and another knife — for has not Greenough my original one? — to kill more sheep; if indeed there be any remaining for slaughter; or to stab and throw overboard another hapless boatman.

To save my life, I cannot prevent my absurd situation from coloring my actions. I constantly remind myself of the centipede which, on being asked how it used its many legs, became suddenly conscious of them and fell over into the ditch.

For example, at breakfast this morning I gravely poured some coffee into Jock's saucer, instead of the left-over cream from the breakfast table. And Edith caught me in the act.

"Nobody home," she announced. "Poor old dear, so nice and once so intelligent! It is sad," she said to Jane, "to see his mind failing by inches. But his heart is all right. If the worst comes to the worst———"

"Don't talk about my mind," I snapped, and then was sorry for it. "I don't feel humorous at breakfast, my dear," I said. "I'm sorry."

But the plain truth is that I am sadly upset. Even what before seemed a plain and obvious duty, to go to the other house to-night and tell

Mr. Bethel on his arrival the exact situation, has been all day a matter for most anxious thought. It had seemed quite simple before. I would say to him: "Sir, I have rented you this house. True, I warned your secretary of certain unpleasant qualities it is supposed to have, but I must also warn you. The building is reported to be haunted. I do not believe this, nor I daresay will you, but I feel that I must tell you."

Or again:

"There is also a popular − or unpopular − idea that some recent sheep-killings around the vicinity are somehow connected with this haunting. The police do not think so, but the more ignorant of the natives do. If this alarms you, I am prepared to pay back your money to you."

Not quite in this fashion but with a similar candor, I have been prepared to clarify my relations with my new tenant. But now what happens? Will Greenough, for instance, credit my entire disinterestedness? Will he not rather believe that I have given but one more evidence of my essential lunacy? Would I not myself, only a few weeks ago, have distrusted any indivdual who came to me with such a tale?

After all, I have told young Gordon. At least I have that to my comfort if anything happens.

But what am I writing? What can happen? "It is sad," says Edith cheerfully, "to see his mind failing him by inches." Perhaps it is. . . .

I have seen Bethel, and I have not told him. He gives me every impression, in spite of his infirmity, of being able to look after himself, and after to-night's experience he is welcome to do so. Let him have his raps and his footsteps; let him find his tea-kettle on the floor, and his faces in the pantry. Let him freeze in cold airs or stew in his own juice. I have done my part.

His car drove in at eight-thirty, and I followed it along the drive. True to her agreement, Annie Cochran had only waited until seven and then had taken a firm departure, and I daresay this threw him into the execrable temper in which I found him. The secretary had assisted him into the house, and I found him in the library, with only one lamp going, huddled in a chair among a clutter of wraps, and introduced myself. He barely acknowledged it.

"Where the devil's the servant?" he barked at me. "I thought there was a woman, or somebody."

"There is a very good woman," I said, "but she goes home before dark. That is," I corrected myself, "she leaves early. I told your secretary that."

122

"Do you suppose she's left a fire? Gordon!" he called. "Go and see if there's a fire. I want some hot water."

He fumbled in a pocket and brought out what I fancy was a beef cube or some similar concoction, and sat with it in his hand.

"Which way does the house face?" he asked, suddenly.

"East. Toward the bay."

"Then I want a back room. Don't like the morning sun. Don't like anything in the morning," he added, and peered up at me through his spectacles.

Young Gordon returned then with a cup of hot water and a spoon, and Mr. Bethel favored me with little or no further attention. He has but one usable hand, and the secretary held the cup while he stirred the tablet in it. Only once did he favor me with direct speech during this proceeding. He glanced up as I stood — he had not asked me to sit down — and said:

"Been having some sheep-killing around here lately, haven't you?"

I may have flushed slightly, but I doubt if he could see it, although his eyes were on me. "Yes," I admitted.

"Saw it in the papers," he said, and went back to his broth.

Then if ever was my time to plunge, but to

save my life I could not do it. That truculent, childish old man, one leg stretched out before him in the relaxation of partial paralysis, one hand contracted in his lap with the tonic spasm of his condition, taking soup under the direction of a pasty-faced boy who grinned at me above his white head, was no recipient of such information as I had to give. And he allowed me no further opportunity; the cup empty, he indicated that he wished to go upstairs, and with a nod in my direction he shuffled out, Gordon supporting him on the infirm side.

I had had some notion of offering my assistance, but I felt that this recognition of his condition would only annoy him; obvious as it was, he had not mentioned it to me, and I guessed that it was a cross borne not only without fortitude, but with a continuing resentment. I followed them to the foot of the stairs however, and part way up, pausing for breath, he must have suspected my presence there for he turned and looked down.

"What do you think is behind this sheep-killing?" he said. Just that. Not good-night. Nothing whatever about the house; nothing about my presence or my approaching departure. "Who's killed them?" he rasped.

"Some maniac, probably."

"A maniac!" he barked, and steadying himself

by Gordon, twisted around so he could see me the better. "Religious tomfoolery, eh? The Blood of the Lamb!"

He cackled drily, staring down at me. Then he turned, without another word, and went on up and out of my sight.

July 8th.

On Halliday's advice, I am not leaving the property, and whenever it is humanly possible, I am in sight of Thomas. Thus to-day I have been weeding Jane's flower beds for her, and with the garage doors open have been ostentatiously oiling the car. To-night, too, I have drawn the table in my room to the window and am there making this day's entry, in full view of any observer who chances to take any interest in my movements.

I am, I am convinced, under espionage. Old Thomas is too frequently in view, as he patters round his day-light tasks, and to-night I have a distinct impression that some observer who takes an interest in my movements is outside, watching my window. Jock believes this also. He is restless, moving from the passage into my room and back again, and twice, standing near me, the short ruff on the back of his neck has risen. . . .

Halliday brought me to-day further details about Carroway's disappearance:

"The hotel clerk ran down to the piers," he says, "and he heard the engine going for some time. The boat didn't start up the beach, but out into the bay, as if Carroway felt the other man had a good start of him, and was trying to cross the bay. Then he either lost the sound of the engine, or it stopped.

"He waited on the slip for a half hour or so and then went back to the hotel. Greenough came in about that time and called up Starr, and they went together to the town slip. But Carroway hadn't shown up, and after a time Greenough decided to go out after him.

"They found the boat pretty well out in the bay — the tide was going out — and empty. They looked around, as well as they could, then Starr got into it and brought it back. But here's the part they're not telling: Peter Geiss says Greenough got some waste and wiped something off the top of the engine box."

"He didn't see what it was?"

"They wouldn't let him near the boat, but he says it was the circle again."

Of any other details there are apparently none. Bob Carroway has apparently gone the way of all flesh, poor lad. And while Greenough or some emissary of his watches me from my own drive, the murderer is perhaps concocting some further deviltry.

In the meantime a veritable panic has, according to Halliday, seized the country-side, and of this we have certain evidence ourselves. The road beyond the Lodge gates, usually a procession of twin lights, is to-night dark and silent. No motor boats with returning picnic parties rumble across the water, throwing us now and then a bit of song. The fishermen, starting out at three in the morning, are going armed and in fear of their lives. And each man suspects the other.

My own position is as unpleasant as possible. To-day Jane said to me:

"I wish you would get a meat knife in Oakville to-day, William."

"What do you mean by a meat knife?"

"Just a good sharp knife," she said, "with a long blade."

"My dear," I said, "anyone buying such a knife in Oakville to-day would be put into jail at once. Personally, I need razor blades, but I shall grow a beard like the sloop's before I purchase any."

"You could send for one, in town."

And I could not tell her that such a proceeding would be even worse than the other.

Jane's own attitude these days is curious. She

is quite convinced, for instance, that she had a premonition of Carroway's death the night she sent me to the slip. As she has no idea that this premonition of hers may be most unpleasant in its consequences to me, to-day I got her to talk about it.

"Just how did it come?"

"I don't know. I had been asleep, I think. Yes, I know I had. I wakened, anyhow, and I seemed to be looking at the slip. There was somebody there, kneeling."

"Kneeling? Saying his prayers, you mean?" with a recollection of the altar.

"I think he was feeling for something, under the float."

There is a certain circumstantial quality to this, one must admit. He had been seen and was being followed, and his knife for some reason was still where he had left it. Or rather, it was not there, since Halliday had that day found it and taken it away. Had it not been for that, poor Carroway might have met his end there on our slip, and not later. But the knife was gone, and there was nothing left but flight.

Just where that flight began no one can say. It seems incredible that he had left his boat moored directly below our boat-house, with Halliday so close at hand. It seems more likely that he ran up the beach a way, and that —

well, *de mortuis nil nisi bonum.* Perhaps I am wrong, but it seems to me that Carroway could more easily have followed him by one of the row-boats from our slip, than follow the method he did, with the loss of time involved.

Still, I myself would not have started out unarmed after a killer, even of sheep, unless I had first raised the alarm and was fairly sure of assistance to follow.

"But I don't see," I said to Jane, "why you felt that there was anything ominous in this dream of yours, or whatever it was."

"I never have them without a reason."

"But that night when you so unjustly accused me of holding up the chapel wall————"

"There was a reason there," she said, coldly. "I thought it quite likely I might have to go and get you."

There may be one comfort to the superstitious in all this; not once, since the night when we lighted the red lamp in the pantry, has it————

Midnight: I have just had rather a curious experience, and I am still considerably shaken.

I had no more than written the above words when I glanced out the window, and distinctly saw a small red light through the window of the den in the main house.

My first thought, so certain was I that the

lamp was carefully hidden in the attic, was of fire. Long before I had seen Mr. Bethel's light, in the room above it, go out, and soon after that young Gordon's had been likewise extinguished.

I went quickly to my window and leaned out. So dark is the night that it hangs outside like an opaque curtain, and as the light almost immediately disappeared, I was left staring into this void, when suddenly Jock on the staircase landing gave vent to an unearthly howl.

The next moment I heard, under the trees and toward the house, the short dry cough of cardiac asthma, and smelled the queer unmistakable odor of Uncle Horace's herbal cigarette.

I have reasoned with myself for the last ten minutes or so. All the evidence is against me; Greenough may be watching me, or having me watched, and some poor devil out under the trees is suffering from the night air. Or old Mr. Bethel, unable to sleep, has somehow dragged himself out for a midnight airing under the trees.

But I saw the lamp. And it is locked in the attic. I myself put it there, and at this moment have the key.

July 9th.

I made an excuse this morning to Annie

Cochran, and she slipped me up the kitchen staircase of the other house and so to the attic. The lamp was as I had left it and the closet locked, and to-day I am asking myself whether, with that curious lack of perspective one finds at night, I did not see instead of the lamp far away, the lighted end of a cigar close at hand.

Annie's report on my tenants is satisfactory on the whole. She doesn't much care for the secretary, but the old man's "bark is worse than his bite." He comes down in the morning, or is helped down, to his breakfast, and she cuts his food for him — he seems to dislike the boy's doing it — reads the paper and then goes to work.

"To work?" I asked. "What sort of work?"

"He's writing a book."

But it appears that he is writing it only in the non-literal sense. He is dictating a book. And it also appears that he has chosen this place because of its isolation, and Annie's orders are that he receives no visitors.

But it also appears that young Gordon is perhaps not as courageous as he made out to me when he came to look over the house, and that he has been "hearing things."

"What sort of things?"

"He didn't say. But he asked me this morning if I'd been in the house last night. 'If you find me here at night, it'll be because I'm paralyzed and can't move,' I said, 'and if you take my advice, you'll not go around hunting if you hear anything.' "

"That must have cheered him considerably."

"I don't know about that. He just looked at me and said, 'What's the game, anyhow? I'll bet a dollar you're in on it.' "

Edith has sprung a surprise on us all. I have noticed for a day or two that she has been taking a keen interest in the mail; yet Edith's mail, with Halliday here, is largely a matter of delicate paper and the large square hand-writing of the modern young woman, and has dealt this summer largely with reports on house-parties, summer resorts, and various young men who seem recognizable to her under such cognomens as Chick, Bud and Curley.

This morning, however her mail included a business-like envelope, and she flung the white, rose and mauve heap aside and pounced on it. A moment later she got up and coming around the table to me, gravely kissed that portion of my head which is gradually emerging, like a shore on an ebb tide, from my hair.

"As one literary artist to another," she said, "I salute you." And placed before me a check for twenty dollars.

She has written a feature article on our

sheep-killing, and has sold it.

"And it took me only two hours," she says triumphantly. After that she was rather silent, computing I dare say how much she can earn, giving four hours a day to it for six days a week. At the rate, then, of ten thousand a year!

"Considerably more than I receive, Edith," I said gravely, and I saw I had been right by the way she started.

She set off at once for the boat-house, but came back later considerably crestfallen, and poured out her troubles to me.

"If he had anything he would give it to me," she wailed. "If I can write and make money———"

"You can't fight the masculine instinct, my dear, to support its woman; not be kept by her."

"And wait for years and years to do it!" she said. "The best years of our lives going by, and — nothing."

"Besides, have you considered this? You will not always find subjects as salable as this one has been."

"Subjects!" she said scornfully. "Why, this place is full of them."

The result of which has been on my part all day an uneasy apprehension as to what she will choose next. Nor am I made easier by a question she asked me just before dinner.

"What became of the Riggs woman?" she asked. "Do you suppose she's still around here?"

"I imagine not. Why?"

"I just wondered," she said, and wandered to that particular corner of the verandah from which she has a distant but apparently satisfactory view of the boat-house. . . .

Perhaps Halliday is right. (Note: In his suggestion that Jane and I take the sloop and go down the coast for a few days.) If any sheep are killed in my absence, or anything more serious should happen, it will serve to rout Greenough's absurd determination to involve me, and provide a complete alibi. At the same time, it will be rest and recreation for Jane, and it may put me in a better frame of mind.

Peter Geiss, he thinks, would go with us as captain and bunk under a pup tent, leaving the cabin to Jane and myself.

(On board the sloop) July 10th. Amazing, the celerity with which youth thinks and acts. To-night Jane and I — and Peter Geiss — are rolling gently to our anchor in Bass Cove, close enough in to be quiet and far enough out to escape the mosquitos. And yet only yesterday the plan was an amorphous thing, floating in the air between Halliday and myself, a mere ghost

of an idea, without material substance.

I am glad to sit in my wicker chair, this Journal on my knee, and rest my body. I have indeed earned my night's repose. Now and then I reach out a languid hand and touch a fishing line, one end of which is tied to the arm of my chair, the other extending into those mysterious depths from which I hope to lure to-morrow's breakfast.

The sloop is tidy. Is even fairly sea-worthy. Her bottom has to-day been scrubbed with a broom, and her sails, slightly mildewed, still present from a distance a certain impressiveness.

"What," I shout at Peter Geiss, "is that small sail in front? Forward, I mean."

"How's that?"

"The sail there, what's its name?" I say, pointing. "*Name?*"

"I'll say it's a shame," he says. "Canvas on this boat cost the old gentleman a lot of money."

By and by, however, I learn the jib and the flying jib. Also that sea water is an unsatisfactory cleansing medium, as witness the supper dishes.

"Why," I demand of Jane, "did Nausicaä wash her garments in the sea, when there was a river at hand?"

"I haven't an idea," she says absently, her eyes

on her alcohol cooking stove. "They weren't overly clean in those days, were they?"

But I think my dear Jane is exceedingly uncertain as to just what days were those of Nausicaä.

We have a small cabin, with four bunks in it, and two of these are now neatly and geometrically made up, ready for the night. In Jane's small closet there is food of all sorts, neat rows of tins and wax-paper packages. If we are washed out to sea we can, I imagine, live indefinitely on deviled ham, sardines and cheese. And I have always my fishing line.

Ah! a tug at it!

July 11th.

I have been playing solitaire to-day, as a cover for my thoughts. For this, I take it, is the great virtue of solitaire, that it insures against frivolous interruption, while at the same time leaving the mind free to wander where it will.

My worries are dropping from me. Helena Lear is with Edith, and no doubt Halliday is camped on their doorstep, as vigilant as a watch dog, and certainly more dependable than Jock. I can see, too, with better perspective how absurd my anxiety has been as to Greenough. It is his business to believe every man guilty until he has proved himself innocent. And am I not now in the act of proving my innocence?

But my problem remains. And trying to solve it is like playing solitaire with a card missing. I have, we will say, lost the knave of clubs out of my pack, and without it the game cannot go on.

Halliday, I know, believes that there is a possible connection between the killer and Uncle Horace's letter. He believes, in other words, that some curious and perhaps monstrous idea lies behind the sheep-killing, and that it may be the same idea to which the letter refers.

"There is something behind it," he asserts. "Something so vital to the man who believes it that he is ready to kill — has killed certainly once and possibly twice — to protect it."

But the nature of the idea, or conviction, he nobly evades.

"And this monstrous idea was to kill sheep, and build a stone altar?"

"How do we know that isn't merely a propitiatory sacrifice, Skipper? A sort of preliminary to the real thing?"

"And what is to be the real thing?"

"What is the wickedest crime you can name, against society?"

"The taking of human life."

"Exactly."

But this, as he says, is as far as he goes. He is,

however, careful to say that his theory has got him somewhere; that is, that there is a definite idea behind what has been happening.

"An insane one, then."

"Not necessarily," he objects. "Your Uncle Horace didn't write that letter to a man he considered insane." . . .

Peter Geiss has his own theory about poor Carroway's death. Carroway, he says, probably located the boat; he could do that by cutting off his engine and listening for the oars. Then, in black darkness, he steered toward it, probably with the idea of driving the fellow back. But Peter does not think that Carroway would have closed in on the murderer, unarmed as he was.

"The chances are," he said to-day, "that the fellow crept up on him, quiet-like, and leaped into the launch."

"But he was unarmed, too," I said remembering the knife under our slip.

It seemed to me that Peter not only heard that with surprising distinctness, but that he shot a stealthy glance at me.

"He had an oar," he said, and fell back into his customary taciturnity.

The nights are wonderful. I have brought my mattress out of the cabin, and shall sleep to-night face up to the stars. We are anchored in Pirate Harbor, that small enclosed anchorage the shore of which has been so frequently dug for treasure that it is pitted like a pock-marked face.

In our fore-rigging hangs our riding light. It should be white, but as in a burst of energy this evening I scraped a supper plate over the side, I also scraped off the lanter. So it is red, our red sailing light. It reminds me of the lamp at home. I thbink about light in general. What do I know about light, anyhow? That it is a wave, a vibration, and that only within a certain fixed range can it be perceived by my human sensorium; that, below the infra-red, and above the ultra-violet, are waves our human eye cannot perceive. Then, all around us are things to which our human senses do not react. How far dare I extend that? From invisible things to invisible beings is not so far, I dare say.

What is reality and what is not? Only what we can see, hear, touch or taste? But that is absurd. Thought is a reality, perhaps the only reality.

But can thought exist independent of the body? The spiritists believe it can. And un doubtedly the universe is full of unheard sounds; all the noises in the world go echoing around our unhearing ears for centuries, and then comes the radio and begins to pick them up for us.

But the radio requires a peculiar sort of receiving instrument, and so with the sights and sounds beyond our normal ken. Jane may be such an instrument. So for all I know may be Peter Geiss, snoring in his pup tent. Even myself———

(Note: I fell asleep here, and the entry is incomplete.)

July 12th.

Just what did Peter Geiss see last night?

If I were asked to name, in order of their psychic quality, the three persons on this boat, I would put Jane first and Peter last.

He is a materialist. Not for him the interesting abstractions, the controversial problems of the universe. The life of the mind, the questions of the soul, are hidden from him. His food, his tobacco, the direction of the wind, the state of the tide, these cover the field of his speculations and anxieties. And yet – Peter saw something last night.

It was about one o'clock in the morning, and he had wakened and crawled out of his pup tent, with, according to him "the feeling that we were in for a blow. There was a cold wind across my feet."

So he rose, and he saw that our red lantern

140

was burning low, and gingerly stepping across me, reached into a locker for the oil can. When he straighted up he saw a shadowy figure standing in the bow of the boat, directly under the lantern.

He thought at first that it was I, but the next moment he had stumbled across me as I lay supine, and the oil can fell and went a-rolling. The noise did not disturb the figure, and Peter gave a long look at it before he howled like a hyena and brought me up all standing.

It was only then that it disappeared. "Just blew to windward," according to Peter. I never saw it at all.

Peter did not go to bed again all night, but sat huddled by the wheel, staring forward, a queer old figure of terror without hope. And I admit I was not much better.

For Peter says that it was that of a man in a dressing gown, and that "it looked like the old gentleman." By which he means my Uncle Horace.

July 13th.

Ellis Landing.

We have had bad news, and are preparing to land and take a motor back.

Edith wires that Halliday has been hurt.

141

She gives no details.

Halliday's condition is not critical, thank God.

We found him (Note: in my bedroom here at the Lodge) with Edith and Helena fussing over him, and with his collar bone broken, the result, not of the attack but of his ditching the car.

For he is the indirect victim of an attack.

On the evening of the 12th he was on his way to the station at Oakville to meet Helena Lear and Edith, who were in town on some mysterious feminine errand which detained them until the late train.

At eleven o'clock, then, he took the car and started off, and as he was early took the longer route through the back country. The one by Sanger's Mill and the Livingstone place. It was near the drive into Livingstones' that a man carrying a sawed-off shot-gun stopped the car and asked for a lift into town. He was, he said, one of Starr's special deputies, watching for the sheep-killer.

It was very dark, and he could only see the outlines of the deputy. But as, all along, he had come across men similarly armed — "The fence corners were full of them," he says — he thought nothing of it, and told the fellow to jump in.

"I hadn't seen him," he said, "but I got an impression of him. You know what I mean. A heavy square type, and he got into the car like that, slowly and deliberately. I think he had a cigar in his mouth, not lighted; he talked like it, anyhow."

Once in the car the man was taciturn. Halliday spoke once or twice, and got only a sort of grunt in reply, and finally he began to be uneasy. He had, he says, the feeling that the fellow's whole body was taut, and that his silence was covering some sort of stealthy motion, "or something," he adds, rather vaguely.

"And of course he had his gun. Lying across his knees as well as I could make out."

They had gone about a mile by that time, and then Halliday began to smell a queer odor.

"He was not trying to anaesthetize me," he is certain. "He'd had it in his pocket, and something had gone wrong; the cork came out, perhaps. Anyhow, all at once it struck me that ether was a queer thing for one of Starr's deputies to be carrying, and I felt I was in for trouble."

He took his left hand quietly from the steering wheel, and began to fumble in the left hand pocket of the car, where he had put his revolver. And although he is confident he made no sound, the fellow must have had ears like a bat, for just then Halliday saw him raise the gun, and as he ducked forward the barrel of it hit the seat back behind him with a sickening thud.

But he had somehow turned the wheel of the car, and the next moment it had left the road. Halliday made a clutch at it, but it was too late; he saw, as the car swung, the lights of another car ahead and coming toward them; then they struck a fence, and the machine turned over.

He had been found, by the people in the other car, unconscious in the wreckage, and brought to the Lodge. No sign of the other man was discovered.

But this story, curious and ominous as it is, is as nothing to my sensations to-day when I visited my small garage, where my car is awaiting insurance adjustment before undergoing repairs.

The point of the matter is this: Greenough has already been to see our invalid, and has assured him that he has been the victim of an ordinary attempt at a hold-up.

"Only difference is," he told Halliday, "that our men around with weapons gave the fellow a chance to carry his gun openly. Gave him a good excuse for a lift, too. Most people around here now aren't stopping their cars for anything or anybody. But of course they'd pick up a deputy."

"I'm not as familiar with crime as you are," Halliday had responded. "But is ether part of the modern hold-up outfit?"

"It's pretty hard to name off-hand anything they don't use," said Greenough, imperturbably. "From silk stockings up."

Which was, I imagine, a bit of unconscious humor.

So Greenough dismisses the possibility of any connection between Halliday's trouble and the unknown malefactor; in a word, my absence has probably not altered his suspicion of me a particle. Or had not, for within the next half hour I propose to show him that an absolute connection exists between the two.

On the right-hand cushion of my car, which during the salvaging of it was thrown upside down into the rear, there is marked an infinitesimal circle in chalk, enclosing a crude triangle. I have sent for Greenough. . . .

Later: Truly the way of the innocent is hard.

Dr. Hayward was making his afternoon call on Halliday when the detective came, and as I feel confident that the doctor is in Greenough's confidence I was glad to spring my little bombshell on them both at the same time. But to-night I am feeling much like Bunyan's Man in an Iron Cage. "I am now a man of despair, and am shut up in it."

Edith was on the verandah when the detective came, and young Gordon was with her. During our absence he has struck up with her an acquaintance of sorts, but she dislikes him extremely. She has, Jane tells me, nick-named him Shifty.

As Hayward was still upstairs, I sparred politely with Greenough for a few minutes. We had had good weather for the trip; fishing was only fair. It was too bad to be brought back as we were. Yes, but if things like that were going on, it was better to be on the ground. "What sort of things?" he asked.

"We have had two murderous attacks, haven't we? One successful, and one not."

"So you class this little affair of young Halliday's with the other?"

"Don't you?"

"Not until I've got something that ties them together, Mr. Porter."

Hayward had come in and stood inside the doorway, gnawing at his fingers and listening.

"But if you found something *did* tie them together?"

"For instance?"

"I'm going to ask you something. Was there

or was there not something drawn on the top of the engine box of the boat from which Carroway disappeared?"

"How do you know that?" he shot at me. And like a fool I said, thinking to protect Peter Geiss: "That doesn't matter, does it? It's the fact I'm after."

"Suppose there were. What would that prove?"

"And suppose I can show you another, and similar mark on my car, made there by Halliday's assailant before he struck at him?"

It was then that Greenough smiled horribly, damnably.

"It's there, is it?" he said, and looked up at Hayward.

"It is there."

He got up, the remains of that smile still plastered on his face, and confronted me.

"That's curious," he said. "I examined that car in the ditch, before they moved it, Mr. Porter. And I've been over it here with the doctor, since. If there's anything there of the sort you describe, it's been put there since yesterday afternoon."

And then I saw where I stood. They believed that, finding Halliday assaulted during my absence, I was attempting to link that assault with the sheep-killing and with Carroway's death, and turn it to my own advantage. In other words, to prove that the reign of terror had gone on in my absence!

A drowning man, swimming exhaustedly toward a log which sinks when he touches it, must have much the same sensation that I had, as I stood there facing Greenough's vile smile and the doctor's searching gaze.

"You can go out and look," I said feebly. "It's there."

I did not go with them. I heard Edith and Gordon follow them out, and then I sat down and faced my situation.

And indeed it has passed the point of philosophical endurance. Even if Carroway's body is not found and no charge of murder can be brought, it is not hard to see what power lies in this detective's hands, backed by his conviction of my guilt. He may not imprison me, but he can cost me my reputation, even my position in the university. He can hound me out of the only life I know and am fitted for, the warm place behind the drain pipe.

It is well enough for Halliday to say that we can assume a counter-offensive. When? With him temporarily crippled, and every act of mine watched and questioned? And, even with all other things equal, how?

Nor do I see, as he does, any possible clue in

young Gordon finding the chalk with which the drawing was done, behind the lawn-roller in the garage, a fact which Edith reported after Hayward and Greenough had gone, or in the scrap of paper in which it was wrapped when found. For one thing, Edith's memory as to what was on the paper may be at fault. Naturally, not knowing my situation, she would observe it only casually.

According to Clara, the only persons visiting the car after it was brought back yesterday morning were Annie Cochran and Thomas, who were there when it was returned; Greenough, who spent some time there while the doctor made his call on Halliday, the doctor himself, who wandered in later to look at it; young Gordon, who she says showed particular interest in it and a sort of ghoulish amusement, and the Livingstones. Or rather, Livingstone only, who appears to have stood in the doorway smoking and surveying it while his wife carried up to the invalid a jar of jellied broth.

But as the garage door was unlocked all night, such speculation is purely futile.

Edith suggests malicious mischief.

"The village children are chalking up circles with triangles all over the fences," she says, "and old Starr came out here yesterday with one between his shoulders. He almost had a stroke when I told him."

Her explanation of the paper found about the chalk and what was on it is equally simple. That in itself, she concludes, proves her contention: "It looked as if children had been playing with a typewriter," she says. And she has reproduced it from memory, as nearly as possible, Greenough having carried it off with him.

It was done, she says, on a typewriter in a curious jumble of capitals and small letters, and the paper was perforated at the side, as if it were from a loose-leaf note-book. Also, it had been torn, so that only a portion of the typing remained.

This portion was, according to her, as follows:

GeLTr, K. 28.

(Note: As will be seen, Edith's memory was extremely good. She made only one error in the ciper. The final number, 28, should, of course, have been 24.)

To-night I have had a long talk with Halliday. It appears that the time of Peter Geiss's apparition, almost exactly coincides with the attack. This, however, does not impress Halliday as it does me.

"You have to remember, Skipper," he says, "that old Geiss has been scared almost out of his wits the last few weeks. And the Carroway affair has carried the terror right out onto his domain, which is the water."

"Then why didn't he see Carroway?"

"Search me," he said, with a shrug that set him wincing. "What's bothering me is why doesn't anybody see Carroway? Eight days, and no body found yet."

When I left him a few minutes ago, he had Edith's memory copy of the paper found in the garage, and was propped up in bed with a pencil.

"If we had the original we'd be better off," he said. "It oughtn't be to hard to find the typewriter in the vicinity that wrote it. And if Greenough isn't crazy with the heat he's looking for it now."

I glanced at my own portable machine, sitting on the table, and he followed my eyes and smiled.

"You've got your best alibi right there," he said, "if this turns out to be a cipher. And I think it is."

He has, it appears, some small knowledge of ciphers, and from the mixture of capitals and small letters he believes he recognizes this one. But it requires a key word, or two key words.

"Even without it," he says, "it could be solved, possibly, if I had enough of it. But with only this scrap —! And I don't get the number added to it."

The idea of this type of cipher, I gather, is to take a word, or two words, containing thirteen letters of the alphabet, no one used twice. Written first in small or lower case size these letters represent the first thirteen letters of the alphabet. The same word or words repeated in capitals becomes the second half of the alphabet.

Thus the words "subnormal diet" become a key in this fashion:

```
subnormaldiet   SUBNORMALDIET
abcdefghijklm   nopqrstuvwxyz
```

But as "subnormal diet" was the only key phrase we could think of, and as it obviously did not fit, I left him still biting the end of his pencil, and came to complete this record. . . .

Renan said that the man who has time to keep a private diary has never understood the immensity of the universe. But I reply to Renan that the man in my position, who does not keep a private diary and thus let off his surplus thoughts, is liable to burst into minute fragments and scatter over the said immensity of the universe!

Sunday, July 15th.
The one pleasure that never palls is the pleasure

of not going to church. . . .

Again, as I recorded once before, a quiet morning and I am still at large. Jane has gone. Sometimes I suspect Jane of throwing a sop to Providence in this matter of church-going; almost, one might say, of bargaining with the Almighty. "I will do thus and so," says Jane to herself, "and in return I have a right to ask thus and so."

Yet she asks little enough; a quiet life, peace, and if not active happiness, that resignation which after the hot days of youth are over, passes for contentment. And as she went out this morning, demurely dressed in the Sabbatical restraint which is a part of her bargain, I felt rather than said a small prayer for her; that she who asks so little may keep what she has.

And Jane is worried. She knows nothing, but she suspects everything. By that, I mean that she is somehow aware, after her own curious fashion, that there is something wrong with her world. She watches me, when I am not looking at her. She has an odd, rather furtive, dislike of Doctor Hayward. And she is almost criminally forwarding Edith's love affair.

Since Halliday was brought here Jane and I have shared her bedroom, and this morning, buttoning my collar, I said:

"The sooner that boy gets back to the boathouse, the better."

"Why?" she demanded, almost militantly.

"Well, if you can't see what's going on under your eyes, my dear———"

"I don't see why it shouldn't go on. There's not too much love in the world."

"Nor enough bread and cheese."

"We didn't have very much when we started, William," she said, looking up at me wistfully.

"And we haven't much more now," I said, and kissed her.

But the plain truth is that Jane's nerves are shaken. She wants Edith settled; she would like nothing better than a speedy marriage, if that would take us back to the city at once. All her old hatred and distrust of this place have been steadily reviving, and the attack on Halliday has about eaten away her resistance.

All life is the resistance of an undiscoverable principle against unceasing forces. And my poor Jane, after years of protected life, is only discovering those unceasing forces. . . .

Later: Poor Carroway's body has been found. The tide was unusually low at two this afternoon and a yawl from Bass Cove, crossing the bay, saw it floating face down, and recovered it, not without difficulty. The poor lad had been tied with the end of an anchor rope, and the anchor thrown over with him. Thus for days the body has been only a few feet beneath the surface, floating at the end of its tragic tether.

From the doctor, making his afternoon call here, we heard the details. He was summoned as soon as the body was brought in, and made a hasty examination. From that it appears that Carroway was beaten over the head first and then thrown into the sea.

"He was probably dead before he touched the water," is Hayward's opinion. "Of course the autopsy will tell that. If there is no water in the middle ear or the lungs, we can be certain."

But from Peter Geiss, who wandered in this afternoon after salvaging certain of his personal possessions from the sloop, we learned other facts. Thus, Peter declares that the man who killed Carroway was a sailor, or at least knew how to use a rope, sailor-fashion.

And as Halliday said to me, aside, this was cheering news, for my best friend could not accuse me of any nautical knowledge.

The body, it seems, was tied with two half-hitches around the wrists; from there the rope extended to the ankle, with similar half-hitches, and to these ends, again, the anchor had been affixed. To my query as to whether such a proceeding would not take considerable time Peter says not.

"Two half-hitches is about the quickest and easiest tie there is," he assures me, "and the best to hold. If it slips one way it holds another."

There is, it seems to me, a certain relish in Peter's account of these gruesome details; a gusto in the telling. Like the ancient Greeks, Peter's literature is purely oral, and he has by accident stumbled on an epic.

But the recovery of the body has roused the neighborhood to fever heat. There have been those, up to now, who have half-believed that Carroway had been the victim of an accident; had somehow stumbled and fallen overboard, and to prove this they brought out the fact that, like many of the men on the waterside, he could not swim.

There were others, too, who still inclined to the belief that some supernatural influence had been at work; that Carroway, indeed, had been the victim of some other-world foul play. But even these superstitious folk cannot now blame the red lamp. Carroway has been murdered, by hands which wielded the oar that struck him, and which tied the half-hitches which "if they slipped one way, held the other."

The anchor presents the only possible clue, and that is a feeble one. There was no anchor in the boat Carroway took out. On the other hand, there is a sort of half-hearted recognition of it by Doctor Hayward as one stolen from his

156

small knock-about sometime late in June.

"Of course, all these anchors are as like as peas," he said this afternoon, "but the boys down at the wharf say it's mine, and they can tell two fish-hooks apart, same size and same kind." . . .

The county authorities have finally roused themselves and the Sheriff, Benchley, is in Oakville. Under the excuse of examining our float Greenough brought him out, and Halliday dressed and went with them, to show where he had found the knife. On their return they stopped in and looked at my car.

When Halliday came back he was grave and quiet. In vain did Edith try to coax him into his usual light-heartedness. While I have no idea as to what happened, I can make a fair guess, for he announced at supper that he was through playing the invalid.

"It's time for me to be up and about," he said.

Benchley has increased the County's reward to twenty-five hundred dollars, and this with Livingstone's makes three thousand. As a result, until twilight frightened them back to their hearths, the vicinity was filled this afternoon with amateur detectives. According to Annie Cochran, one of them was skulking around the hedge of the main house when Mr. Bethel saw him and drove him off.

Just what that irritable and exclusive gentleman makes of the situation, I do not know. He must have learned, through Gordon, of our trouble here, but he makes no sign. Now and then, but not often, I see him on the terrace, and if he acknowledges my finger to my cap, I do not see it.

He is so consistently unpleasant that one must respect it, as consistency of any sort is respected. . . .

My own position is rather strengthened than weakened by to-day's developments, and I imagine Greenough himself is somewhat at sea. Not only am I no sailor, and obviously no sailor, but I am not a physically muscular man. In the pursuit of English literature the wear and tear is on trouser seats rather than on muscles; in ten years my one annual physical orgy has been putting up the fly-screens each April.

I could no more strangle a man that I could bull-dog a steer.

And, unless Greenough is more beset with prejudices and theory than I think he is, he must know this. He has, in addition, a slowly growing list of qualifications, all of which the murderer must possess, and few of which are mine. Thus:

The murderer is physically strong. I am not.

The murderer (or at least Halliday's assailant) wore a soft dark hat, well pulled down. I have here in the country a golf cap and a summer straw. No other. The murderer had a sailor's knowledge of a rope. I haven't the slightest knowledge of a rope, except that it is used on Mondays to hang out the washing.

On only two points do I plead guilty, and there with reservations. For the murderer shows a knowledge of the country-side, not only equal to my own, but better. And Halliday says he got into the car as would a man of middle life, rather than youth. I am middle-aged, — if that be not the next period just ahead and never quite reached, until some day we waken to find that we have passed it in the night and are now old, and taking an ingenujous pride in that age.

July 16th.

I am facing an unusual quandary, which is: shall I or shall I not attend poor Carroway's funeral to-morrow? What is the customary etiquette under the circumstances? Does the suspected agent of the death remain decorously absent, the only one in the entire neighborhood so missing? Or does he go, with a countenance carefully set to show exactly the polite amount

of concern, and be suspected as the dog returning to his vomit?

There is an old theory — I would like to
question Greenough about it, if I dared — that
your true murderer has an avid curiosity as to
the work of his hands; that, against all
prudence, he returns to it. Under these .cir-
cumstances, what shall I do?

Compromise, probably, send more flowers
than I can afford, and stay at home. The same
sort of compromise which I effected with my
soul yesterday, when I gave Jane a rather larger
amount than usual for the collection plate. . . .

One of the reporters who has been hanging
around the vicinity since the recovery of the
body approached me to-day on a possible connection between the murder and the attack on
Halliday. I found him coming out of the
garage, but as Greenough had carefully erased
the symbol on the seat cushion, I doubt if he
had found anything valuable.

He pried me with polite questions, but I
evaded him as well as I could.

"But don't you, personally, believe there is
some connection?" he insisted.

"I should have to have some proof of such a
connection."

"And you have none?" he asked, eyeing me
closely.

"I imagine you know at least as much about it as I do. Have you found any?"

Perhaps my attitude had annoyed him, or perhaps he merely had the discoverer's pride in achievement, for he put away the handful of yellow paper, on which he had made no notes, and smiled.

"I haven't found any connection," he said. "But I have found something your detectives missed, Mr. Porter. I have found where the fellow hid after the crash, when the other car was rescuing Mr. Halliday."

But the odd part of that discovery to my mind is not that hiding place, nor Greenough's failure to locate it. As a matter of fact, I doubt if Greenough has ever looked for it. He seems to have taken for granted that Halliday's assailant merely escaped the wreck and made off in the dark.

No. The point that strikes me, and struck Halliday when I told him is the intimate knowledge of that location shown, and the quickness with which he took advantage of it.

(Note: In view of what we now know, I imagine this is an error. The chances seem to be that he was thrown near the mouth of the culvert, and that the lights of the on-coming car showed it to him.)

Crossing the road, according to the reporter,

161

and about fifteen feet from where the car was ditched, is a small culvert. Hardly a culvert, either, but a largish clay pipe designed to carry the drainage of the higher fields on one side to the lower on the other.

"Have you searched this pipe?" I asked.

"I looked in. If I'd had a pair of overalls I'd have gone in. But as the only clothes I have with me are on me ." he smiled again. "It's a good job for a ferret," he said.

He gave me up reluctantly, at last, and prepared to go.

"So you think it's only an ordinary case of hold-up?" he asked.

"I think it's a damned unpleasant case of hold-up," I replied, and he went away. But I have been thinking of his phrase since his departure.

How much of the present world disorganization lies in that very use of the word "ordinary!" Time was when no hold-up was ordinary, and an act of physical violence or a murder caused a shock that swept us all. Is it true, then, that one cannot turn the minds of a people to killing, as in the recent war, and then expect them at once, when the crisis is over, to regard life as precious? And is this the reason Greenough spoke of its being a "queer time in the world?"

Is every criminal then merely seeking escape from reality?

But why the word "criminal"? Was not I myself seeking to escape it, when on June 16th I wrote in this very Journal:

"Yet what is it that I want? My little rut is comfortable; so long have I lain in it that now my very body has conformed." . . .

For the rest of this afternoon, I have made my will! "To my dearly beloved wife, Jane Porter, I bequeath, etc."

There is something strangely comforting in making a will; it is as if one has completed the last rites, and now, with such complacence as may be, faces whatever is to come. Like Ishmael in "Moby Dick," I survive myself; my death and burial are locked up in my desk. I am "like a quiet ghost with a clear conscience, sitting inside the bars of a snug family vault."

A ghost, too, I begin to feel, among other ghosts. . . .

Ignore it as I will, there is a certain weight in the slowly accumulating mass of evidence at my disposal, a weight and a consistency which have commenced to influence me. I am bound to admit that, if I were able to conceive of the survival of intelligence beyond death, I could also conceive that poor old Horace has been on hand during some of our recent experiences.

Not Thomas's "George," the spirit evoked by Mrs. Riggs and still surviving in the lamp; not some malicious demon, frightening honest folk by ringing bells and pinching women in the dark. But a mind like my own, only greater in its wider knowledge, and painfully trying in its bodiless state to communicate that knowledge to me.

The sum total of evidence is rather startling.

(a) Jane's photograph, taken on Class Day.

(b) Jock's refusal to enter the main house, persisted in to this time.

(c) My own curious telepathic message, relative to the letter.

(d) Jane's experience under the red lamp in the pantry. (Doubtful.)

(e) Halliday's lights over the marsh. (Again doubtful. It may have been the unknown, finding the boat-house occupied and seeking a way to the beach.)

(f) My own experience in hearing Uncle Horace's peculiar cough and smelling the odor of his asthmatic pastilles, or cigarettes.

(g) Jock's peculiar conduct at the same time.

(h) Peter Geiss's vision on the sloop, and his identification of it. (Yet Peter is a staunch supporter of "George." Had he been looking for such a visitation would he not naturally have seen George?)

(i) And the fact that this vision corresponds in time with the attack on Halliday.

In this attempt to refresh my memory I have not included Jane's premonition the night Carroway was murdered, or her dislike and distrust of the house. Nor have I included the vague stories of haunting told by Mrs. Livingstone, Annie Cochran or Thomas. Of the latter, they are not only beyhond my personal experience or contact, but they are, if the word may be used in such a connection, apparently without motive.

With Jane, too, I feel that a faculty which enabled her to rise in the morning without seeing her clock, may be extended further without touching the supernatural. I grant her a strange power, possessed doubtless by many criminals and a few human beings, of being able to see and hear what cannot be seen and heard by normal eyes and ears. But as I grant this same faculty to Jock, it seems to me to be rather a question of ordinary limitations than of a peephole, as I may put it, into another world.

On the other hand, I must not disregard the fact that Jane seems an essential part of the phenomena which I have recorded. On the two occasions when I have had the strongest impression of some disembodied presence, she has been asleep nearby. In the case of the photograph, it was Jane who operated the camera; in the pantry of the main house, it was Jane who saw the face behind her, reflected in the window. And so on.

I am driven to wondering if, in some states, Jane herself does not provide the medium for these manifestations. Whether she does not throw off some excess of vital matter, in which the poor naked and disembodied intelligence may clothe itself.

But that is to accept the whole theory of spiritism, and I am not prepared to do that; to travel with Cameron and little Pettingill, weighing the dying with the one and claiming that the purely chemical loss of weight is the weight of the soul; and sitting in the dark with the other, asking non-physical intelligences to commit various physical acts! Putting their belief in eternity into the grasping hands of a paid medium, and seeing God in the pulling of a black thread.

Which reminds me of an amusing conversation at luncheon to-day, Halliday's last meal with us before returning to the boat-house.

"What becomes of all the mediums?" Edith asked suddenly, apropos of nothing at all.

"What becomes of all the hairpins, and dead birds?" I asked, not too originally.

"But it is queer," she persisted. "These

women come and make a *furore*. Then all at once they disappear."

"They get discovered and then quit," Halliday said. "And of course, even a medium must die in time. Not that they actually die, of course. They simply go into the fourth dimension."

"And what's the fourth dimension?"

"Why, don't you know?" he asked. "The simplest thing in the world. It's the cube of a cube. And once you get into it you can turn yourself inside out like a glove. Not that I see any particular use in that, but it might be interesting."

Edith, it appears, intends to write an article on mediums!

July 17th.

I do not like young Gordon. He has little enough time to himself — only, I gather, an hour or so after luncheon, while Mr. Bethel sleeps — but he spends that here, if possible.

Edith snubs him, but he is as thick-skinned as one of the porpoises which rolls itself in the bay.

"Why, if you're so clever," I overheard her today, "don't you go out and do something? Use your brains."

167

"It takes brains to do what I'm doing," he said, "and don't you forget it."

But as to what he is doing he is discreetly silent. There is a book under way, but he parries any attempt to discuss it. Also, he seems to delight in investing Mr. Bethel with a considerable amount of mystery.

"The Boss is having one of his fits to-day," he will say.

"What sort of fits?"

"That would be telling," he says craftily, and ostentatiously changes the subject.

Edith, who has a very feminine curiosity, has questioned Annie Cochran but without much result. The "fit" days, so far as we can make out, are merely days when the invalid is less well than others, and mostly keeps his bed. Annie Cochran, however, has her own explanation of them; she believes that those days follow nights when "George" has been particularly active, and when presumably Mr. Bethel has not been sleeping on his good ear.

And as proof of this, she produces the fact that twice now, having left her tea-kettle empty on top of the stove, she has found it full in the morning. As Mr. Bethel cannot get downstairs unassisted, and as the secretary has always stoutly maintained that he has not left his room all night, Annie Cochran falls back on "George"; and, one must admit, not without reason. . . .

Poor Carroway was laid away yesterday, after the largest funeral in the history of these parts. And so ends one chapter in our drama. Ends, that is, for him. What is to come after no one can say.

One thing has tended somewhat to relieve the local strain. No sheep have been killed for eighteen days, and the altar in the field still remains without oblation. There are, I believe, one or two summer people who still make it the objective of an early morning excursion, hoping to find on it who knows what horrid sacrifice. But they have only their walk for their pains.

Maggie Morrison, who passes it every morning in her truck, makes a daily report of it to Clara, and so it filters to the family.

"Clara says the altar is still empty."

"I suspect her of longing to lay a chicken on it, herself. There is something pantheistic about her."

Jane — or Edith, as it may be — is silent, reflecting on the meaning of pantheistic.

It is Maggie, too, who brings us much of our local news. To-day, for instance, she informs us that the detective has gone away, "bag and baggage," from the hotel, and probably this accounts for the lighter tone of this entry. I am reprieved, at least until some other sheep are killed. . . .

Later: Halliday and I, late this afternoon, made an examination of the culvert, or pipe, in which our unknown hid after the accident. We chose a late hour, in-order to avoid the procession of cars which winds along our back roads — the further back the better — during the afternoons.

In this we were successful, for although, like my own, the general sentiment is one of reprieve, there are few still who trust themselves out after twilight. Mr. Logan, the rector of the Oakville Episcopal church, Saint Jude's, had an experience in point the other night: Calling late on a dying parishioner he ran out of gasoline on the main road, some six miles from home. He endeavored to stop various cars as they flew past, but in the general terror no one would pick him up, and after being fired at by one excited motorist he gave it up and walked back to the rectory.

We must have presented a curious study for any observer, working with guilty haste, and I in particular emerging from the pipe covered with mud and a heterogeneous collection of leaves and grasses. Not only was Halliday too broad in the shoulders for easy access, but his injury forbade the necessary gymnastics. There was a time when, half in and half out of the pipe, I could hear him laughing consumedly.

But I found nothing, save that undoubtedly someone had preceded me into it. A man skilled in such matters might have read a story into the various marks and depressions, but they were not for me.

I retreated, inch by inch, and was again free as to my legs but a prisoner as to the remainder of my body, when Halliday called that a car was coming. I had three choices; one was to remain in my present shameful state; another was to emerge and face the public eye, looking as though I had been tarred and feathered; and the third was to retire into my burrow.

I retired. With that peculiar venom with which fate has been pursuing me, the car stopped over me, and Starr spoke.

"Looking over the scene of your trouble?" he said.

"Looking for the clues you fellows can't find," Halliday retorted, easily.

I could hear Starr snort, and then chuckle drily as he let in his clutch again. "I'll give you a dollar for every clue you find," he called, and the car moved on.

When Halliday gave me the signal I emerged feebly into the open air, and stood upright.

"That was a narrow squeak," I said.

But he was looking after the disappearing car. "Yes," he said. "But I think it was a mistake. I should have told him you were there."

The net result of the search was not encouraging. True, Halliday picked up, outside the pipe, half of the lens of an eye-glass, but there is no proof that it belonged to his assailant. On the other hand, I myself had made a discovery of a certain amount of importance. Halliday had said that the man he had picked up had seemed to be a heavy man, broadly and squarely built.

But my experience showed me that no very heavy man could have entered the pipe. We have, in effect, to recast our picture of the murderer; a man of medium size, we will say, compactly if muscularly built.

To-night, sitting down to make this entry, I have missed my fountain pen, and as it has my initials on it we must recover it to-morrow if possible. It would be extremely unpleasant under the circumstances for Starr, for instance, in a burst of zeal to find it in the pipe.

True, Peter Geiss could swear that, at the moment Halliday was attacked he and I were looking for a ghost in the fore-rigging of the sloop. But I am at this disadvantage, that they give me no opportunity to defend myself, for they make no accusation. Their method is that damnable one of watchful waiting; Greenough's psychological idea that, given enough rope a criminal will hang himself.

July 18th

Edith and Halliday went this morning to recover my fountain pen, Edith in spite of our protests determined to crawl into the pipe for it. To this end she put on my mechanic's overall in which I oil and grease my car, and very sweet indeed she looked in it.

But the pen was not there. She found the cap of it, embedded in the mud, but not the pen itself. It looks as though Starr has lost no time!

Edith, I believe, suspects something. There is a growing gravity and maturity in her; she tries to show me, by small caresses and attentions, that she believes in me and loves me. But she knows that there is something wrong.

And she has, I think, quarreled with Halliday. There was nothing on the surface to show it, on their return to-day, but he declined her invitation to luncheon and went off, whistling rather ostentatiously, to his bacon and beans at the boat-house. This afternoon, while Mr. Bethel slept, she accepted young Gordon's invitation to go canoeing, and had the audacity to take the canoe, so to speak, from under poor Halliday's nose. According to Jane, she needs a good shaking.

There is, I understand, no definite engagement between them.

"Much as I — care for her," Halliday said to me, while he was still invalided here, "and I guess you know how it is with me, Skipper — I'm not going to tie her down until I've something to offer her beside myself. She's young, and I'm not going to take that advantage of her."

"But you do care for her?"

"Care for her? Oh, my God!" he said, and groaned, poor lad.

Three years, he has figured, maybe four. "Three with luck." And what Edith cannot understand is that he does not dare trust himself for that length of time. The urge that is in him is so different from hers; sentiment and attachment on her side, and strong young passion on his. Heigh-ho!

When one thinks that a mere ten thousand dollars or so would stop all these heart-aches, and that there are men to whom ten thousand dollars is only a new car, well — heigh-ho again! . . .

I must not forget to enter that Halliday last

night believes he saw the red lamp burning, in the den behind the library of the main house. He told me the details this morning as he waited for Edith to don my overalls.

It was his first night, after his accident, at the boathouse, and he could not sleep.

"I had a good bit of pain," he said, "and at one o'clock I got up and went outside. There was a sort of dull red light coming from the windows of the library of the other house, and I watched it for awhile. It was extremely faint, and at first I thought it might be a fire; then, as it didn't grow any, I saw it must be a light of some sort."

He knew the stories of the red lamp, but he also knew I had locked it away, so after a time he started up toward the house. He was about half way up the lawn when it went out, suddenly, and left him staring.

But he was curious, and he went on. He made a complete circuit of the building, but there was no movement or sound from within, and so he turned and went back again. He believes the light was in the den, not the library, for he saw only a diffused reddish glare, as though it came from behind. He could not, through any of the three long French windows which open onto the terrace, see the source of that glare.

Here, then, is corroboration of my own impression of some few nights ago, but with a difference. For I saw the light itself, a momentary flash as though a breeze had for an instant pushed open the heavy curtains at the den windows, and then had let them fall again.

I am convinced that young Gordon has never seen the light, or he would have spoken of it. He is fluent enough about what he calls the "spooky" quality of the house. It is unlikely that Mr. Bethel, imprisoned in his upper room, can have any knowledge of it. Yet here we have two dispassionate observers, seeing at different times and under different circumstances, a light apparently of spontaneous origin and no known cause.

Cameron says (Note: "Experiments in Psychical Phenomena," a book I had sent for some days before.) that the production of lights is very common; he quotes the appearance of bluish-green lights in the experiments with Mary Outland, the brilliant star-like white lights of Mrs. Riggs, and the luminous effulgence which was frequently seen hanging over the head of the Polish medium, Markowitz.

But in no case is the production of red light mentioned, and in every instance this spontaneous production of light is in the presence of a medium.

In the case of Markowitz, for instance, I find on referring to him:

"Following the appearance of the effulgence, usually came the materialization. Sometimes there emerged from between the curtains of the cabinet, while the medium was in sight and securely held, — a large white face; again it would be a small hand and arm which apparently came, not from between the curtains, but through the material itself."

But this is no field of conjecture for a man about to go to bed. My nerves are not at their best, anyhow, and in spite of myself. I find that from behind the slight breeze which is waving my curtains, I am expecting something extremely unpleasant to appear.

July 19th

A sudden and terrifying storm outside. Above the howling of the wind I can hear the surf beating against the shore. Halliday reports, over the telephone, that the float is in danger and that the run-way has broken loose. But there is nothing to do. I have just been out, and I do not propose to be soaked again.

(Note: The approach of the storm had made Jane very nervous, and I had driven in to Doctor Hayward's for a sleeping medicine for her.)

Jock is as bad as Jane, and should have a narcotic also! He is moving uneasily from place to place, now and then emitting a dismal howl, and Clara is sitting forlornly at the foot of the staircase, under the impression that it is the only place free from metal in the house, and thus less likely to attract the lightning.

It is indeed a night for dark deeds. And for dark thoughts. . . .

I wonder if I have any justification for my suspicions? Why should Hayward, preparing to go out to an obstetric case, start me along a new and probably unjustified line of thought? Surely, of all men in the world, he has the best right to carry ether. I must be careful not to do as Greenough has done, allow my necessity for finding the guilty man to run away with my judgment.

And yet, in spite of myself, I cannot help feeling that Hayward fulfills many of the requirements. He alone, of all the people hereabout, is free to move about the country at night without suspicion. He knew Uncle Horace "as well as anybody." He is — and God forgive me if I am wrong — enough of a sailor to know and use the half-hitch.

There are other points, also. He is about my age, if anything older, but he is a muscular man. And he is, like all general practitioners in the country, by way of being a surgeon also. He would know how to find the jugular vein of a sheep. . . .

I have re-read this. Possibly Greenough is right after all, and I am a trifle mad. For why sheep? Sheep and a stone altar! And only an hour or so ago he was saying to me, in his professional voice: "Tell her to take plenty of water with it, and not to be impatient. These things take an hour or so to get in their work."

"In all earnestness I appeal to you to consider the enormity of the idea," wrote poor old Horace, more than a year ago. But while killing sheep is unpleasant, even sad, there is no particular enormity in it. I pass by a leg of springtime lamb without considering that a tragedy lies behind it. The murder of Carroway, too, cannot come under the strictures of that letter; it was done as a matter of protection.

Nearest of all to the possibilities suggested by the letter comes the attack on Halliday, and if the sheep-killer did that, why not have put his devilish symbol on the car during that silent ride of a mile before he prepared to strike? Why have crept in later and done it?

But here again – the doctor had access to the car, after Greenough had examined it. He went in alone, according to Clara, and was there some time.

Was it, then, the doctor's typewriter which wrote the cipher over which Halliday has been puzzling? The GeLTr, K. 28?

July 20th.
Maggie Morrison disappeared last night; disappeared as completely as though she had been wiped from the face of the earth by the storm.

Livingstone telephoned me the facts at seven this morning, and Halliday and I took the car and went over. We have been out with the searching party all day, but without result.

After luncheon young Gordon joined us, sent by Mr. Bethel, who had not heard the news until that hour. It was all we three could do to keep Edith from starting out also, but it was not work for a woman.

To-night the search is still going on. Starr has sworn in more deputies, and the entire country-side is aroused.

Jane has been ill all day, and has kept her bed.

July 21st.
No trace of the unfortunate girl to-night, and all hope of finding her alive is slowly being abandoned. . . .

180

I can now record such facts as we know, relative to the mystery.

The girl went in to Oakville yesterday to do some shopping, and remained for dinner with Thomas and his wife. In spite of Thomas's prophecy of a storm she insisted on staying over for a moving picture, and it was therefore ten-thirty when, alone in the farm truck, she started out of town.

Nothing more is known of her movements, save that she got as far as the Hilburn Road, about two hundred yards beyond the Livingstones' gate. The truck was found there yesterday morning at daylight by an early laborer on the Morrison farm, who however thought that she had abandoned it there during the storm the night before, and neglected to report it.

At the farm house itself there was no uneasiness, as the family supposed the girl had remained in town. But when the hour came for her to start out with her milk delivery, and she had not arrived, inquiries were set on foot.

The truck shows no signs of any struggle, and that robbery was not the motive of whatever has happened is shown by the fact that the missing girl's pocketbook was found behind the seat of the truck, where she usually placed it.

Greenough and the Sheriff were on the ground when we got there, as well as a small knot of country folk, kept at a distance by a deputy or two, and already a small posse, hastily recruited, was beating the wood nearby. Such clues as there may have been, however, had been obliterated by the storm. There was no trace of the dreaded symbol in chalk. . . .

Halliday was reconstructed the story, in view of his own experience.

"The fellow was waiting," he said, "and hailed her, as he hailed me. He knew nobody would pass a man caught out in a storm like that. He got in, and closed the storm curtains, and of course she hadn't a chance in the world."

He does not therefore agree with the general conviction, that we are dealing with a sexual crime. And that word "general" does not include all of the population; there are many, I understand, among the more ignorant who have put together the almost uncanny violence of the elements that night, a night indeed for demons, and the complete disappearance of the unfortunate girl, and are building out of it and their own superstitious fears a theory that the girl's body will never be found; that she has been, indeed, spirited away.

It has its elements of strangeness, at that. Possibly five hundred men and boys have been searching steadily since yesterday morning; the back country, where it happened, is fairly open; the sea, with its salt marshes, both of which would give unlimited opportunity for concealment, is fully six miles by road from where the truck was found. . . .

Much talk is going around as to a story from the light-house on the extreme tip of Robinson's Point today. As is to be expected, the superstitious are making considerable capital of it. And I myself am not disposed to dismiss it without considerable thought.

The story is as follows:

On the night of the tragedy, a flying night bird of some sort broke one of those windows of the light-house which protect the light itself. The keeper and the second keeper repaired it as best they could, but the terrific gusts of the wind made them uneasy, and they remained on watch.

(Note: In light-houses of a certain type there is a small aperture, running down through the successive floors of the building, and through which, as the light revolves, the weights of the clock-work mechanism of the lamp slowly descend.

It should also be said that the Robinson Point light is a red flash, timed at ten seconds.)

They sat, high in the air, in the room just beneath the light, now and then glancing up to see that all was well. The storm increased in violence, and as the sea came up the surf beat on the rocks below with a crashing only equalled by the thunder itself. As is usual in the high tide of the full moon, the low portion of the point to landward, and the keeper's houses, the engine shed, boathouse and oil storage tank were soon cut off from the mainland by a strip of angry ocean.

Nevertheless, they were comfortable enough, and the under-keeper had actually fallen asleep, at eleven o'clock, when there came a sudden lull in the storm. It was that time, which I well remember, when there came one of those ominous and quivering pauses in the attack which seem, not a promise of peace, but a gathering together of all the powers of wind, sea and sky for one final and tremendous effort.

And in that pause Ward, the light-keeper, heard something below in the tower. He touched his assistant on the shoulder and he sat up. Both of them then distinctly heard footsteps on the lowest flight of stairs, five floors below.

They were alone in the tower; cut off from the mainland by a rushing strip of tide, and no boat could have landed through the surf. And outside was that unearthly quiet which was more sinister than the storm itself. Neither one of them moved or spoke, but the keeper remembers that, as the steps came on inexorably, a cold air began to eddy around the small circular room, and that he looked up at the red light apprehensively.

The act, one sees, was the habit of a life-time. Even then, with his body fairly frozen with terror of what was on the staircase, he looked up.

At the top of the second flight the steps pauses, and both keepers drew a breath. Then they heard a small dry cough, and the steps recommenced on the third level.

Up and up. The stairs curved round the inside wall of the tower, and they knew they would not see what was climbing until it was fairly on them. They sat there, their eyes glued to the door, and heard the steps coming up the last round. Whatever it was, it was on them. It reached the top, and the next step would bring it into view.

Then the storm burst again, in an explosion that fairly set the tower rocking, and simultaneously the electric lights in the room went out.

It was then that the assistant keeper swears that something touched him; something cold; but there seems to be no doubt, whether that is true or not, that the whole room was filled with the cold eddying wind referred to before.

I prefer to trust the head-keeper's statement.

Ward is an unemotional type, and this is what he says:

"I was scared enough, but when the lights went out I looked up at the lamp. It's an oil burner, and it was all right. Old Faithful, we call it. Well, you have to understand that we weren't entirely in the dark, even then; some of the red light from above came down, and I could see where Jim was standing. I couldn't see him, y'understand, but I could see where he was. And there was a third party in the room, over near the stairdoor. That is, he was there one minute; the next he was gone."

They did not make an immediate investigation. True to their type, they ran up and inspected the lamp, but it was "sitting pretty," as Ward says. They had candles, for it was not unusual for storms to put the Oakville light company out of service, and keeping close together they went down through the successive floors of the tower. They found nothing, and the outer door was still closed and bolted.

In view of so detailed and corroborative a statement, the final support of my early scepticism has had a severe blow. . . .

What would be the change, should we enter another world, with the same faculties we have now, but no limitations in their use? For after all, it is the brain that sees, and the human eye is only a faulty window, which shows us but a tiny portion of the universe; the ear hears only a modicum of sound. To carry with us that strange thing of which the brain is only an instrument for our poor physical use, and thus to hear all things, see all things, perhaps even know all things.

And thus equipped with limitless faculties, who would dare to leave out the emotions? To sorrow, then, to love, even perhaps to hate. And who shall laugh at the poor ghost who, knowing and suffering all things, makes its desperate attempt to avert a wickedness? To convey, through the thick mantle of the flesh, a knowledge that is not conveyable. To stand by, wringing its pale amorphous hands, while crimes go on and unnecessary wretchedness inhabits the earth?

Nothing bodily accounts for personality. Back of everything physical, and greater than anything physical, is the mind. And mind is not an attribute of matter.

July 22nd.

The body has not been found, and the Sheriff has raised the reward to five thousand dollars. This with Livingstone's original five hundred for the sheep-killer, which is to go to the finder of the murderer as being in all probability the same individual, raises the reward to fifty-five hundred dollars.

To-day, however, certain information acquired by Halliday has shifted the scene of the search to the salt marshes and the bay, and to-night, as I glance from my window I can see lanterns moving in the marsh beyond the main house, and up and down the shore. Jane has made coffee, and those of the searchers who come up this way from the beach have been stopping in.

Every bit of woodland in the county, according to the Sheriff, has been beaten without result, and to-morrow they will drag the bay.

We get a curious reaction from the men who are searching. The police, of course, see in it nothing unusual, and are prosecuting the case with vigor. But the fishermen, always a superstitious crowd, seem to me only half-hearted in the search.

The story from the light-house has convinced them once more of the diabolical nature of whatever is at work among us, and there is current also a tale from some passing motorist that the red lamp was burning in the main house at midnight the night of the 19th.

Coming up from our salt marsh, there is more than one who has made a wide detour to avoid the other house. . . .

Halliday's discovery, made to-day, is as follows: He calculated just how far the truck would have to go after it was hailed, before it stopped, and went back to that point, which was not far from the entrance to the Livingstone drive. Already the crowd of searchers and sensation hunters had pretty well destroyed any clue that might have been left, but about twenty yards from the gates he found marks in the mud indicating that, not only had the truck been backed to that point, but it had been turned there and headed back toward Oakville and the bay.

Just where it left the road again, if at all, is a question. I believe Halliday has taken a scraping from the wheels and proposes to have it analyzed. He finds something suspicious in it. I cannot say what.

I have spent to-day reorganizing my household. None of the women, including Clara, are to leave it after nightfall unaccompanied, and although no entrance into any house has yet been attempted, Halliday and I have spent the late afternoon tightening window locks and adding new bolts where they are necessary.

I took advantage of the opportunity to tell Halliday my suspicions about the doctor. He was so astonished that he let go of a window sash, dropping it on my fingers.

"The doctor!" he said. "Never in this world, Skipper."

And when I had put forth all my evidence he was still sceptical.

"I admit, of course, that the weight of it is rather startling," he said slowly. "But it wasn't the doctor I picked up. I'd know him, even in the dark."

"I'm not so certain of that, Halliday. But I think Maggie Morrison would have."

"Meaning———?"

"That I don't believe she would have stopped that truck at night for anyone she didn't know. You have to consider the character of the girl; she was as timid as a rabbit about some things. Superstitious, too. I say she would have gone by, after your experience, unless she had had a particular reason for stopping. And I still think she recognized this man, possibly by the lightning, which was practically incessant, and so she stopped."

"You're right in one thing, probably," he said. "She had a reason for stopping."

Edith has been recalcitrant about not leaving the house in the evening, but has finally agreed to it.

"I can write," she says resignedly. "I haven't really buckled down to it yet."

But nothing is more clear than that Edith's dreams of opulence are slowly fading. Her article on "The Beach at Low Tide" has been returned to her, and the Morrison mystery is being covered as spot news by those who are doing it as a part of the day's work, and on a salary basis.

Jane has entirely recovered, and has to-day resumed work on her tapestry, with us a barometer of normality. She has even agreed to dine at the Livingstones to-night, not particularly to my delight.

"Come over and dine," Mrs. Livingstone telephoned, "and let's have a little bridge. I've had the horrors for three days."

"You don't object to my wearing my revolver, as a part of my evening outfit?"

"Everybody's doing it," she said. "This house has been turned into an arsenal."

But in the midst of death we are in life. Clara, going to turn down my bed last night, saw two feet projecting from beneath it, and let out a series of wild shrieks.

Needless to say, they were my boots, hastily discarded for a pair of dry ones. . . .

Later: Doctor Hayward stopped in this evening for a final professional visit to Jane, and on an impulse I showed him Uncle Horace's letter. I may be mistaken, but it seemed to me that, under pretense of reading it a second time, he was playing for time.

"Curious!" he said, when he passed it back to me. "What do you make of it?"

"The last part of it is fairly clear. He was in danger, and knew it."

"But the rest of it?" he said. "What does he say? The wickedness of the idea. What idea?"

"You haven't any opinion on that yourself?"

"No," he said slowly. "I can't say that I have." The tension, or whatever it was, seemed to relax then. "As a matter of fact," he said, "I thought it was addressed to me, when I commenced it. We'd had a long argument not long before his death, on euthanasia. I believed in putting the unfit out of the world; he didn't. But of course the end of it settles that."

He laughed again, but the end of a thumb, hesitated, and then got his hat.

"Danger!" he said. "And the police! No, that wasn't for me."

"And you still believe he died of heart disease?"

"It was his heart, all right," he said, and going out, climbed heavily into his car. He seemed abstracted, and made no reply to my good-night.

I can read into this what I like. His manner was not that of a guilty man; on the other hand, it was not entirely natural, either. He was both watchful and self-conscious. And I do not believe he read the letter twice. ...

One of the evening newspapers to-night prints a photostatic copy of the cipher found in our garage, and offers a prize for its solution.

Edith's memory is shown to have been faulty in only one particular. The cipher, as published reads:

GeLTr, K.*24*.

July 23rd.

Mrs. Livingstone has given me something to think about. ...

The dinner went off very well. A trifle too much food and service, according to Jane, for a meal *en famille* in the country.

"One can see they have not always had money," says Jane, with the calm superiority of one who has never had it.

But the bridge was irritating. It is always a mistake to seat four people at a table, and place cards before them, when their minds are full of another and totally different matter. Thus: I would deal and bid a spade, for example, and wait patiently for Livingstone to sort his cards. In the pause, conversation between the women would be going on. Finally Livingstone would say:

"Who dealt?"

"I did," I reply, as patiently as possible. "And bid a spade."

"A heart," from him.

"You'll have to say two hearts."

"All right," he assents reluctantly. "Two hearts."

Then we wait. Mrs. Livingstone finishes what she is saying and pickes up her cards.

"Let's see," she says, "did anybody do anything?"

"I dealt," I say, "and bid————"

"It wasn't your deal, was it? I'm perfectly sure I dealt that last hand."

"We have the blue cards," I explain. "Now I have bid a spade, and Mr. Livingstone has bid two hearts. If you want to declare anything————"

"I don't," she says promptly, and starts laying out the dummy. We restrin her by main force, and Jane looks bewildered.

"I'm afraid I'm a little mixed," she says. "You bid two spades, Mr. Livingstone?"

After two hours of that sort of thing last night I was ready to go out and bite a hole in one of the porch pillars. But Jane at that point tactfully ended the game and saved my reason.

Nevertheless, the evening was not without a peculiar interest of its own. While Mr. Livingstone took Jane to see his hot-houses I had a few moments alone with his wife, and I received what is to me a new angle on the whole mysterious business.

We were in the library, and I was wandering around looking at Livingstone's books. They were the usual uncut editions a man thinks he should have on his shelves, but reserves for his old age to read; Darwin, Huxley and Haeckel, de Maupassant (in English), Tennyson, Wordsworth and Shelley, and of course, Emerson, among others.

In one corner, however, was a large and well-worn collection of books of an entirely different character. They were, as a matter of fact, books on psychic subjects, and as I glanced up from them Mrs. Livingstone was watching me, gravely.

"If you do not know what you believe on these matters," I said, "you must certainly know the opinions of others."

"And you?" she said. "Are you still a cynic? A carrion crow?"

I turned and faced her.

"I don't know what I am."

"Ah! You have heard the light-house story?"

"Yes."

She said nothing for a moment, then:

"What about your new tenant? Your Mr. Bethel? Has he made any complaint?"

"Not yet. As a matter of fact I have talked to him only once."

"And that was———?"

"Mostly about hot water and a beef cube," I admitted. "And the direction in which the house faces. He struck me as an extremely irritable and material type."

" 'Irritable and material,' " she repeated thoughtfully. "And yet I suppose you know they are saying that he is using the red lamp."

"The red lamp is locked away. So far as I know, he doesn't even suspect its existence."

For some reason or other that puzzled her.

"But it's been seen burning," she protested, after a blank pause.

"It is locked in a closet on the upper floor, Mrs. Livingstone, and I have the key. What is more, I heard that story some time ago, and investigated. So far as I can tell, it has not been disturbed since I put it there. Of course, he may have brought another similar lamp, but that's going rather far, isn't it?"

"Annie Cochran would know."

"I'll ask her, if you like. But privately, I believe that if she so much as saw such a lamp, she would run shrieking from the place."

She picked up some knitting at her elbow and worked at it thoughtfully.

"You have changed since I last talked to you," she said at last. "What has brought about that change, Mr. Porter?"

"A good bit has happened since then."

She looked up at me searchingly.

"Including the light-house."

"Including the light-house," I agreed, soberly. It was then she put down her knitting.

"Why has he come back?" she asked, watching me intently. "Why is he earth-bound? Have you no idea?"

"I haven't an idea what you mean by earth-bound."

"Just what I appear to mean, you know it," she said.

But after a moment, during which she continued her curiously searching gaze at me, she picked up her work again, with a smile.

"There is always a reason," she said. "You can laugh if you like; Liv does. But I know what I know. There is always a reason when they come back like this. A very good reason."

But beyond that she refused to go. Whether she has an inkling of this "reason" to which she attributes what she refers to as his "coming back" I have no idea.

The conversation, as I record it, seems as

extraordinary as the entire situation; two intelligent people, a man and a woman, discussing the return of a spirit to earth, much as they might that of a friend from Europe:

"What brought him back?"

"Goodness knows! Some sort of business, perhaps."

Some of the humor of the thing occurred to me on the way home and, with no disrespect, I chuckled.

"What in the world are you laughing at?" Jane demanded.

"Sheer relief that that's over," I said.

It was then that Jane made the remark about the Livingstones not always having had money.

July 24th.

The truck, according to Halliday's analysis, had been driven through heavy leaf mould. But a second drenching rain toward morning, and still continuing, discourages him. Into the bargain, the cars of searchers and summer tourists alike have made it practically impossible to identify any trail.

He has given his information and the result of the report to Greenough, but that gentleman appears to think he requires no assistance.

"If you amateurs would keep out," he

198

grumbled, "we would get somewhere with this case. Some day one of you is going to be missing, and I'll have more trouble on my hands."

From which one may gather that Mr. Greenough feels that we are not through with the situation.

Greenough himself is frankly puzzled. Whether his espionage of me assures him that my single excursion the night of the tragedy was to Doctor Hayward's office and back again, or whether he believes that this new catastrophe bears no relation to the sheep-killing, I do not know.

But the fact remains that, when we met today, he showed me more vicility than he has shown in our casual encounters recently. But I have reason to believe that I am still being carefully watched, especially at night, and that his vigilance has increased since the loss of my fountain pen.

He has, in his mind, definitely connected me with Carroway and it is, I daresay, only needed to establish some connection between this recent mystery and the ones that have preceded it, to set him at my heels again.

As a matter of fact, until the body is found or some such connection is established, he has no case in law against anybody, according to Halliday.

"There can be no murder without a body," says Halliday. "The law of *corpus delicti*, you know. He either has to find the Morrison girl, or failing that, pin his case to Carroway."

He (Halliday) and Edith have taken the car and gone out this evening. Jane is very uneasy, but I feel that they will be safe enough.

The best time to travel is immediately after a railroad accident.

July 25th.

And now where are we?

We can no longer doubt that the same hand which throttled Carroway and attacked Halliday, has brought about the disappearance and almost certain murder of Maggie Morrison.

Halliday knows it. Edith knows it. I know it. But what use are we to make of our knowledge? What effect, for instance, will it have on my own serio-comic position? Could Greenough arrest me on suspicion? Although Halliday laughs at that, he is, I think, a trifle uncertain. He feels, as I do, that before long Greenough will have to satisfy the public by an arrest of some sort, and that I am the only person against whom he has the shadow of a case.

We held a three-cornered conference at the boat-house this afternoon, while Jane slept after luncheon, and for the first time Edith was taken fully into our confidence. She went a trifle pale, but she slipped a hand into mine as a vote of confidence.

"You," she said, "the gentlest soul on earth, hiding a knife under that float there, and going out at night in a boat to kill somebody! Why, you can't even row a boat, properly!"

The small laugh which followed helped us all.

What developed last night is as follows: Halliday got out of the car at the spot where the truck was found, and had Edith go back and approach slowly, along the road from town. Approximately, the conditions were the same as those of the night of the disappearance, save that no rain was falling.

Halliday, it appears, was searching for that spot, back among the trees, where the unknown had waited, secure from observation but still able to see the truck's lights far enough away to be able to run out and hail it before it had passed.

After two or three experiments he found the proper location, and there commenced a sort of intensive search with the pocket flash, with Edith in the car, to warn him of any approach, and the lights out.

(Note: Perhaps it is as well, to record here a conversation with Halliday, which took place a day or so before.

In that, I recall, he stated that the first man who takes a case blazes the trail for any others who may come after. The situation more or less crystallizes under his handling of it. This he claims is the weakness of the French system which follows one direction until it ends in a blind alley, before it takes up another, and the strength of Scotland Yard, where into a central office is brought from varying sources all collectible material, which is there assorted and clarified.

"Greenough's mistake here," he said, "is that he has directed all his efforts toward finding the body, under the impression that that will yield the necessary clues. That's all well enough, but time is going by, has gone by, and he has nobody. And in the meantime rain is wiping out some possible clues, and the murderer himself is free to pick up the others."

He insisted that there would be clues, of one sort or another.

"There is no such thing as a perfect crime," he said, "and of course the general idea that a clue is some mysterious phenomenon which it requires super-human powers to understand, is all bosh. Clues are practically always trivial, because it is only the trivial things the criminal overlooks. He takes care of the big ones."

It may be as well to add, too, that the reason he did not make this investigation earlier was that, until the search shifted to the sea and the marshes, the vicinity where the truck was found was still the focal point, and was rarely without its constable, or its group of curious on-lookers.)

Not under the tree he had selected, but perhaps a dozen feet away from it, he found, well trampled into the ground, a small screw cap, made of tin; exactly similar, he tells me, to those used on the cans of certain makes of ether, and underneath which there is a cork.

"In my case, he was unlucky," he explains. "He went through the same procedure, and took the cap off before he hailed me, but the cork came out. He had better luck this last time."

As to his discovery of the murderer's infernal symbol, he is more reticent. He had some sort of a "hunch" to examine the trees themselves, he says simply.

"What do you mean by a 'hunch'?"

"I don't know. Just an idea, I suppose."

"You thought there might be something on a tree?"

"I don't know that I thought about it at all, Skipper. I just turned the flash up, and there it was."

Perhaps I am wrong, but his explanation does not quite satisfy me, nor, I think, does it satisfy himself. With all his keen intelligence he is strictly conventional; I think he believes it would somehow invalidate his manhood to confess that his "hunch" might have been a guidance by some unseen source.

But the triangle enclosed in a circle was there, on a tree only thirty feet back from the road.

July 26th.

Annie Cochran says absolutely that there is neither a red lamp nor a red lantern in the other house.

I stopped her this morning and asked her. . . .

The day has brought no developments in the Morrison case, which has settled down more or less into a routine. The searchers are fewer each day; the fishermen have gone back to their nets and trawls, and to-day will probably see the last of the attempts to drag likely spots on the bay.

There are many now who believe that this time the anchor rope is shorter, and that the body, securely anchored to the ooze at the bottom of the bay, will not be uncovered by the lowest tide.

But if the day has brought no developments outside, it has brought one or two to us here.

For one thing, the morning mail returned to me through the dead letter office my letter of thanks to the young woman in Salem, Ohio, an event which would puzzle me more, did I not suspect the lady of using a fictitious name, for all her apparent frankness.

For another, Jane has at last unbosomed herself. She maintains that on the night of the nineteenth she saw Maggie Morrison, clairvoyantly. Rather, on the morning of the twentieth, for granted that she has actually had another of her curious psychic experiences, there is a discrepancy in time here as marked as the interval between Uncle Horace's death and her vision of him lying on the library floor.

Maggie Morrison disappeared presumably at eleven o'clock the night of the 19th; Jane's vision occurred at three the morning of the 20th, or four hours later. . . .

This morning, at eleven o'clock, Jane left the cottage for the first time in days, giving as an excuse that she meant to look over Warren Halliday's clothing and bring back such as required mending.

"I need a little attention of that sort myself," I observed. "I don't mind competing with a tapestry — after all, that is art, and what am I to art? — but I resent competing with a younger and handsomer man."

She gave me the smile with which every wife greets an old familiar jocularity of every husband, and left me to my reading.

When an hour, however, had gone by and she had not returned, I began to grow uneasy. Halliday, I knew, was out on the bay, and in such times as these any small deviation from the normal is upsetting. I started after her, therefore, and was startled not to find her in the living quarters or on the verandah. But when I called she answered from below, and going down I found her among the boats.

"Well!" I said. "And are you going fishing?"

"I was just wandering about," she said. "There's another boat, isn't there?"

"Halliday's out in it. Why?"

But she pretended not to hear me, and went up the steps again. Even then she made various excuses not to leave at once. She went inside, and I could hear her straightening the small living room. When there was nothing more to do she came out again.

"I don't think he has cooked a thing since it happened," she said. "Suppose we wait for him, and take him back to luncheon?"

She is no actress, is Jane, and it began to dawn on me that she was determined to wait for

Halliday's return, and that she had one of her hidden reasons for it. It was there, sitting on the boat-house verandah, that she finally told her story, which is detailed in the extreme.

"You remember," she said, "the night of Maggie's disappearance, that a storm was threatening, and that I was nervous. I felt queer – I can't describe it, William. I had a sort of premonition, I think, anyhow, I didn't want to go to bed, and when I told you that you started off to Doctor Hayward's for a powder."

"You had meant deliberately to stay awake?"

"Yes. Once in awhile something terrifies me, and I am afraid even to wink for fear something happens while my eyes are closed. It was like that.

"Edith was writing something or other, shut in her room, and after you had gone the storm began to come up, and I felt queer and jumpy. I went around the windows downstairs, and then went into the living room and sat down to wait for you."

"Let's see. What time was that?"

"It must have been ten o'clock; maybe a little later. Then – I hate to tell you this, William. It sounds so silly."

"I've been thinking some pretty foolish things myself, lately, my dear," I said, gravely. "Go ahead."

"Jock was very strange, from the moment we went in there. He sat and stared at that old parlor organ. I———"

"At the parlor organ! What in the world———"

"At the parlor organ," she said positively. "Or rather, above and behind it, where it sits across the corner. And after awhile, I thought I saw something there."

"What sort of 'something'?"

"I can't tell you," she said, and shivered. "That is it wasn't really anything. It was like a mist. I could just tell there was something there, and then Jock lifted up his head and howled at it, and — I don't even remember getting upstairs, William."

Now, so far, this runs fairly true to form; the usual strange combination of the grotesque — witness the parlor organ! — overstrained nerves due to the approach of an electrical storm, and Jock, absently staring at nothing at all and preparing to give the storm howl for howl.

It is the remainder of Jane's story which seems worthy of consideration, in view of her previous average of hits.

She went to sleep, sinking fathoms deep into unconsciousness, but at three o'clock she wakened, suddenly and fully, and sat up in her bed. But she was not in a bed at all. She was in a boat, and Maggie Morrison also was in it, lying at her feet. After a time — she has no idea how long — the vision faded, and she was still sitting up in her bed.

Such details as I can draw from her are as follows:

"Did you see Uncle Horace in the same way?"

"Wakening out of a sleep? Yes."

"Was there the same sort of light?"

"Not a light exactly. It doesn't come from anywhere. I can't describe it exactly; the things I see are luminous."

She has, however, her strict limitations; she speaks of a boat, but whether it was quiet or in motion she has no idea; asked if she and the girl were alone, she thinks not, but can give no reason for so thinking. Asked as to why she believed the girl was dead, she says: "I *felt* that she was dead," and then qualifies that by adding: "Besides, I never have these visions unless some one has died."

This, like most broad statements, is an error, but in this case the general developments bear her out. I myself believe that, if she saw the Morrison girl at all, she saw her dead, as she says.

She saw no rope on the body or in the boat, and there was no sign of injury on the girl.

"She looked very peaceful," says Jane, and sets me to shuddering.

On one point, however, she is entirely definite. She maintains that there were pieces of cloth tied around the oar-locks of the boat. "White cloth," she adds, as an after thought.

"Why cloth?"

"To keep the oars from making a noise," says my Jane, who has been in a row-boat perhaps a half dozen times in all her life! . . .

We sat on the verandah while Halliday came in with the boat; he had been out, I daresay, on some scouting business of his own, and I confess to a sort of terror that by some unlucky chance we might find the oar-locks of this very boat, wrapped with white cloth, "to keep the oars from making a noise." But they showed no stigma of crime.

"Why," I said to Jane, as Halliday tied his boat and came with his splendid stride up the run-way, "why did you come down here to look at *our* boats, my dear?"

She showed a faint distress.

"I don't know, William. I just had a feeling that I had to come."

I have not asked her why she has suppressed this experience for so long. Carrying it down with her to pour my breakfast coffee, going with it through the day, and at night mounting the stairs with it and so to bed. Brushing her hair meticulously, and settling Jock for the night; going in to kiss Edith and tuck her into her fresh white bed, and then closing her door and shutting herself away with it for the night. And always with the guilty feeling that she was withholding that which should be known.

For she no more doubts that Maggie Morrison was killed and thrown into the sea from a boat with muffled oar-locks, than she doubts her own existence. But coupled with that certainty has been her dread of possible publicity, and that ever present feeling of hers that whatever power she has is somehow shameful.

My poor Jane.

July 27th.

The blow has fallen again, and this time almost at our very door. That it is not murder is not due to any lack of intention, but to weakness in execution. I have spent a large portion of the day in urging Edith and Jane to go back to town, but without result.

"Not unless you go," Jane said firmly, and Edith and I exchanged glances.

As a matter of fact, last night's events have left me in a more precarious position than before, and I feel that any move on my part

211

would only precipitate matters. Greenough has given out a statement to the reporters that an early arrest may be expected, and I do not for the life of me understand why he has not pounced already.

I imagine the only thing that has saved me, so far, has been the single fact that Peter Geiss knows I was on the sloop the night and hour when Halliday was attacked. That puzzles him. . . .

To record last night's strange affair in sequence:

I could not sleep, a condition which is growing chronic with me lately, and at or about midnight I went downstairs and outside. The night was extremely dark; I paced back and forward along the drive, keeping at first close to the Lodge, but gradually extending my steps as I grew accustomed to the darkness.

After twenty minutes or so of this, and at the extreme of my swing toward the other house, I heard some sort of movement in that direction, and stopped to listen. It was a cautious disturbance of the shrubbery, and I swung in among the trees and stood listening. It was not repeated, however, and I turned to go back.

I had, however, lost my way, and for some brief time I floundered about. At last I found the sun-dial, by striking against it, and thus orienting myself, turned about and struck back toward the Lodge.

I had not gone ten feet before I heard the bell ringing.

(Note: A large bell on the kitchen porch of the main house and used in times before the telephone was installed, to summon the gardener. It is rung by pulling a rope attached to it.)

It rang sharply twice and then abruptly stopped, and the sudden silence seemed somehow ominous, like the stillness after a shriek.

There were no lights in the main house, and no further sounds came from it. I daresay at such times one does not think; one acts automatically. Someone has said, "With the spinal cord. Not the brain." I do not recall thinking at all, but I do recall trying to feel my way through the trees, and that I ran into one and was partially stunned for an instant.

The house was still completely dark and silent. I felt my way with more caution, skirted the shrubbery, and at last found the railing leading up the steps to the kitchen. Here I was on safer ground, and I crossed the small porch to the door with increased confidence, only to stumble over something and almost fall. I knew at once what it was, and I felt suddenly ill, although my brain was as active as ever in my life. "In the pit of his stomach man is always a coward." But I found some matches in my dressing gown pocket, and striking one bent over a figure lying prone at my feet. It was young Gordon, unconscious and bleeding from a blow on the head, and securely tied with a rope. I was still stooping over him, fumbling for another match, when a flash-light shone in my face, fairly blinding me. It played on me for a moment, and then on the boy stretched on the floor and now slightly moving.

"What's happened?" said a voice from behind it, and with relief I recognized it as the doctor's.

"He's hurt," I said, rising dizzily. "Struck on the head, I think."

"Open the door there and turn on the lights. I'll carry him in."

I did as he told me, being still somewhat unsteady, and as he laid the boy on the floor and straightened I was aware that his eyes, as they rested on me, were hostile and suspicious.

Immediately, however, he went to work on the boy, examining him first and then removing the rope.

"He's only stunned," he said, and leaving him lying as he was, began to move about the room. Just inside the door was the poker from the kitchen range, and this, with the rope, he laid

214

aside carefully. Then he went outside, and with his flash examined the bell.

"Just where were you, Porter, when this happened?" he asked.

"In the grounds, by the sun-dial. I couldn't sleep. When I heard the bell I came on a run."

"It was the boy who pulled the bell?"

"I haven't an idea."

He went back to his patient, and examined the wound in the scalp more carefully. After that he dressed it, the boy by that time moving about and groaning, but still only partially conscious. I gave such help as I could, getting water and so on, and when the dressing was done the doctor disappeared, and returned with a cushion. Keeping the boy supine, he slipped it under his head. Then he straightened.

"You'd better notify the old man," he said. "I'll stay here, if you don't mind."

And from the look he gave me, I gathered that he had no intention of leaving me with the boy.

I made my way upstairs to the room over the den, and knocked for some time before I was heard. Then Mr. Bethel called out, startled, and I asked if I could come in. I heard him making heavy work of getting out of bed, and finally he shot the bolt and opening the door an inch or two glared out at me.

"What the devil's the matter?"

"Nothing serious," I said. "There's been a little trouble downstairs, and we thought you'd better be told."

"A fire!"

"Not a fire," I reassured him, and gave him a brief account of what had occurred.

He was not particularly gracious; demanded to know what the boy was doing outside at that hour, and seemed to feel that, with a doctor already in the house, his responsibility was ended. As there was actually nothing he could do, I helped him back to his bed and left him sitting on the side, an unpleasant but helpless figure.

As I went out he asked me to bring him a cup of hot water!

The boy was conscious when I went back to the kitchen, staring around him, and particularly concentrating on the doctor and myself. He put his hand to his head and felt the bandage.

"Where'd I get that?" he asked thickly.

After a time he tried to get up, and the doctor put him into a chair.

"Now, Gordon," he said, "what happened to you? Try and think."

"He hit me," he said finally. "The dirty devil!"

"Who hit you?"

But he was still too dazed for coherent thought. He improved rapidly after that, however, although he complained of severe headache. He became garrulous, too, as happens after concussion, but out of his maunderings we were able to secure a fairly connected story.

He had been unable to sleep, because of certain noises in his room. He glanced at me. "You were right, old dear," he said elegantly, "when you said the place has an unpleasant reputation. I'll tell the world it's unpleasant."

He had got up, and gone down to the kitchen for something to eat. After that, reluctant to go up to his room again, he had wandered out onto the kitchen steps and sat there. It was then that he heard someone stealthily approaching the house.

He listened, and finally he heard a window of the old gun room next to the laundry being raised. He stared that way, and insists he saw a dark figure there. The next moment it was gone, and he was certain there was someone in the house.

He had, apparently, turned to enter the house and head off the intruder, but was struck down in the doorway. On the matter of ringing the bell he was rather vague at first, not remembering that he had done so, but later saying he had had his hand on the rope, when the blow came.

Hayward listened to this intently. Then he turned to me.

"And you were where, Porter?"

"By the sun-dial. On the other side of it. I had started toward home."

"Do you mean to say that, after that bell rang, this man Gordon speaks of had time to tie him and escape, before you got here?"

"I've told you the facts. It isn't a simple matter to get here from the sun-dial, in the dark."

I remembered the hot water then, and finding some in the tea-kettle carried it up to Mr. Bethel. He showed me more civility this time, inquired after the boy, and even offered his pocket flask, lying on his bedside table. There was a revolver beside it, and he saw me glance at it and smiled grimly.

"What with the sounds inside your house, and the things that are happening outside, I think it best to be prepared for anything."

So, in spite of young Gordon's prophecy, he too has been hearing things. . . .

In spite of the doctor's attitude and my own fears, I cannot see to-day that a dispassionate examination of the evidence would really involve me.

Gordon saw a man enter the gun room window, and was attacked from the kitchen by that man. It must be perfectly evident to Greenough, on hearing the doctor's story, that had I for any reason desired to make some nefarious entrance into the house, I need not have resorted to a window. I have keys to every door, and can produce them.

Thomas, however, who seems to have his own methods of acquiring information, to-day tells a fact which, in my ignorance of such matters, I had not noticed last night. He states that the doctor reports the boy as having been tied in the same manner as poor Carroway; in two half-hitches around the wrists, a turn or two about the body and arms, and ending in two half-hitches at the ankle.

The rope, it appears, was not brought for the purpose, but had been left lying on the top of Annie Cochran's laundry basket in the kitchen, when she went home last night.

Later: Greenough and Doctor Hayward have driven past, on their way to the main house. I have telephoned to Halliday, and he is on his way here. I may need him.

July 28th.

After all, things passed off yesterday better than I had hoped. The detective concedes that, while in daylight it is a simple matter to reach the main house from the sun-dial, it is not an easy one at night. And I think he was puzzled when I said:

"After all, the real mystery to me is how Doctor Hayward, who says he was passing on the main road in his car, could reach the house so soon after I did."

"He had his car."

"But he didn't drive in. You left it outside the Lodge gates, doctor, didn't you?"

"I didn't know just where the bell was ringing."

"But you knew there was such a bell on the main house. Everyone around here knows that. Even at that, you made very good time. I had only had time to light one match and see the boy, when you turned your flash-light on me."

I imagine, and Halliday agrees with me, that whatever Greenough had in mind when he came, the new element thus introduced caused him to hesitate. And to add to his hesitation, the doctor, from the breezy unctuousness of his entrance, took to twitching and gnawing his finger tips.

"I don't suppose you are intimating that I knocked the boy down, Porter," he said, "but it sounds like it. As a matter of fact, I didn't even know him; never saw him, to my knowledge, until last night."

"I'm not intimating anything. I'm in a peculiar position; that's all. And you have been considerably more than intimating that I was where I had no business to be last night. I had, you see, exactly as much reason to be there as you had. Rather more, I imagine."

I was perhaps a trifle excited, but heaven knows I had a right to be.

"I know what you have in mind, Mr. Greenough, and I'm glad to have this chance to lay my cards on the table. Ask my wife why I was on the float, the night Carroway was killed in the bay. She'll tell you I was in bed, until she roused me and sent me down to the beach. Ask Peter Geiss where I was at the hour when Halliday was attacked; he can tell you. Ask the newspaper reporter who told me, right here, about the culvert under the road where Halliday's car overturned; and ask Halliday himself about our excursion to examine it, and my losing my fountain pen there. And then ask yourself if I would open the gun room window of the main house to make an entrance when I have in this desk a key to every door in the place."

Greenough smiled drily.

"That's a pretty strong defense, considering that you haven't been accused," he said. "As a

221

matter of fact, we hadn't found your fountain pen, Mr. Porter. I'm afraid we overlooked something there!" ...

Since they have gone, I feel, although he has not said so, that Halliday believes I have made a tactical error. And I dare say, in one way, I may have. I have given my defense to the opposition, and not only that; I realize that my list of witnesses is painfully weak; my wife, my niece's lover, and Peter Geiss!

And Peter Geiss, by local repute, is, like some of the weak sisters of the world, to be bought with a price. ...

Nevertheless, I feel a great sense of relief. I have at least made a hole in that web of circumstantial evidence which has seemed to be closing around me, and sent the detective scurrying back to the center of it again, to spin such new threads as he is able.

July 29th.

To-day has been quiet. Those constant reminders of the latest tragedy, the boats dragging the bay, have disappeared, and once more we see gay little picnic parties, chugging across the water to Robinson's Point or thereabouts, laden with hampers and, I dare say, with flasks.

Edith came down to luncheon in her best

pink frock, with a hat to match, and made shameless eyes at me during that meal. The cause of this sudden attention developed later, when she took the car — and Halliday — and went to the light-house. Over the purpose behind this unexpected display of interest in our coast-guard service she draws a discreet veil.

For the rest of the day, there is nothing to record. Jane and I took a brief walk this afternoon, and noticed a man clearing the woods on Nylie's farm, across the road. We stopped and watched him for a time, and he seemed curiously inexpert at the job. But perhaps I am too ready to suspect Greenough's fine hand in everything I see.

I confess, however, to a certain unholy joy when Jock made a most ungentlemanly attack on him, and was only called off with real difficulty. . . .

Young Gordon, although still confined to his room, is up and about again.

To-day I asked Hayward, who had been to see him, if I might visit him, but he shook his head.

"He is still in an excitable condition," he said. "Better give him a day or two more."

As, however, Annie Cochran reports him in excellent shape, although moody and irritable,

I can only feel that the doctor has his own reasons for keeping me away from him. At the same time, I must be careful not to allow suspicion to carry me too far. Mr. Bethel states flatly that the boy has no idea of who attacked him and himself suggests Thomas! ...

My talk with Mr. Bethel last night was interesting and not without an unusual quality of its own. He chose to be civil, and rather more than that. I felt that the alarm of my entrance once over, he not only greeted me with a sense of relief, but kept me as long as possible. And he voiced something of the sort before I left.

"My infirmity cuts me off from my kind," he said. "I am dependent on the indulgence of others, and that is a poor thing."

As it was the first time he had referred to his condition, I ventured to ask how he managed without Gordon. It seemed to me that the small laugh he gave was ironical.

"Paid solicitude!" he said. "I can manage without it. I make heavy weather of it, but I manage." My offer to assist him upstairs before I left, however, met with a decided negative. He was not going up yet; when he did, it would be a slow process, but he had done it the last night or so, "somehow." My last impression of him is of a helpless and yet indefinably militant figure in a dimly lighted room, sitting upright in its chair, one withered hand palm upwards, on his knee, and the other not too far from the revolver. . . .

I am puzzled over that picture, as I am over the one which I saw from the terrace window, as I approached. He gave the same impression then as he did when I left, of a man waiting for something.

As I looked in at him, he was facing toward the hall and the dining room door, directly across, with a concentration so great that my light tap at first did not reach his ears. And during the entire conversation which followed, every now and again I was conscious of a sudden abstraction on his part, an intent listening, that made me nervous in spite of myself.

But the conversation was both interesting and enlightening. He was, through the secretary and Annie Cochran, acquainted with the general outline of what has been going on, and even of the stories current about the house itself, especially as to the red lamp.

"I dare say my statement that the red lamp is locked away," he said whimsically, "would not greatly assist the situation. As I understand it, they would simply say that this was some further evidence of its abnormal powers."

I gather that, like young Gordon, he has heard certain sounds in the house at night, but does not intend to be stampeded by them, to use his own words. He has some theory of a disturbance of molecular activity, by some undiscovered natural law, which I could not follow closely. But in the discussion of superstition in general which followed, I was a trifle disconcerted to find him laying much of it to the Christian religion; that our present theology had given birth to the wide-spread belief in evil spirits and in sorcery. He went even further, and classed the adoration of saints as polytheism, and the worship of sacred relics as fetichism.

Strangely enough, I had at that moment one of those curious sensations which I have heard referred to as a failure of the two sides of the brain to synchronize.

(Note: Lear, who has read this, advises me that this is now an exploded idea, and that only one side of the human brain functions at all.)

I had the feeling that sometime, somewhere, eons ago, I had sat in a dimly lighted room and heard those same words. And that I had had the same instinctive revolt from them.

But the impression was fleeting, and seeing perhaps that our views did not coincide, he added that I must not believe that he disregarded the spiritual side of the individual, or of the universe. And he quoted Virgil's *Spiritus inter alit* with a certain unction.

"Soul animating matter!" he said. "It is a great thought, Mr. Porter. And I have reached that time in life when what is to come is assuming more importance than that which has gone."

Then he dismissed the subject, and went back again to the local situation, this time taking up the crimes themselves. He sees no necessary connection between the disappearance of Maggie Morrison and the tragedy of Carroway, and on this I did not enlighten him. On his saying, however, that in my place he would not feel safe in keeping Jane and Edith here, I told him at some length of my own involvement, and this brought about a discussion of Greenough and his methods.

He smiled drily over my account of the detective's psychological attitude.

"Psychology," he said, "the study of men and motives, is a science in itself. With all due respect to the gentleman in question, I imagine that his chief psychological resource would be that portion of the third degree which consists in knocking a man unconscious, and then obtaining his confession before he has entirely recovered his senses. I would rather trust your young friend at the boat-house. At least he appears to be using a certain independence of thought."

He broke off there, as he had once or twice before, and seemed again to be listening. But in a moment he picked up the talk again. The mention of unconsciousness had brought Gordon to my mind, and his first words on recovering. It was then that I inquired if the secretary had recognized, or thought he recognized, his assailant that night, and that Mr. Bethel replied in the negative.

"At least," he said, "he has not said so to me. But he is a queer boy; moody and sometimes sullen. A good secretary, but an indifferent companion."

As to the strange affair of the attack on Gordon, he himself with Annie Cochran's assistance, examined the gun room the next morning. The lock of the window was broken, but he fancied that was a matter of old standing. He was having it repaired.

"The boy's story seems to be borne out by the facts," he said. "There were indications, as you probably know, that someone had entered by the window. But what strikes me as strange is that whoever did so should have known his way so well. Gordon says no light was turned on, yet this fellow puts his hand on the only weapon about, the poker, without difficulty." He turned and glanced at me. "How long have you known Thomas, the gardener?" he asked.

"Too long to think he would do a thing like that," I said, rather warmly.

"I dare say. And, although I think Thomas is not fond of Gordon, that would be carrying a distaste rather far, I imagine."

He has no anxiety for himself, or at least so he said; I am personally not so certain. For as I looked back from the terrace on my way out, he was once more facing toward the hall, and — I somehow felt — watching it.

July 30th.

I have to-day borrowed some of Mrs. Livingstone's books on psychic research, and intend to go into them thoroughly. If there is any proof in a mass of evidence, it is certainly here.

On the other hand, one must remember that the hope of survival is the strongest desire of the human heart. How many, if they felt that this life was all, would care to go on with it?

Analyzing my last night's experience, however, I can find nothing in my mind before I went to sleep, to account for it. I ate a light dinner, and spent the evening after Jane retired, with this Journal. The night was quiet, and my last waking thought was concerning the wood-cutter across the road, who seems so singularly inactive except when someone leaves the Lodge, or appears at one of its windows.

One thing I have traced, however. It is distinctly possible that the herbal, aromatic odor I noticed at the end of the experience was due to the leaves he collected yesterday, and which I find have smouldered throughout the night. . . .

It was after midnight when, just as I was dozing off, Jane came to my door and asked me if I would mind sleeping in her room.

"I can fix you a bed on the couch," she said, avoiding my eyes. "I'm nervous to-night, for some reason."

I went at once, trailing my bedding with me, and while she prepared the couch I observed her. She was very white, and I saw that her hands were shaking, but she refused my offer of some brandy with her usual evasive answer.

"I'm all right," she said. "I just don't like being alone."

She fell asleep almost at once, like one exhausted, but the change of beds had fully roused me, and I lay for some time staring into the darkness. I do not know when it was that I began to have the feeling that we were not alone in the room, but I imagine fully half an hour had passed.

I saw nothing, but I had the sensation of

being stealthily watched, and with it something of horror rather than of fear. I was rigid with it. Then something seemed to tug at my coverings, and the next moment they had slid to the floor. Almost immediately after that there came a rush of air through the room, a curtain billowed over my face, and the door into the hall swung open. Then all was silent, save for a low whine from Jock, outside in the hall.

How much of this to-day to allot to my nerves I do not know. Undoubtedly Jane's nervousness had affected me; equally undoubtedly bed clothing has a tendency to slip from a couch. I have quietly experimented to-day. A gale of wind would blow out a curtain and open an unlatched door.

On the other hand, I am as certain to-day as I have been certain of anything recently, that I had bolted the door when I entered the room. But it was not bolted in the morning.

If I have indeed actually had a psychic experience, it seems singularly purposeless. Up to this time I have imagined, correctly or not, that these inexplicable occurrences have had a concealed but definite objective, if such a phrase may be used. But in this case there is apparently nothing.

Otherwise the night was quiet, without new developments. Greenough continues his work, handicapped by the usual difficulty besetting a detective in the country, that his every move is known and watched. Jane herself wakened this morning, after a quiet sleep, and although she is languid, the present intense heat may easily account for that.

We have had, however, a development of our own, and this from Edith!

It appears that this morning, seeing Doctor Hayward pass on his round of morning calls, she went to his office and, on his housekeeper reporting him out, asked permission to go into his office and there leave him a note.

"A note?" I inquired. "What sort of a note?"

"Any sort of note," said Edith. "As it happens, I asked him to tea to-morrow. It was all I could think of."

But what she really did was to type a few lines on his typewriter, tear the paper out and put in in the small vanity case which is as much a part of her as the nose she powders from it.

(As a net result of which audacious performance Halliday now informs me that the cipher words were not written on the doctor's machine.)

A careful comparison under a magnifying glass shows this so that even I can recognize it. So there we are again.

If we are to believe that the chalk which

marked my car was brought in that paper, we must grant that the doctor did not mark the car. Or in other words, that our contra-offensive is not to be launched, as yet, and that our only course is to continue rather ignominiously in our trenches.

July 31st.

Halliday has found the boat.

At least he has found a boat which answers Jane's description. To-day he took me to see it.

It lies in the small creek which extends through the marsh half a mile north of the boathouse, and just beyond Robinson's Point.

(Note: This creek is really a narrow estuary from the bay, almost entirely overgrown and its entrance hidden by reeds, and is only a few hundred feet in length. At its upper end, where the boat lay, the swamp ends and woodland commences. Although on another estate, the woodland is a continuation of our own.)

The boat, evidently an old and abandoned one, gives some evidence of recent use. That is, although it contains some water, there is very little, whereas, as Halliday says, after the recent rains it might well be full.

The oar-locks are wrapped with dingy white cotton cloth, and to prevent their being stolen, or the boat taken away, the oars had been skillfully hidden in the marsh. Halliday located them but left them as they were; but with his pen-knife he cut away a small bit of the muffling on the oar-lock, for later possible identification.

During the search for the Morrison girl undoubtedly this boat was discovered and examined; there are numerous foot prints on the bank which effectually prevent any clue being discovered among them. But the discovery of an entirely sea-worthy boat, in so remote a location, with only the light-house in sight and that at a considerable distance, is in itself suspicious.

It was in this boat, Halliday believes, that the murderer fled onto the bay from our slip the night Carroway discovered him, and from it too that he later climbed into Carroway's launch and attacked him.

Small wonder that the boy's face set hard as he examined it.

Yet, for one must find some humor nowadays or go mad, there was something humorous in the careful indirection by which we reached it. We made rather ostentatious preparations to go fishing, Halliday working with hooks and sinkers, and I hopelessly entangled in coils of line.

Later, we rowed across the bay and anchored by the whistle buoy, where we fished assiduously for some time. Our approach to the mouth of the creek was therefore of a most desultory sort, but once around Robinson's Point, we abandoned caution and rowed rapidly.

The mouth of the creek was well closed with water weeds, but we poled the boat through them and over a shoal, into the deeper water beyond. Then, with a look around, we settled to the oars again.

Had Greenough been able to see us, from start to finish, he would have had some basis for his suspicions of me.

Whether Halliday's later discovery has any significance or not we are not certain. Believing that, on the night of the girl's murder she was brought in the truck to the water front, and coupling this with the finding of the boat, he left me sheltered from observation in the woodland and started through it toward the main road.

In a half hour or so he came back again, and reported that he had found the track of wheels driven through the woods, and that in one place a barbed wire fence had been taken down and boards placed over it, to permit the passage of a car across it.

This is, I imagine, fair presumptive evidence,

although it brings us no nearer the identity of the criminal than we were before. And it has this disadvantage, that the villagers have always exerted a right of pre-emption over the fallen timber in the woods hereabout, as I know to my cost, and that the trail may be nothing more nor less than that of some thrifty individual, seeking fuel for his cooking stove.

One thing, however, may be valuable. Edith, who knows a number of unsuspected housewifely things, insists that the strips which wrapped the oar-locks are of a fine grade of material.

"Look for somebody," she says, "who uses linen sheets on his bed, and doesn't care that they cost twenty-five dollars a pair nowadays."

From which I gather, among other things, that our little Edith has been pricing the equipment of a home. . . .

To-night that old sea-chest which in the boat-house holds on its top the law books which were to occupy Halliday's leisure this summer, and which so far seem to be used chiefly to hold open his doors on windy days — the old sea-chest contains to date the four clues which are our sole ammunition in the putative expedition against Greenough. They are:

(a) Half of a broken lens from a pair of eye-glasses.

(b) A scrap of paper, containing a cryptic bit of typing in large and small letters.

(c) The small cap of an ether can.

(d) A fragment of white cloth.

Had it not been for Halliday's unwittingly placing a weapon in the enemy's hands we should also have had:

(e) A very sharp knife, with a plain wooden handle and a blade approximately six inches long.

August 1st.

I am now convinced that any attempt to solve these crimes by the discovery of an underlying motive is a mistake. Nor will Greenough's study of psychology help him here, unless he be expert in its psychopathic developments.

One cannot piece together into a rational whole the fragmentary impulses of a lunatic. . . .

An incendiary fire was started beneath the boat-house last night, or rather toward morning. An assortment of what was apparently oil-soaked waste was placed in one of the pails from the sloop, and a candle lighted and placed in it. Over this was laid such lumber as was left from the repair of the pier.

Had Halliday been asleep the entire building

might have burned. As it happened, he had been in the woods near where we found the boat, on a chance that its proprietor might pay it a visit. He discovered the fire from some distance and by hard running, reached it in time to extinguish it.

He notified Greenough early this morning, but that gentleman was extremely noncommittal. He stood with his hands in his pockets, kicking over the ashes of the fire.

"What's the big idea, Mr. Halliday?" he inquired.

"I don't get that," said Halliday, belligerently.

"Don't you?" said Greenough, and after kicking the ashes once more, took an unruffled departure.

The best we can make of that is that the detective believes the whole thing a clumsy but concerted plan, on Halliday's part and mine; that we have endeavored to show that, although his watchers would be able to testify that I had not left the house last night, the unknown is still at work.

Nor can I entirely blame him for that. Whoever built the fire knew that Halliday was out at the time. But Halliday could not so state without betraying his knowledge of the boat, a matter he wishes to keep to himself as long as possible.

Small wonder that the detective, estimating from its charred remains the amount of lumber heaped over the flame, was sceptical.

"You are a good sleeper, Mr. Halliday!" he observed. . . .

A new month begins to-day, and like Pepys, it behooves me to take stock of myself. In spite of my best endeavors, some of my anxiety has crept into this record during the last month; and not always anxiety for myself. Alone, I could take off my coat and fight this thing out, but I am handicapped by Edith and Jane.

Edith will not go and leave Halliday; Jane will not consider abandoning me here, although she has no idea of the true situation.

"If you want to go back to town," she says, "I'll go too, of course. But if you are talking about staying here alone, for some silly reason, I won't even consider it. You wouldn't have a clean shirt, after the first week."

But, even if I felt that no action would be precipitated by the police, in case of such a move, I have a responsibility I cannot evade. The responsibility to my tenant.

I have, by a reduced rent and an alluring advertisement, brought here an elderly paralytic and his young secretary. And, evade the issue as I may, the fact remains that the last two acts of violence have been on my property.

From the beginning, indeed, the most casual survey of the situation shows me that Twin Hollows has been a sort of focal point. It was on this property that Nylie saw the sheep-killer hunt sanctuary; not on it, but adjacent to it, is still hidden the boat, and it was from my own float that he first escaped from Carroway and later killed him; it was even very possibly his flash-light that Halliday saw, the night of his arrival when, finding the boat-house occupied, he worked his way through the salt marsh toward the sea.

More recently the radius of his activity has been narrowed to the property itself. The secretary sees him outside a window; he enters the house and attacks him from within. And a few days later, possibly having overseen Halliday's discovery of his boat, he attempts to drive him away by setting fire to the boat-house. . . .

I am tempted to ask Mr. Bethel to cancel his lease; to return him his money, entire, and relieve me of responsibility.

What would he say, I wonder?

August 2nd.
I write and read, and now and then make a fugitive excursion into Jane's room, from

240

behind her curtains to watch my watcher at work. In spite of himself he has achieved something, and will doubtless go back to the city somewhat the better for an unexpectedly athletic summer.

I have been reading Mrs. Livingstone's books, and a pretty lot of nonsense I find them. If there is anything in this question of survival, surely we cannot expect to find it in physical phenomena. Why not better accept that the nervous force which actuates the body may, in certain individuals, extend beyond the periphery of that body?

Nevertheless, it is as well that I brought away from the other house the book I found there on the desk, on "Eugenia Riggs and the Oakville Phenomena." It is no reading for Mr. Bethel, under the circumstances.

One finds, for instance, that the small panelled room which we call the den was used for her seances. That panelling in itself sounds suspicious. But stop! It was not panelled at that time; I recall when poor old Horace found that oak panelling and gleefully installed it in what had been the old kitchen of the original farm house.

An investigation, made just now, has supplemented my memory. The photograph (Note: Plate I, "Eugenia Riggs and the Oakville

Phenomena") shows a plastered wall, and one or two crude water colors on it. Possibly the spirit paintings of the text.

It also shows that the cabinet, so called, was not a cabinet at all, but a dark curtain on a heavy pole, which extends across a blank corner. In the picture these curtains are thrown back, showing a small stand on which are the stage properties of "George," a bell, a pan of something, a glass, and a small bunch of flowers. On the floor, ready for his ghostly hand, is a guitar. The wall is certainly plastered.

An inset shows the pan, set on its edge to allow photography, and with the title: "Imprint of hand in putty. Dec. 2nd 1902. Notice lack of usual whorls and ridges." But in spite of this rather militant caption, I find I am unimpressed. Rather am I wondering whether somewhere in the back-ground there was not a Mr. Riggs, with a short broad thumb and a bent little finger, who was not ignorant of the lack of the usual whorls and ridges in a pair of rubber gloves.

But it is no book for Mr. Bethel. Mrs. Riggs meets Markowitz on his own ground and fairly beats him. True, he produces a broad face and an arm which comes through the soiled stuff of the curtain. But she does that, and more; she shows, under very dim red light — and anyone who has tried to see by it knows how negligible that is — hands which may be touched and held.

"The hand," says one witness, "came out from the cabinet and advanced toward me. I could see no body, but the billowing of the curtain indicated some unearthly presence behind it. I asked permission to touch it and the medium agreed, provided I did it without force. I then took the hand and held it for a perceptible moment, when it seemed to dissolve away and slip from my grasp."

One may be sure it dissolved away! And that as speedily as possible.

But, considering that plastered wall, the entire evidence in the book, gathered together, forms a surprising whole. One must take off one's hat to the Riggs family, provided there were two of them, or to whomsoever assisted the lady. Especially since the windows were "shuttered and bolted, and small strings of bells, which would ring at the slightest touch, were hung across them."

One does not wonder, since Annie Cochran probably had access to the book, that she found her tea-kettle moved about, and had her bed clothing shamelessly taken from her.

Halliday, who is an early riser, burst in on us this morning at the breakfast table, fairly bristling with excitement.

"Good morning, everybody!" he sang out. "And how about a picnic to-day? Ginger ale and fried chicken, I to provide the ginger ale?"

"Sit down, man, and pull yourself together," Edith said, eyeing him. "William, fetch the aromatic spirits of ammonia. He will be all right presently."

"What do I receive for a piece of very cheering news?" he demanded.

"Who's to judge whether it's cheering or not?"

"Well, I leave it to all of you," he said. "Greenough's gone. Benchley came over yesterday and threw him off the case. At least, that's what they say at the post-office. Thirteen days he's been fooling around, and he couldn't get over the hump."

"If only he had stayed a little longer," Edith said regretfully, "and somebody had killed him! It's rotten bad luck, that's all."

The conversation had little or no meaning for Jane. She was, I could see, puzzled by our excitement and unable to understand our relief. "Surely they have left somebody," she said. "We ought not to be left without protection.

Who knows when something will break out again, and then where are we?"

"Where indeed?" said Halliday, and he and Edith two-stepped into the living room, where Edith sat down at the organ and played execrably a few bars of "Shall We Gather at the River?"

"Latest song hit," she called. "Words and music here, twenty-five cents."

"I think you are all a trifle mad," Jane said, and went out to do her morning ordering. . . .

The move is a totally unexpected one. Yesterday, as Halliday said, the Sheriff came over to the hotel and was closeted for an hour or two with Greenough. A bell boy reports that, on carrying some cracked ice to the room, he found Greenough sitting morosely by a table, and Benchley at the window, staring out. Half an hour later the Sheriff left, passing out of the hotel without so much as a nod to anyone, and within the hour Greenough was paying his bill in the lobby and ordering a car to take him to the train.

Our own relief is enormous, but there is much grumbling among the summer folk as well as the natives. Starr is the usual variety of small-town constable, and it seems extraordinary that the case should be left in his care. It is of course possible that another man is to be sent in Greenough's place, but if so we have no intimation of it. . . .

Later: Incredible, the rapidity with which news circulates here. The immediate result of Greenough's departure has been rather to revive the interest in the situation than otherwise. I dare say as long as the police were on the case the people more or less lay back and depended on them; now they are thrown once more onto their own resources, and a variety of opinions and even of clues are being exchanged at that central clearing house, the post-office. Thus:

This morning the cows of a man named Vaughan were found huddled in a corner of the field, giving every evidence of having been run to death during the night.

(To the common sense suggestion of a dog being the culprit, pitying glances.)

A stranger three days ago tried to buy a large knife in hardware store.

(Later shown to be the Livingstone's new butler seeking a carving knife.)

The second keeper at the light-house has resigned, declaring the tower is haunted.

(This is true, so far as the resignation goes. He has, it appears, asked to be transferred. But Ward says there has been no repetition of the strange affair the night of the storm.)

A car driven recklessly and without lights has been seen twice near the Hilburn Road, both times after midnight.

(There seems a certain authenticity in this; the car, however, shows its lights until fairly close to another car, when it shuts them off entirely. There may be, of course, some defect in the dimmers.) . . .

My own relief is beyond words. Looking in my shaving mirror to-day, I am startled at the change in me the last few weeks. The Lears are coming out to dinner to-night. More power to them.

August 4th.

The party last night was a great success. Lear had brought me out a bottle of claret, and with candles on the table and six wine glasses, hastily borrowed from Annie Cochran at the main house, we took on quite a festive air. Lear looked a trifle puzzled when, at Edith's suggestion, she, Halliday and myself drank to "the absent one!" But otherwise all was well.

We divided after the meal, Jane and Helena to talk, Edith and Halliday for the boat-house and a canoe, and Lear and I to pace the drive with our cigars.

Lear's quiet face and general dependability,

and perhaps the need of a fresh mind on the conditions here, impelled me to tell my story, to which he listened without interruption.

His opinion is that we have to do with a homicidal maniac, and that the sheep-killing was preliminary to the rest, "a propitiation," he puts it.

"Of course, I am no psychiatrist," he said, "but what other explanation have you?"

"None at all," I admitted. "Of course, if I meant to commit a series of crimes, I might find it useful to establish my insanity first. I doubt if any jury, once convinced that the murderer and the sheep-killer are the same, would doubt his essential lunacy."

"On the other hand," Lear said, in his cold academic voice, "the man who sets out to commit such a series of crimes as this *is* unbalanced. He doesn't have to kill sheep to make a plea of that sort. He may present an entirely rational face to the world, but something has slipped, you can depend on it."

The supernatural angle of the case he put aside with a gesture.

"I won't even argue it," he said. "There may be something to it; I'm not denying that. But it's not stuff to be meddled with; when the Lord means to open that veil he will do it. And I am no peeping Tom."

He said further that Helena has taken up the ouija board, and sits for hours "with anyone she can entrap," getting absurd messages which sound well and mean nothing.

"In your place," he said, "I would forget it. If you get really to the point where you think you have something, send for Cameron and let him look into it. But keep out of it yourself, Porter. It's bad medicine."

I took them to the eleven o'clock train, and have only just returned. But I think it would amuse Lear, in spite of his hands-off attitude, to know that as I drove into the garage and shut off the lights and the engine, in the very act of getting out of the car I heard once more that peculiar dry cough, the faint slow foot-fall, and smelled again that curious herbal odor which I shall, all the days of my life, associate with my Uncle Horace.

So unexpected was it, coming on top of the happiest evening of the summer, that I stood for a moment immovable. Then I leaped from the terrifying darkness of the garage out into the moonlight, and there confronted young Gordon, standing outside and quietly smoking.

"Hello!" I said, when I could speak. "Out again, I see."

"Yes. That place gets my goat," he replied. "I guess I'm jumpy, since the other night."

He looked badly, and I asked him if he cared to sit down before starting back. But he refused.

"I'll get hell if he finds I've left the house," he said elegantly.

I turned and walked back with him toward the house, and seeing him secretly amused about something, asked him what it was, whereupon he said that he was thinking of the way I had shot out of the garage.

"Put something over on you there, didn't I?"

"You startled me. What do you mean?"

"I guess you know," he said, with his side-long glance. "That cough."

"You mean, the light-house story?"

He fell again into one of his secret convulsions of mirth.

"No, I don't mean the light-house," he said, and turning abruptly, struck off through the trees.

I can take from this as much or as little as I will. Is it possible that Gordon has heard the cough in the house, and associates it with the other sounds of which he has complained to Annie Cochran? Or has he merely been told of it, and with his perverted idea of humor, been deliberately alarming me with it?

If I am to believe my recent reading, according to tradition the discarnate frequently do, after death, the things they did most frequently in life; your hunter returns on horse-back, and is seen along on country roads; ladies of ancient time who lighted themselves to bed with candles seem to go on perennially retiring to God knows what unearthly couch, with the same everlasting candle in their hands.

But to record, in all seriousness, the possibility that they carry with them, without the flesh, the weaknesses of that flesh, is beyond my power of credulity.

August 5th.
I returned the wine glasses to Annie Cochran this morning, and as a result have been attempting ever since to reconcile what she says with the facts as we know them. . . .

Annie Cochran declares that young Gordon has been in the habit of slipping out of the house at night; that he commenced to do it shortly after his arrival, and has done it ever since; that, indeed, he was not sitting on the kitchen steps before he was attacked, but had been out in the car, and was trying to get back into the house.

She also believes that Mr. Bethel suspects it, and has been on the alert, especially since the night of the attack.

"There's been bad blood between them, ever since that night," she said. "They talk a bit when I'm in the dining room, but once I'm out of it, they're as glum as oysters."

She also suspects Mr. Bethel of being afraid of Gordon. On the nights when she assisted him upstairs, while the secretary was still invalided, she always heard him bolt his door as soon as he was inside.

"And the nights he stayed down," she added, "he had me bring down that revolver of his. He laid it to the fellow who got in by the gun room window, but I've got my own ideas about it."

Her reasons for not telling the detective are peculiarly feminine. He had antagonized her early by some high-handed method of his own, and "he was getting paid for finding things out. I wasn't."

But her other reason is curious, and shows a depth of loyalty to me which is unexpected and rather touching.

"I didn't see the use of dragging this place in," she says. "It's got a bad enough name already. And there's a lot of talk going on; some of it makes me sick."

From the way she avoided my eyes and rattled at her stove, I am left to conjecture that my wood-cutter — who by the way is missing today — has not passed unnoticed, and that possibly either Starr or Nylie has been talking. Probably Nylie. In any event, Annie Cochran, and very likely the entire vicinity, has evidently known that I have been under surveillance; a miserable thought, only relieved by Annie's loyalty.

"What makes you think he had been off the place, the night he was hurt?"

"He said he couldn't sleep, didn't he? And he got up and went downstairs to get something to eat, and then went outside?"

"So he said."

"Well, as far as I can make out, he was dressed from top to toe. He didn't need to do that to get down to the pantry."

And we had missed that! Hayward, Greenough and I had checked up that story, according to our several abilities, and had never noticed that discrepancy. "I sent his clothes to be cleaned the next day," she said, "and I noticed it then."

But her real contribution, if I may call it that, lay in the garage, and after tip-toeing to the hall and listening to the sound of Mr. Bethel's dictation from within, she drew me outside.

(Note: The small garage for the main house sits behind the kitchen, and not far from the kitchen door. There are two methods of access to it, one by the drive past the Lodge, which curves around the house, and the other by what we knew as "the lane," a dirt road leading through the woodland, which extends toward Robinson's Point, and which strikes the macadam highway further along.)

"So far as I know," she said, "that car's only been out twice since they came, and that was to take Thomas home one time, and me another, the night of the storm. But it's been out, just the same."

"Wouldn't the old man hear it?"

"He might and he mightn't. Suppose it was rolled along the lane and started? He wouldn't hear it there, would he?"

To support her contention she showed me a number of marks in the lane, certainly suspicious but by no means evidential. It is nothing unusual for motorists to strike into the woodland along the lane, under the impression that it is a public road, and to be brought up all standing at the house.

But against all this, at least as pointing to young Gordon as our possible criminal, is what is to me an insuperable obstacle. We know that the crimes are connected with the killing of the sheep. It is not possible to doubt this. And the sheep were killed and the altar built before Mr. Bethel brought Gordon into the neighborhood. Annie Cochran has a certain support for her contention, but not enough.

And she dislikes the boy extremely. Probably she unwittingly revealed the reason for her attack on him just before I left.

"There's something wrong about him," she said. "When a man's dishonest he thinks everybody else is."

"Surely he doesn't say that about you."

"Well, he's taken to locking his room and carrying the key about with him. I never took a thing of anybody else's in my life."

As Halliday went to twon early to-day, taking the scrap of paper with the cipher to an expert he knows there, I have not been able to discuss this new angle with him. Quite aside from the discrepancy in dates, however, Gordon not arriving until after the reign of terror was well under way, the chief stumbling block is the attack on the boy himself. . . .

Suppose the boy does slip out at night, and take the car? He is young, and I imagine pretty much a prisoner all day. He takes dictation all morning, types after luncheon while Mr. Bethel sleeps, and at four o'clock again is ready with his book and pencil. The few moments he has spent with Edith now and then are plainly stolen.

August 6th.

Halliday's expert was not particularly helpful, I

gather. We have this to our advantage, however, if advantage it be; the typing was done on a Remington machine.

As I had expected, he does not take Annie Cochran's story very seriously, but he bases his scepticism rather on the beginning of the terror before the boy came, than on the attack on the boy himself.

"After all," he says, "how do we know that it wasn't the old man himself who knocked him out? I imagine he has considerable strength in that one arm of his."

"It's difficult, but I'll suppose it."

"Suppose the old chap heard him outside," he went on, "trying to get back into the house, and thought it was somebody else. The killer, we'll say. He'd be pretty well justified in banging him on the head with a poker."

"Granting he could have got there, which I doubt, how could he have tied him?"

"One point for you!" he said. "And one more theory hanged with its own rope. Still, you'll admit it's a nice idea to play with; Mr. Bethel kills a burglar with a poker, sees it is his secretary, rings the bell and calls help, and then gets up to his room and pretends to be asleep."

"It was Gordon who rang the bell."

"Oh well, have it your own way!" he said disgustedly, "But it was a pretty thing while it lasted. And it's my opinion still that there is more in it than meets the eye." ...

Aside from this blind alley, up which Annie Cochran started us, we are all more nearly normal than we have been since the early days of the summer. I rise, shave and bathe and go to my breakfast, no longer with the feeling that it may be, figuratively speaking, my last.

Jane is at the table, fresh in the crisp ginghams she affects, and which in their turn are no crisper than the bacon. She must have been sadly puzzled the last few weeks; she shows such evident relief now. Sometime during the meal Edith, who has been awaiting her turn at our solitary tub, breezes into the room surrounded by her usual aura, pats Jock, kisses Jane and takes from me the society portion of the morning paper, after a casual glance at the mail. Any step outside, Thomas preparing to wash the verandah, or the boy who has taken poor Maggie's place, brings a faint color to her face. But in case it turns out to be Halliday, she is cavalier in the extreme.

"Morning," she says airily, and it may be adds: "Where on earth did you get that shirt?"

"What's the matter with this shirt?"

"Nothing at all," she says, resuming her breakfast. "I just thought maybe someone had given it to you. It isn't exactly the sort of shirt one buys, is it?"

Her glance appeals to me; I am for a moment the arbiter between them.

"It is a perfectly good shirt," I say with decision, and am accused of sex solidarity and poor taste, both apparently equal sins in Edith's eyes.

It is the apotheosis of the trivial; small things once more make up our lives, and we find pleasure in them. Clara brings in more bacon, catches a reflection of our morning cheerfulness and smiles with us, and even Jock, hearing unaccustomed laughter, joins in with sharp staccato barks.

We are not worried by the uncertainty of the prospect before us; the long period ahead of Edith and Halliday before they can marry; that next year, and the year after that, and God knows how many years to come, I shall be pouring the priceless treasures of the English language into ears that will not hear; that my vacation is more than half over, and that its net result so far is a loss to me of some odd pounds of weight.

We are once more safely behind the drain pipe.

August 7th.

Edith has to-day received the large sum of ten dollars for the light-house story. While she is

258

still far from the opulence she has anticipated, there has been great excitement here to-day, on receipt of the check.

She has kept a carbon copy, and has let me read it. It is well enough done, in her breezy fashion, but I find she has used the story of the so-called ghost at Twin Hollows as a basis to work from, and that she uses my name as the owner of the property. Quite aside from a distaste for seeing my name in print, I feel that the mere fact of its publication will give it a substantiality it has hitherto lacked.

It is characteristic of the average mind often to question what it hears, but to believe whole-heartedly what it reads. . . .

I find that Halliday has been quietly working along the lines opened up by Annie Cochran. He is convinced that Gordon has been going out at nights, clandestinely, and using the car to do so.

"I don't blame him for that," he said to-day. "The car's there, and not being used. And — I'm not keen about Gordon — but from such views as I have had of Mr. Bethel, a little of him would go a long way. Gordon's disconnected the speedometer, by the way. But there's something else."

He thinks it was Gordon who set fire to the boat-house. He found a bit of waste outside the garage, hanging on a limb of blue spruce there, and a similar scrap on the raised walk over the marsh to the boat-house.

"Of course that isn't evidence, Skipper," he said, "except as a trout in the milk might be. But the stuff's there, and it needs some thinking about."

"But why?" I asked. "There has to be a reason."

"I can go a long way for one," he said thoughtfully, "and imagine he knows I've been working on the case and wants to get rid of me. But I grant that's not good. Burning me out wouldn't do that, unless he hoped I was inside! But that is to imply that he is guilty of the crimes, and I don't believe it."

But he added, as an after thought:

"There's one curious thing, though. That is, it may be curious; I'm not sure. The machine he's using is a Remington."

August 8th.

This has been a nerve-racking day. I for one am willing to cry quits, to compromise with crime, and to say, in effect, that if the murderer leaves us alone we will not disturb him.

And yet the reason for my moral surrender does not lie in any event to-day on which I can place my hand. I cannot say that for this reason, or for that, I am through. Discouraged. Ready to go to the mountains and come back from a walk with a withered bunch of wild flowers held in my clenched hand, or to sit on some piazza with my after-dinner cigar and talk politics in the presence of the universe. Or to go back to town and help Jane select a new wall-paper for my study.

My condition probably arises from sheer confusion. For the life of me I cannot see where the results of Halliday's search can lead us, nor I think does he. . . .

Edith this morning, at Halliday's request, telephoned to Gordon and asked him to lunch with us. He accepted, after a brief hesitation, and promptly at one o'clock came down the drive, clad in white flannels and with an additional dose of pomade on his hair.

Whether he was suspicious or not we cannot tell. I know that, watching him from a window, part way down the drive he came to a dead stop and then turned, as if he had some idea of going back on some pretext or other. But he evidently thought better of it, looked at his watch, and came on again.

He made a poor impression on us, furtively watching Jane's choice of fork or spoon and otherwise bestowing most of his attention on

Edith. Such attention, that is, as he bestowed on anybody at the beginning. He was what a novelist loves to call *distrait,* although any question about himself roused him to a faint enthusiasm. He has, I suspect, an inordinate vanity.

"I'm a sort of wanderer," he said once, apropos of some question or statement of mine. "I stay in a place long enough to look about me and then I get the itch to move on. Restless," he added.

And restless he was. From where he sat he had his back to the windows, but more than once he managed to turn and look out. I had the felling that the small room enclosed him too much; that he felt somehow trapped. And more than once I found his eyes on me, and felt that he suspected me of some purpose he was attempting to discover.

His nervousness finally infected me, and even Jane began to show signs of distress. The small lunch party, for some reason she could not understand, was going badly. Only Edith played up well; she pushed back her plate at last, and with her elbows on the table and her chin in her hands, said:

"And now, tell us about the night you were hurt."

He was lighting a cigarette at the moment,

and he halted, the match held in mid-air, and glanced from her to me.

"I'll do that," he said, with his twisted smile, "if Mr. Porter will tell me how he and the doctor both happened to be such Johnnies on the spot."

But he carried that no further, and although the covert insolence of the speech brought the color to Edith's face, she continued to smile.

"There isn't much to tell," he went on. "The fellow got into the house all right; I turned to go in by the door and head him off, and that's all I remember."

"But you rang the bell first, didn't you?"

Whether because he hated to acknowledge that call for help, or for some reason none of us can determine to-night, he hesitated.

"Yes," he said finally. "I was pretty well excited, but I suppose I did."

On the subject of the house itself he was more fluent, showing a considerable curiosity as to its history, and inquiring with more particularity than delicacy as to the circumstances surrounding Uncle Horace's death.

"The Cochran woman has a line of talk about it," he gave as his explanation. "Seems to think he was done in, or something."

I told him of the doctor's verdict of heart failure, and he seemed to be considering that.

But almost immediately he asked me if I had tried hearing the bell as far away as the highroad, "with a motor engine going."

"I don't believe it could be done," he said, with his sideways glance at me. "He's got good ears, the doctor."

He said something before he left about looking for another job, as this one was too confining, and the old man not easy to live with. "I only took it for the summer," he said, "and I'm about fed up with it. It's too confining. And he'd let that car of his rot before he'd let me take it out."

With which clumsy attempt to alibi himself regarding the car, he took his departure. Edith believes that in some manner he knows that the car has been examined, and she may be right....

Halliday's investigation of his room during his absence proceeded without difficulty. With my keys and Annie Cochran's connivance he made an easy entry, Mr. Bethel having retired for his after-luncheon siesta.

At first glance the room offered nothing, and leaving Annie Cochran on guard outside, under pretense of cleaning the passage, Halliday made a more intensive search. The bed disclosed nothing, nor did the closet; his suitcase was locked, and over it Halliday spent more time than was entirely safe.

"Toward the end," he says, "I was pretty shaky. I kept thinking I heard him, and of course the more I hurried the more I bungled the thing."

He got it open at last without breaking the lock, and found in it the note-book.

(Note: I find I have given no description of the note-book in the original Journal. As it played a considerable part in the approaching tragedy, it deserves some attention.

It was a small compact volume of the loose-leaf type, a sort of diary, but not regularly kept. Most of the entries, due to the complication of the cipher, were very brief. One or two, however, occupied almost a page, and all of them had been typed.

Needless to say, the cipher was the one we had found on the scrap of paper picked up in my garage.)

The discovery of the note-book with its cipher sent his excitement to fever pitch. He ran through it for the code word, but was unable to find it. Then, replacing the book and leaving the suitcase as he had found it, he set to work more carefully on the room itself.

The coil of rope and the knife were behind a row of books on the bookshelf, a packet of typing paper and a box of carbon sheets thrown over them with apparent casualness, to conceal them still further.

So closely had he calculated the time that he had barely restored them to their places when Gordon slammed the entrance door downstairs, and he says:

"If he had come straight up we'd have been caught. I could have got out, but I don't believe I could have locked the door. But he stopped there a second or two, and I just made it."

He had not time to make the back staircase, however. Annie Cochran opened the linen-closet door, and he bolted in there. He heard Gordon unlock his room and enter it, and almost immediately re-appear and demand of Annie Cochran if she had been in it during his absence. An angry dispute followed, within a foot or two of the linen-closet, not the less acrimonious because of its lowered voices, and of an almost hysterical quality in Gordon's.

Every particle of his veneer had dropped from him, and the threats he made if he should find she had been in his room are not even to be recorded here. . . .

And now, once again, where are we? We have, as against Gordon:

(a) The knife and the coil of rope.

(b) Our belief that he uses the car, clandestinely, at night.

(c) At least an indication that he set the fire

266

under the boat-house.

(d) The cipher, found in my garage.

(e) The note-book, in the same cipher. A man does not record his thoughts in this manner, unless he wishes to keep them hidden.

(f) The linen strips muffling the oar-locks, and suggested to Halliday to-day by his place of concealment. The inventory of the main house shows a certain number of linen sheets. If one is missing it will prove a strong factor in connecting him with the boat.

(g) The locking of his bedroom.

(h) Last and not least, an unpleasant personality. Halliday uses the word "degenerate," but I am not prepared to go so far.

As against all this, however, we have:

(a) The attack on him at the kitchen door, and the manner in which he was tied, corresponding to the rope about Carroway.

(b) The sheep-killing and murder of Carroway, taking place as they did before his arrival.

(c) The fact that Halliday cannot identify him as the man he picked up in his car.

(d) The distinguishing mark by which the criminal has signed his crimes, so to speak, is the circle and triangle, drawn in chalk; while this is not vital, Halliday found no chalk in the room. . . .

I have put to Halliday the boy's veiled inquiry about the doctor. It is impossible for us to experiment with the bell, but he thinks it could be distinctly heard from the main road.

On the other hand, the arrival of Hayward on the scene almost as soon as I had got there is extremely puzzling. We have to-night paced off the distance, in view of my statement that I had lighted only one match when the doctor's flashlight was turned on me.

There seems to be no doubt that Hayward was on the property that night. But I do not accept the possibility, suggested by Halliday, that as he was in Greenough's confidence he had been watching me. A man does not, I imagine, go out on such an errand with his medical bag in his hand, and the doctor had carried his bag. I recall distinctly his taking from it the dressings for Gordon's head.

August 9th.

Leonardo da Vinci said: "Patience serves as a protection against wrongs as clothes do against cold. For if you put on more cloth as the cold increases it will have no power to hurt you."

But I have put on all the extra patience I can find in my mental closet, and I am still uncomfortable.

Whether Jane has noticed our ostracism I do not know, but I have, and so I think has Edith. So marked has it become that to-day I greeted Mrs. Livingstone with a warmth that slightly puzzled her.

Nothing else new to-day. Halliday watched the main house last night, but no one left it. Annie Cochran reports that Mr. Bethel is suspicious of Gordon, and that the feud between them still continues. He declines the secretary's assistance as much as possible.

That he is not certain, however, is shown by the care with which he now has the house locked up at night.

"He waits in the library," she says, "until I've locked all the doors and windows. Then I bring him the keys, except the one to the kitchen door. He lets me have that to get in with in the morning."

He is showing considerable courage, to my mind. . . .

Mrs. Livingstone was slightly ruffled on her arrival. It appears she had tried to leave her cards and Livingstone's on the old gentleman at the main house, but was finally compelled to put them under the door, although she could hear voices in the library.

But she recovered sufficiently to tell us a new story, illustrative of the general state of the local mind. She says that three nights ago Hadly, who keeps the hardware store in Oakville, when passing the cemetery where Carroway is buried, saw a figure walking slowly past the grave. It stopped, looked at the mound and then moved on, fading into nothing at the clump of evergreens beyond it.

Hadly seems to have made no further investigation!

It is unfortunate, however, that Edith's story appeared to-day, evidently syndicated and receiving wide publicity. The confirmation is sufficient to send off most of the summer visitors, looking back over their shoulders, like Hadly, as they run.

August 10th.

At midnight last night Halliday wakened me by throwing pebbles against the screen of my window. He was standing close underneath, and asked me to put on something and work my way quietly toward the other house.

"What's wrong?" I asked.

"He's getting ready to go out, I think. He put his light out at eleven, and turned it on again a few minutes ago."

Halliday moved away, and as quickly as possible I dressed and followed him. He was under the trees, waiting, when I joined him, and together we worked quietly across the garden and toward the garage, coming out beyond it, toward the lane. Here, while concealed ourselves, we had a full view of the house, but the light was out again and for a time it looked as though nothing more were to happen.

Halliday's plan was as follows: In case Gordon took the car, I was to follow it on foot at a safe distance as he went along the lane, while Halliday himself ran for my car. He would meet me at the fork of the road, and I would be able to tell him which of the two roads Gordon had taken.

We stood together, well hidden in the shrubbery, for some time. A slight wind had come up, and we could hear small waves lapping against the piles of the pier, and the monotonous wail of the whistling buoy beyond Robinson's Point, always an eerie sound. Halliday, who has not had much sleep for a night or two, fell to yawning, and I was not much better off, when I heard some sort of stealthy movement in the woodland to our left. I touched Halliday on the arm, to find him rigid and bending foward, staring toward the house.

"He's coming," he said. "Quiet!" The boy was raising his window screen, with all possible caution. Even when it was accomplished he stood so long, probably listening and watching, that I began to think he had changed his mind and gone back to bed, but as events showed, he had done nothing of the sort.

Up to this moment I had not suspected the use of the rope, although I believe Halliday had. I know my gaze was fixed on the kitchen door, with now and then a glance at the windows of the laundry and the gun room; or rather, in their direction. The darkness was extreme. But now I heard a faint scraping against the wall of the house itself and realized that he was coming down by means of the rope.

His coming was as stealthy as the preliminaries had been. He was probably half way down, coming hand over hand, before I had interpreted the sound.

I was not even aware that he had reached the ground, when I saw him, a blacker shadow among other shadows, near at hand. But he did not come directly toward the garage; he walked along under the walls of the west wing to the gun room window and stood there. Then, with extreme caution, he raised it an inch or two, as if to reassure himself that it had been unlocked from within, and closed it again.

From there, with somewhat less caution, he moved to the corner of the house and seemed to be surveying the water front and the boat-house. We had our only real view of him then, as he stood silhouetted on the top of the rise. (Note: The main house stands, as I think I have already recorded, rather higher than the remainder of the property.) But suddenly something alarmed him. Neither Halliday nor I saw or heard anything, but evidently he did, and realized too his exposed position.

He dropped to the ground. So unexpected was his sudden disappearance, that I gasped; it was not until I heard him creeping along the ground that I understood his manoeuvre. He lost no time in his retreat, nor did he attempt to use the rope again. He raised the unlocked window, crept over the sill, and closed it again, all with surprising rapidity and silence, and sooner than we could have expected we heard him drawing up the rope from his room overhead. . . .

No interpretation of this is possible without taking into consideration the really horrible stealth of the boy's manner. He was engaged on some nefarious business of his own, whether we can connect that with the crimes or not.

As to the extremely dramatic manner in which he chose to escape from the house, when he had already unlocked the gun room window, Halliday is divided between two theories, of which he himself favors the second.

"He may be merely dramatizing himself; you'll find a certain type of degenerate mind which is always acting for its own benefit. Or — and this is more likely — our old friend Bethel is suspicious and is watching him. The old man's door commands his. He locks his door from the inside, uses his rope, and is free to go where he pleases.

"But," he added, after a pause, "he unlocks the gun room window, too, so he can beat a retreat if he has to. That's the best I can do, and if it isn't correct it ought to be!"

To-day I am convinced beyond doubt that Gordon is our criminal, and I think even Halliday is shaken. I am no detective, but it seems to me that the boy, coming here during the height of the excitement about the sheep-killer and young Carroway, found the way already paved for a career of secret crime, and adopting the methods and the symbol of some still undiscovered religious maniac, has carried on, one may say, under his banner.

My psychiatric friends have discussed with me the neurotic aftermath of the war; the search for the sensational, the wooing of fugitive and secret pleasures, often brutal and violent; and the apotheosis of the criminal. They quote, too, von Krafft-Ebing's theory that the instinct to kill is purely a legacy from the past, atavistic and more or less non-deliberate. In other words, that killing is inherent in all of us, and that to the ill-balanced the destruction of the artificial inhibition, from any cause, turns them loose on the world, hereditary slayers and doers of violence.

It would, accepting that, be possible to see in young Gordon the heir, not only to his own past, but to the crimes which preceded his arrival here; to see also that gradual process of identification by which he assumed his predecessor's attributes and even te symbol by which he signed his deeds. I believe that in such cases the mental degeneration sometimes continues to the point of complete loss of personality; in that case, accepting this theory, it may even be that the boy now believes that he killed Carroway, and takes a secret and gloating pleasure in it.

A theory which I shall be happy to place at Greenough's disposal, if the opportunity arrives. It should be one after his own heart.

Certainly one fact at least supports the idea. Halliday may be right, and the attack on him not have been made by Gordon. But there seems no reason to doubt that, some time on the day before we got back, he crept into my garage and put the infernal symbol where we found it.

We have discussed to-day at some length the desirability of notifying the police once more. But our recent experience with them is not reassuring. On the other hand, I feel strongly that Mr. Bethel should be warned. But Halliday argues against it.

"He knows something already," he says. "He is on guard, and the boy knows it. Then you have to remember that the game, so far, has been to strike in the dark, and run. That is, if you are correct, Skipper, and it *is* a game, without motive."

Probably he is right. There would be little chance for him if he attacked the old man; he is too well known to be on bad terms with him. Such a warning, also, might alarm Mr. Bethel to the point of getting rid of him, and after all the only chance we have is to let him go a certain length, and then, with our proofs, call in the police.

But I am very uneasy to-night as I make this entry. I have not Halliday's easy optimism that he "won't get away with anything without our knowing it."

August 11th.

To-day is bright and sunny, and I am in a better mood. Edith came down this morning to an enormous stack of mail, and stared at it incredulously.

"Great heavens," she said, "not *bills!*"

As it turned out, however, they were not bills. Her article has brought out a curious fact; almost everybody has a ghost-story, and is anxious to tell it to somebody else; even the most incredulous of us, apparently, has some incident stored in his memory not capable of explanation. And a visible percentage of these victims of thrills and shivers have written to her about the ghost in the light tower.

She and Halliday are reading them on the verandah at this moment. Each has a heap of them, and such bits as this are to be heard:

"Here's a wonder," says Halliday. "Hold my hand, won't you, while I read it to you? There's some ghostly thing touching my neck at this minute."

"It's a spider," says Edith, coolly. "You can wait. Listen to this!" And so on. . . .

Which reminds me that I had a visit last night from "Cuckoo" Hadly, our village Don Juan, who sells hardware over his counter to pretty village matrons, and who was dubbed "Cuckoo" some years ago by a summer visitor who saw a resemblance to Byron in him, and evidently knew the quotation.

(Note: "The cuckoo shows melancholia, not

madness. Like Byron, he goes about wailing his sad lot, and now and then dropping an egg into someone else's nest.")

Hadly was slightly sheepish. He knows, and he knows I know, that his road home at night lies nowhere near the cemetery. At the same time, he had something to tell me, and was determined to go through with it.

"I guess you've heard the story, Mr. Porter," he said. "I don't suppose I'll ever hear the last of it. But there's a mistake being made, and I thought if Miss Edith was going to write it up, we'd better have it straight."

It appears, then, that it was not near Carroway's grave that Hadly saw the figure, but in the old part of the cemetery, and that there are some facts which he has not given out.

The cemetery is surrounded by a white fence, and inside it is shrubbery. Hadly, it seems, was not alone, but was standing in the road, "talking to a friend." If, as I imagine, the friend was a woman, it was surely a safe place for a rendezvous!

It was the "friend" who saw the light, and who accounts for the suppression of this portion of the tale. It shone through the shrubbery, a small blue-white light about two feet from the ground, and directly in front of the headstone of one George Pierce, who died in the late seventeen hundreds.

Hadly did not see the light, but the "friend" persisting, he crept through the shrubbery to take a look around. It was then that he saw the figure, moving slowly and deliberately toward the trees.

He seems to have no doubt that he saw an apparition, or that the information belongs to me, the reason he gives for the latter being that George Pierce is the gentleman who was, according to local tradition, shot and killed while attempting to escape the Excise in the old farm house which is now a part of Twin Hollows.

I have entered this here, because the day seems given over to the supernatural. We have breakfasted with the spirit world, and seem about to lunch with it.

Everything continues quiet at the other house. . . .

Jane and I to-day returned the Livingstones' call. Although it seems absurd, I have never quite abandoned the hope of finding, in Uncle Horace's unfinished letter, a clue to the present mystery.

I therefore took it with me, hoping for an opportunity to show it to Mrs. Livingstone. But none came. Dr. Hayward was there when we arrived and remained after we left. Perhaps, because my own world is awry, I think the universe is so.

But it seemed to me that we were shown in to what almost amounted to a situation; that Livingstone, usually dapper and calm, was flushed, and that Mrs. Livingstone was on the verge of tears. The doctor, standing by the window, hardly acknowledged our entrance, and remained standing, glowering and biting his fingers, until we left.

He is, I understand, soon to leave for a holiday.

August 12th.

(No entry.)

August 13th.

(No entry.)

August 14th.

To-morrow Hayward says I shall be able to see Greenough; the first intimation I have had that he is back in the neighborhood.

But I feel that my consciousness of my own innocence will be as nothing against Greenough's sheer determination to prove me guilty.

And yet, guilty of what? Of a bullet buried in the floor of my own house, and a broken window! We have had no further crime. Nothing is altered, save my own feeling that a net is closing around me, and that some malignant fate is sitting spider fashion in the center of it, waiting to pounce on me and destroy me.

Yesterday, being allowed to read, I found that with the single exception of the red light, my experience is fairly true to type in such matters; thousands of people have apparently gone through the same sort of thing, and have been neither the better nor the worse for it afterwards.

They saw, they believed, and then dismissed it, to be dug up out of their memories later to assist somebody to write a book, or to entertain a dinner table. But in my case, what?

My only hope, apparently, is to convince Greenough that I saw this thing; to show him the steps by which I was led to fire the shot; to put him, if I can, in my place for an hour or two.

Suppose, like a lawyer preparing a brief, I make my statement here, and to-morrow read it to him? At least I can make this entry full and explicit. It passes the time, and he may be willing to listen. . . .

This is the 14th. It was, then, the early evening of the 11th, when Annie Cochran stopped at the Lodge on her way home and asked to see me at the kitchen door.

"I'm leaving, Mr. Porter," she said. "I don't like to make trouble for you, but I can't stand that secretary."

"What has he done, Annie?"

"Done!" she said, and sniffed. "He's watching me, for one thing. I never go upstairs but he's at my heels. But that's not all. He's going to make trouble for Mr. Bethel. You mark my words. And Mr. Bethel knows it; he's scared tonight."

There had been a quarrel, she said, at dinner, carefully camouflaged while she was in the room, but breaking out again the moment she left it. So far as she could make out, it had to do with the secretary's leaving the house at night, and his insistence that he go out when and how he liked. But there was something beneath that, she thought. "That wasn't enough for the fuss they were making," she said. "There was murder in that boy's face, Mr. Porter."

Mr. Bethel, she thought, was trying to quiet him, but he refused to be quieted. Finally Gordon got up and flung open the pantry door, finding her inside it, and he said, according to her: "Listening, are you? Well, you'd better watch out, or you'll get something you don't expect." Then he went into the hall, got his hat and slammed out of the house, leaving the paralytic sunk in his chair.

"He's gone? Where?"

"He didn't say. He just took the car and went."

She was uneasy; she had construed what he said as a threat against her of a serious sort, and I drove her into Oakville myself. On the way I tried to persuade her to return to her employment for a time at least, on the ground that we might need her, and she finally agreed.

It was perhaps nine o'clock when I returned, to find the rector and his wife calling, and to sit through an hour and a half of gently unctuous conversation, while my uneasiness constantly increased, and my sense of guilt and responsibility. If we had warned the old man he would have been at least prepared to take care of himself in an emergency, but we had foolishly kept our knowledge to ourselves, and even allowing for exaggeration on Annie Cochran's part, there seemed no doubt that such an emergency might be at hand.

At 10:30 our visitors took their departure, and leaving Jane prepared to retire and Edith to answer some of her letters, I wandered with apparent aimlessness down to the boat-house. Halliday was not there, and as the dory was missing I knew he was somewhere out on the water. After waiting until eleven, my restlessness was extreme and I walked up and around the main house, to find the garage doors open and the car still out.

Had there been any indication of life in the building, I think I would have wakened Mr. Bethel and warned him; stayed with him, perhaps, until that murderous young devil was safely settled for the night. But his room was dark and his windows closed, so I thought better of it. But I did ascertain that the gun room windows were locked, and that if the boy effected an entrance at all, it would be by some less surreptitious method.

Thus reassured, I went back to the boathouse, and soon after Halliday rowed quietly in and tied the dory. He had rowed up, he said, to see if the boat was still there. It had not been disturbed, so far as he could tell.

I told him my story, but he was less anxious than I had expected.

"It's not the game," he said. "If Gordon is the killer, we've got to consider that he doesn't kill our of anger. That's different. He's cool and deliberate; he plans his stuff ahead and goes through with it. I don't even think he gets any thrill out of crime itself; the real secret joy is in baffling discovery. And he knows this: after the quarrel to-night, if old Bethel fell down the stairs and broke his neck, he would be blamed for it."

But he thrust his army automatic in his pocket nevertheless, and we started toward the house, with no particular plan in mind, but a fixed determination to protect Mr. Bethel "in case of any trouble," as Halliday put it.

We had almost reached the end of the walk over the marsh when he halted suddenly and stared to the right.

"There was a light over there," he said. "In the woods. Wait a minute; maybe it will show again."

It did show, above the head of Robinson's Point apparently, in that lonely strip of woodland which leads to the hiding place of the boat.

(Note: In explanation of our conclusion, that we had seen one of the lights of the car as Gordon drove down through the trees, I can only give again the difficulty of distinguishing at night a small light comparatively close at hand from a large one some distance away.)

Halliday watched it, and then passed his revolver to me, first taking off the safety catch.

"Don't fall over anything," he warned me. "and don't shoot until you see the whites of his eyes! I'm going over there, Skipper."

He set off on a steady lope, heading for the

light but obliged to make a long detour around the marsh. I myself, holding the revolver gingerly, started on to the house.

I was feeling, comparatively speaking, relaxed. I felt, as did Halliday, that Gordon was near Robinson's Point; my duty, as I saw it, was simply to stand guard until Halliday returned and we could make some plan; in case of trouble later to get into the house, if possible.

This thought, that we might want to get into the house, bothered me. My keys were at the Lodge, and I could hardly hope to secure them without disturbing Jane. I made, as a result, another round of the windows, and was brought up short by the fact that one of the gun rooms windows, certainly closed and locked before, now stood open.

It was the more startling, because I had but that moment ascertained that the garage doors still stood wide, and that the car was still missing.

I daresay every man has occasional doubts of his physical courage; I know that, after the sinking of the Titanic, I was obsessed with the fear that I might have fought like a demon to get into a lifeboat. But I daresay too that every man has a sort of spare reservoir of courage, on which he can draw in the emergency, when it comes. Yet I shall not pretend, even to myself, that I pulled up my shoulders, examined my weapon, and then boldly entered that window.

I crawled in, with knees that shook under me and a definite nausea in the pit of my stomach. And to make matters worse there was a slow footstep somewhere near, which I was a second or so in identifying as a drip from the old shower next door.

I had no doubt whatever that Gordon had returned, and the very fact that he had come without the car made that return sinister. I groped for the door into the passage and stood there listening, but there was no sound whatever, save the leak of the tap; I remember that as I passed the open door of the shower room I looked in, and a gleaming eye nearly lost me my equilibrium, until I remembered Edith's piece of phosphorescent wood. All this, it must be noted, was in complete darkness.

I reached the dining room without incident, and there a new throught struck me. Annie Cochran had represented the old gentleman as distinctly alarmed, and I myself had seen him some time before, more or less on guard, with a revolver. Suppose he saw a strange figure emerge from his dining room and start up the staircase? It seemed to me that he would have every right to shoot me first and investigate me afterwards.

It was while I hesitated there, near the sideboard, that I was first conscious of a cold air blowing around me. So distinct was it that my first thought was that some stealthy movement had opened the door to the passage behind me. Almost immediately on that there was a tremendous crash as though some heavy object had struck the dining room table, and following that the door into the hall burst open, slamming back against the wall outside. This was followed by complete silence.

So shaken were my nerves by all this that my next consecutive thinking found me once more in the gun room, ready to beat a retreat. But here I managed somehow to pull myself together, and to return to my original errand in the house. Convinced that the slamming of the door would have roused Mr. Bethel — if indeed anything were to rouse him again; and by this time, shaken as I was, I was prepared for the worst — the main staircase was not feasible.

I made my way, therefore, into the passage again to the servants' staircase and crept up it, one stair at a time, with the revolver clutched in my hand.

I have no idea how long all this took. Possibly ten minutes from the time I entered the house.

Perhaps even more. I was subconsciously aware, I know, that it was too soon to look for Halliday's return, and in a way I was playing for time.

At the top of the kitchen staircase was a door, opening onto the main hall, and this I cautiously opened.

Save for the ticking of the tall clock on the staircase landing the house was entirely silent. The silence and the closed door gave me back my ebbing courage, and I advanced a step or two along the hall. Here I was close to Gordon's room, and I felt for and tried the knob carefully. It was locked, and listening outside I could hear no movement from within. The relief I gathered from this was enormous, and although my position was still unpleasant enough, the fear of tragedy began to leave me.

There remained, I figured, merely to ascertain that Mr. Bethel's door was closed and locked, and I could beat a retreat which I felt was by no means ignominious. I made my way, therefore, to his door and tried it. It was fastened also, and I heard him move within; the heavy creak of his bed-spring, no doubt as he lay uneasily awake, waiting for the boy's return.

I hesitated there, wondering whether to call to him and tell him he was not alone and helpless, or to retire, satisfied that he was awake and prepared for any trouble that might come. But there were no further sounds from beyond the door, and I turned away and prepared to retrace my steps.

It was then that I became conscious of a light somewhere below. Not a light, rather, but where before had been absolute darkness there was now something else; a faint illumination which outlined the staircase well, and which was reddish in color.

(Note: It is worthy of consideration that when, later on, Halliday and I made our experiment with the red lamp, lighting it in the den and opening the door into the corridor, we secured much the same effect, save that in the experiment the resulting glow seemed stronger than the one recorded here.)

And I will swear that a figure was standing at the foot of the stairs, apparently facing toward me and looking up. Or rather, not a figure, but a face; the light was so faint that no portions of the body were visible. I will swear that it moved, not toward the dining room and a possible exit by the window of the gun room, as Halliday suggests, but still upturned, toward the library, and that within a foot or two of that door it disappeared.

I will swear that the red glow persisted for a moment or so after that disappeared and then slowly faded away. And I will also swear that I had no more intention of firing my revolver at that figure than I had of leaping down the staircase after it. Mr. Greenough would have done no less, in my situation, and might very possibly have done considerably more. The first knowledge that I had pulled the trigger came with the sound of the shot itself. I was certainly not aiming at the figure. If Mr. Greenough examines the mark left by the bullet, he will find, as Halliday and I did, that my bullet went almost directly down, and is embedded in the baseboard of the hall, near the den door. . . .

As a matter of fact, the whole sequence of events, ending with the shot, had stunned me. I heard Mr. Bethel in his room, calling out, and someone outside shouting from the terrace. Almost immediately there was a crash of breaking glass in the library, as Halliday smashed a window with a porch chair, and the next moment was in the house and fumbling for the light switch inside the library door.

When he ran into the hall I told him what had happened, and he immediately set about his search. As Mr. Bethel was still demanding, beyond his door, to know what was wrong, I went back to reassure him, but it required some time to induce him to unlock the door.

Thus it was Halliday who made the first investigation downstairs.

He is confident no one escaped from the library, unless in that brief time while he was feeling for a light. But it is to be remembered that the floor near the window was covered with broken glass; no escape by that method could have been noiseless. At the same time, any theory of departure by the windows of the den is impossible, since we found all these windows closed and locked on the inside.

I am convinced that the intruder was not the secretary. As a matter of fact, he drove in a half hour later, saw the lights in the house and hammered for admission, and surveyed our group in the hall with an amazement which, under any other circumstances, would be humorous. And I am also convinced that it was not the doctor. Mr. Bethel showing signs of collapse, Halliday telephoned to Hayward. He replied at once. Had he been at the house that night, he could not have made it. . . .

I have no explanation whatever of the fact that Halliday and Hayward later on found the gun room window closed and locked, save that the intruder may have entered by it while I was working my way into the dining room; and that the cold air, the crash at the table, and the bursting open of the door in the hall, which so alarmed me, may have marked his passage through the room.

At the same time, no statement of the situation that night should fail to point out, loath as I am to believe in the supernatural, that for many years this house has had a reputation for similar phenomena; the bursting open of the door and the cold wind are merely repetition of many similar unexplained occurrences. So also is the reddish color of the light I saw.

The disappearance of the figure and the blank darkness which followed that disappearance are difficult to account for, under any natural law at present known. I am not a spiritist, but it is to be remembered that only a second or so elapsed between Mr. Halliday's entrance by the broken window and his turning on of the lights.

Neither he nor I heard in that interval any movement; yet an escape over the broken glass of the window would certainly have made some sound. As I have said, the windows in the den were found to be closed and locked on the inside.

(End of memorandum for Mr. Greenough.)

August 15th.
Up to-day, but not allowed out of my room.

Jock spends most of his time with me, whether from devotion or interest in the appetizing trays Jane sends up, I am slightly uncertain.

Edith suspects the latter, and has taken to calling him old dog Tray. She reproaches me bitterly for my faculty of getting myself into difficult situations, and quoted to me to-day those immortal words of Lewis Carroll, with a small amendment of her own:

" 'You are old, Father William,' his young niece said.

'And your hair has become very white.

'And yet you incessantly stand on your head.

'Do you think, at your age, it is right?' "

In preparation for the detective's visit she has laid out my best silk pajamas, and her reason for doing so sounds like her:

"No man is really at his best without his trousers," she observed. "But there's a sort of moral support about silk pajamas. It puts you out of the house-breaking class, anyhow."

"Not at all," I retorted. "Only our best house-breakers can afford them, these days."

But it shows her strength and my weakness, that I am now wearing them....

Greenough has come and gone. What he thinks of things now I cannot say, but at least I am, as I have had occasion more than once to record here, still at liberty. The fact that the revolver I used was Halliday's, and Halliday's supporting statement, no doubt are in my favor.

At the same time, it is clear that, although he listened carefully to my preliminary statement relative to our suspicions against Gordon, he was not greatly impressed by it.

"How did you and Mr. Halliday reconcile that theory with the sheep-killing?" he asked, when I had finished. "He wasn't here, then, was he?"

"No, that has puzzled us, of course."

"Then again," he went on, eyeing me, "he himself was knocked down and tied. I don't suppose you accuse him of that, too?"

"I've told you," I said impatiently, "that we haven't a case; it's a theory. That's all. Take for instance that rope—"

"Oh, come now, Mr. Porter! I've slipped out of my room at night over a wood-shed; so have you, probably."

Coming down to the night of the 11th, he listened to my written statement without comment, save that he smiled somewhat over what he called my "ingenious conclusion." He also passed lightly over my picture of what followed; of Halliday's entrance, of Bethel brought down and sitting huddled in a chair in the library, somewhat dazed and showing signs of collapse. And of Gordon's return and our sudden realization of my predicament.

"Just what predicament?"

"I was in the house because I knew Gordon had a rope and a knife in his room. If we let him up there, and he did away with them, it left me in pretty poor shape."

"So you kept him downstairs! By force, he says."

"I wouldn't call it force. But we were three to his one, of course."

"In other words, you telephoned to the doctor, but you didn't telephone to Starr until Gordon came in and found you there."

"If you want to put it that way, yes."

"You broke into the house and found somebody there who had no business there. But you didn't think of calling on the police."

"What I felt we needed was not a policeman, but a medium."

He condescended to smile at that, but he was back to the matter again like a needle to the pole.

"Gordon says that Hayward and Halliday went off somewhere, after telephoning Starr, and that you held the gun on him. Is that correct?"

"I still had the revolver. I didn't point it at him, if that's what you mean. As for Halliday and Hayward, they were going through the house. That's all."

"And they found the gun room window closed and locked?"

"So they say. I wasn't present."

"How do you account for that, if that's the way you entered?"

"I don't account for it."

"I suppose you have keys to the house?"

"I have."

"But you entered by this window?"

"Great heavens, man!" I said impatiently. "I don't carry those keys with me. I wasn't trying to get into the house. I went in because the window was open. And if you think I liked doing it, I'm here to tell you I didn't."

"You can't account for the window being locked, later?"

"I cannot. Why should I have locked it, if that's what you are trying to intimate? I had to get out again."

He abandoned that for the time.

"The point is this, Mr. Porter," he said. "You and Halliday have laid considerable emphasis on that knife. It was because Gordon had it that you were in the house, I understand."

"Had it and might use it," I amended.

"It was, in your opinion, either on him or in the room upstairs. But as it turned out, it was neither on him nor in his room. He denies ever owning such a knife."

"Halliday saw it. He's lying."

"It's your belief, then, that on this murderous errand of his, which was to end up at the house, he disposed of the very weapon which you had expected him to use?"

"I haven't said that, but I think it probable."

"Why? Why should he? He could have had no idea the house was to be entered, or his room searched. He came back, smoking a cigarette I understand, to find you and Halliday in the hall, a window broken and a bullet imbedded in the floor. That doesn't sound like a man who has been out hiding the evidences of his crimes."

He asked me abruptly after that how long I had known Halliday, and his relationship to the family. Then he attacked Halliday's statement that he thought he had seen the lights of a car by Robinson's Point, and had started for that.

"Mr. Halliday," he said, "says that he believed that this car was Mr. Bethel's and started toward it, giving you his revolver and leaving you alone; that he found no car there, and turned back. To support this statement, he says that a boat, lying in the creek there, had excited his suspicions because the oar-locks were wrapped. Muffled oar-locks are not uncommon things."

"The position of the boat was suspicious."

"Perhaps," he said. "But that was a matter for me to determine, not Mr. Halliday. As to the strips he maintains were wrapped around the oar-locks, I am not saying they were not there; but I am saying that they were gone when I went over the next morning to examine the boat."

What he had hoped to gain by that I do not know. He shifted rapidly, perhaps in the hope of somehow trapping me; our reasons for hoping to connect Gordon with the crimes, since one of them had taken place before his arrival; when I had first missed my fountain pen; exactly where I was standing when the revolver was fired; when I had taken off the safety catch; where I was when Halliday broke the window. And from that, without a pause, back to the gun room window and had me repeat my story about finding it open, and entering by it.

"Yet you thought," he said, "that this boy, whom you consider a degenerate and a murderer, was inside. In a few minutes you expected Halliday back, but you did not wait for him. Is that right?"

"It is."

"Then you thought, in all probability, that the boy had this knife with him."

"I didn't think about it at all," I said. "If I

had, I'm not sure I would have gone in."

"But later on the boy returns, and you won't let him upstairs, because the knife is there. Is that right?"

Looking back over the interview, he seemed to be anxious to break down my story, rather than to be following any idea of his own. Halliday stated it fairly well when I reported the examination to him.

"He's got nothing," he said. "Nothing but you. And that's where his system breaks down; it might work, if you were guilty, but it isn't worth a tinker's dam, since you're not."

One rather curious thing he added, however, in view of Greenough's questions about the knife.

(Note: I was not present when Starr followed by Gordon, Halliday and Doctor Hayward, went upstairs to examine Gordon's room. During the interval of waiting for the constable I had been conscious of an approaching nervous chill, the beginning of the illness which laid me up for the following three days.)

"Gordon was as surprised as I was," he says, "when Starr didn't find the knife. It was too good to be true; he could hardly believe it."

Downstairs to-day for the first time.

As I had expected, Mr. Bethel intends to give up the house. He has so notified Thomas and Annie Cochran, and has sent me a note asking me to see him to-night.

The note was left by Gordon, and as I happened to be in the hall, it was I who received it.

He stiffened when he saw me, it being our first encounter since the other night.

"Mr. Bethel sent this," he said briefly, and started to go. On the verandah, however, he stooped and turned around. "Pretty dirty work the other night," he said, watching me. "And I'm not forgetting it."

He waited, apparently expecting a reply. On receiving none he stood studying me for a moment, — a most uncomfortable moment for me. Then he smiled, his curious sneering smile.

"I'm not afraid, you know," he said. "I can take care of myself. I'm not worrying."

He thrust his hands into his pockets and turned, not toward the other house, but toward the road. Near the gates he began to whistle, and thus theatrically assuring me that he was at ease, started toward Oakville.

I have learned to-day that he is leaving Mr. Bethel, and has gone to the city to look for another position.

The boy puzzles me. Here I am, more or less a specialist in boys; for more years than I care to remember I have known them, collectively and individually, but here is a new type.

He is weak; compared to that prognathous portion of Halliday's face, for instance, he has no lower jaw. He completely lacks personality; he could, according to somebody's description of a similar type, be stood up against a white-washed wall and erased with a good rubber. He is, one would say, almost too weak to be vicious.

But nature apparently gives to these otherwise defenseless creatures of hers a sort of low cunning with which to protect themselves. He has that cunning.

He is not in love with Edith, I think, although that vain young woman probably believes that he is. He is interested in her, as the only young and feminine creature within his present *milieu*; for the same reason he hates Halliday, quite apart from the other night, as representing what he is not and would like to be. At the same time, he hates the world, because he feels himself incapable of coping with it.

But just how far does he carry this secret longing of his to escape his own inferiority? To the length of crime? Granted the desire so to escape it, has he the ability? Can he make his possible dream of being a master criminal come true? I think not....

Other things go on much as before. Greenough after three days of no further discoveries has gone again. The situation at the main house the other night has, thank God, not reached the press. The boat, with the mufflings gone from the oar-locks, still lies in the creek beyond Robinson's Point, and the sole proof of such muffling, if the point is even brought up again, lies in the boat-house along with the broken lens, the bit of Gordon's cipher and the small screw cap of an ether can.

Our lovers move about their ordinary duties with an eye out, as one may say, each for the other. Vague as the future is, they have each other, and only this morning I saw Edith with a basket of mending, from which looked forth what greatly resembled a masculine undergarment in need of buttons. Shades of twenty years ago, when each sex politely assumed that the other went, so to speak, undergarmentless!

They cannot turn the clock on. But there are times when there is a sort of despair in Halliday's face, and sometimes I see Edith sitting alone, her hands folded, looking three or four years ahead with a sort of tragic patience. So much, she seems to think, may happen in three or four years.

She asked him, the other day, out of a clear sky, if he had been gone over by a doctor recently.

And the reward, on which she had so blithely counted, seems as far away as ever. As far away as her dreams of earning a fortune with her pen. She has had another rejection or two, and the heart has gone out of her.

But she has had her moment. Mail still continues to come in. Which reminds me that she received a curious letter yesterday. Because it may be construed to have a bearing on our situation I record it here, but as a matter of fact, one must make certain allowances; Edith's articles used my name in full, and a small amount of investigation by the professional mediumistic underground would supply some of the remainder. The Jane, for example, is quite easily accounted for.

But the remainder leaves me considerably puzzled. The boat, for instance. And that strange condition of Mr. — at the end, a heart which is normal apparently failing him, so that he would have fallen had he not been caught. For all the world as though — but I must pull myself together. The letter from Salem was not authentic; why should I believe this?

Evanston, Illinois.
August 12, 1922.

"Dear Madam:

"I have read with great interest your account of the strange occurrence at the light-house at Robinson's Point, and would like to tell you of something which occurred here that same night and, allowing for the difference in time, at about the same hour.

"I am not a spiritualist, but following a small dinner here, it was suggested that we try table levitation, and against my husband's protests, this was arranged for.

"My husband, I may say, is not psychic in any way, and was greatly bored with the proceeding. We were not surprised, therefore, when after sitting in darkness for ten minutes or so, he fell asleep and began to breathe heavily.

"I tried to rouse him but was unable to, when the opinion was given that he was in a trance state. As none of us were familiar with that condition, and as he began to groan heavily, I was greatly alarmed. There was a doctor in the party, however, and on his saying that his pulse was all right, we sat quiet and waited.

"He then said 'Jane, *Jane*' in an agon-

305

ized voice, and as my name is not Jane there was some amusement, especially when he added: 'She is asleep. I cannot rouse her.' Almost immediately after that, however, he said 'Robinson's Point,' and something about a boat there. (We think now that the allusion may have been to the light-house you mention.) After that he was quiet for a time and I begged to be allowed to waken him, but just as we had turned on the lights again he got up, with his eyes still closed, and leaning over the table, seemed to be staring at the gentleman across from him. (A Mr. Lewis, a very nice man, with whom my husband plays golf a great deal.)

"'I have not changed my attitude,' he said, in a really terrible voice. 'I repudiate you and all your works. I am not afraid of you. The thing is monstrous, and society should be warned against you.'

"I have forgotten to say that he had kept his right hand closed, as though he had something in it. He made a gesture as though he threw this something away, and then looked at Mr. Lewis again and said: 'I have warned you; I shall tell the police.'

"He seemed to be in a state of great excitement, and hardly able to breathe. He fell back into the chair, and our doctor friend reached over and felt his pulse. He says now that, although his heart is perfectly sound, it had almost stopped. Indeed, he would have fallen had the doctor not caught him. In a short time he came around and seemed to think he had been asleep. He felt, however, very wretched the next day.

"This may not interest you, but the mention of Robinson's Point in your article, and the similarity in time, has struck me as a strange coincidence. I am signing this in full, as an evidence of good faith, but I must ask you not to use it for publication."

(Note: I have since secured the writer's consent to the use of this letter, on condition that I withhold the signature.) . . .

"An element which works beyond our guess; Soul, the unsounded sea," says Browning. A poet's idea only, perhaps, but wasn't it Montaigne who said that all our philosophy is but sophisticated poetry?

What a joyous time little Pettingill would have with all this! Trotting about, a note-book in hand, adding up a glimpse here, a look there, until he had a complete panoramic view of all eternity. But the real question is, what would

Cameron say? Not for him the amorous Hadly in the churchyard — a spot by the way, if our spiritists are right, not quite so exclusive as Hadly seems to have considered it — nor a tea-kettle moving about. His the coldly scientific method; the medium in a box, tied hand and foot; scales of weighing; cameras; note-books; witnesses.

Not for him Pettingill's wide view into eternity, but a narrow slit, guarded by little bells on strings, through which the poor ghost must creep if he come at all.

I wonder what would happen if I could induce him to come here?

August 17th.

One lives and learns.

Mr. Bethel last night lifted a small corner of the mystery and showed me a few of the wheels within. With the net result that we are where we were before. . . .

He telephoned me at nine o'clock last night, the first time I have known him to use the telephone, and asked me to see him.

(Note: I have, I think, not mentioned in the Journal that the three buildings, the Lodge, main house and boat-house, are on one telephone. As this fact plays an important part

308

later, it requires explanation.)

I found him alone in the library, but with certain changes from the last time I had seen him thus. The windows were closed and locked, and the heavy curtains drawn across them; both the rear and front doors in the hall were bolted, and when I was finally obliged to ring, I could hear the old man dragging himself slowly into the hall and there stopping.

"Who is it?" he called.

"Porter."

I was on the terrace, and he opened that door for me, working laboriously with his single useful hand. Once inside, he left me to close it for myself, and went back into the library. When I followed him it was to find him seated, with the revolver close at hand as before. He was a strange, half-sinister figure as he sat there, but when he spoke it was as the querulous invalid of our first meeting.

"I don't like your house, Mr. Porter," he barked at me, without preliminary.

"I don't like it myself," I admitted. "I am thinking of adding to the insurance and then setting a match to it. After you are out, of course," I added.

That brought a sort of dry chuckle from him, but the next moment he was back to the attack. He supposed he was responsible for the balance of the rent, but wasn't I morally responsible if he couldn't live there? I had known the stories about the house, and yet had let it to him. There was a question there.

"There is no question," I said. "I have no idea of holding you up for the balance of the rent."

It seemed to me, however, that he hardly heard me. He was listening again, as he had before, and when he spoke it was on a totally different matter.

"You find me rather on guard," he said. "I am alone in the house."

"Where's Gordon?"

"He went into the city this morning. He has not come back."

And there was something in the way he made the statement that caused me to look at him quickly.

"You mean that he has gone for good?"

"No. I wish to God he had."

There was fear in that, and I realized then that all the place showed fear, the locked and bolted house, the dim light — only one lamp going, and that on the desk — the revolver, and the old man's twisted body, crouched and watchful.

"I am afraid of him, Mr. Porter," he said. "I think he means to kill me."

"Nonsense!"

"I wish it were."

"Can't you get rid of him?"

"Don't you suppose I've tried?"

His story, if story it can be called, that rambling discourse broken into by his fits of listening, even once of sending me out to take a look around, is as follows:

He had picked the boy up in the city, knowing little or nothing about him, and from the time they arrived he had not quite trusted him. After a time, too, he began to suspect that he was getting out of the house at night, and possibly using the car.

"Not guilty in itself, perhaps," he said, "but it left me alone, for one thing. And it is not a house in which one cares to be alone." He glanced at me. "And for another, – well, I needn't tell *you* what has been going on."

But he was not, at first, really suspicious of these night excursions, save for his resentment at being left there, alone and helpless, with a killer loose in the neighborhood. He kept a watch, therefore, not so much over the boy as over the house and himself in his absence.

"If he left a door or window open," he said, "I was at the mercy of anybody who chose to enter."

And this, he says, was the situation on the night of the 26th of July. He had gone to the boy's room and found it empty, and had after some debate decided to work his way downstairs and lock him out.

"And myself in," he said.

It took him a long time to do it; he says too that he was very nervous; there were sounds, especially in the dining room. Nothing he could account for, but they upset him still further, and by the time he reached the kitchen he was in a bad way. He had to sit down there.

It was while he was sitting there that he heard sounds on the porch, and somebody at the door knob. From that on he says he was beyond coherent thinking, but he had no doubt in the world, because of the stealthiness of the movement, that the thing he had feared was happening. It seems never to have occurred to him that it was Gordon.

He dragged himself to the stove, found the poker, and as the door opened struck with all his strength.

"It was only when he made a leap for the bell that I knew what I had done."

He was sticken. He felt the boy's pulse and knew he was not dead, but off somewhere near the sun-dial he heard some one moving, and that alarmed him still more.

"A man never knows his cowardice," he said wryly, "until he is put to the test. I have very little idea of what I did next; my only clear recollection is of finding myself in my room. I don't remember getting there."

But — and this is the point — the boy suspected him. He was sure of it. There had been a complete change in his attitude since that time. And watching that change, studying Gordon as he had felt obliged to, he had felt that something underlay all this. In other words, gradually he had begun to associate the boy with the other crimes.

"He is weak," he said, "weak and vicious. And there is that curious mental state called identification; the weak see the crimes committed by the strong, admire them, admire the criminal. Then they begin to ape them, as Gordon may have aped your sheep-killer, finally even identifying himself with this unknown, adopting his symbol, or whatever one chooses to call it."

I listened carefully, trying to fit this new light on Gordon's injury with the evidence as I knew it. True, the weak link in our chain against him had been that he himself had been attacked. And this was now solved in a perfectly matter-of-fact manner. But there was some discrepancy there, something which eluded me until I had gone over in my mind the events of the night of the 26th in their sequence. Then I found it.

"Pure invention, I feel certain. Had he accused me he knew the matter of his night excursions would come out. That was the last thing he wanted."

It was my next remark, however, which has left us, as I wrote at the beginning of this entry, just where we were before.

"You haven't said anything about the rope, Mr. Bethel. That has always————"

"Rope!" he said slowly. "What rope?"

"He was tied hand and foot when I found him."

He glanced at me, and then down at his helpless hand.

"It's a very long time since I have been able to tie a rope, Mr. Porter," he said quietly.

I remained with him until an hour or so after the last train from the city had arrived, but there was no sign of Gordon. I offered to remain for the night with him, but he declined. He would not go to bed, however, and I left him there at last, his revolver within reach. . . .

Of that later talk there is one matter of real importance to record.

I have a strange picture in my mind, bearing on the relations of these two, the old man and the boy, and leading up to it; each watching the other, the old man terrified, the boy deadly. And on the surface, before Annie Cochran, all well enough between them; dictation taken, and the book growing. Small surface differences, perhaps, but underneath suspicion on one side and revenge and hatred on the other.

Then Gordon took to locking his room. It was Annie Cochran who told Bethel, and from that time on that locked room played its own part between them; the old man asking himself what was hidden in it, the secretary with his sneering smile quietly carrying the key. It grew, I gathered, to have a peculiar place in the old man's imagination; he wandered down the passage to it more than once; finally Annie Cochran caught him there, trying the knob, and he had made some excuse and gone away.

But the night young Gordon flung out of the house, the same night I saw the figure at the foot of the stairs, Annie Cochran had come to him before leaving, with a key in her hand.

"I thought you might like this, sir," she said. "I find it fits Mr. Gordon's door."

Then she had gone, and he went to the room and entered it. The knife and the rope were there, and *he took them.*

"What was I to say that night, when the constable came down and reported nothing there? In ten minutes, or an hour, you were going to leave me here with him. He was watching me; he knew."

And I daresay he was right. No matter what statement had been made relative to the rope and the knife, there was no reason for Gordon's arrest that night. In ten minutes, or an hour, they would have been left together, and who knows what might have happened?

August 18th.

Gordon came back early this morning. I invented an errand to the house soon after breakfast, but found that Mr. Bethel was still sleeping — as well he might — and that preparations for to-morrow's departure were well under way.

While Gordon was busy on the lower floor, Thomas and I made a tour of the house, with a view to closing it. I have instructed him to paint and put up the window boards which close the windows on the lower floor; I shall know no peace until the place is sealed, and left to its demons or its ghosts.

But I took advantage of my legitimate presence on the upper floor to examine the locked closet in which I had stored the red lamp. It is still there, and apparently has not been disturbed. . . .

Halliday to-day advised for me a period of masterly inactivity. Not that he calls it so, but that is what he means.

"I have an idea, Skipper," he said, "that this calling Greenough off the case was sheer bluff. Every move he made was being watched, and unless I miss my guess you'll find he's at Bass Cove, or some place nearby, under another name. I thought I saw his Ford a night or so ago."

What I finally gathered is that Halliday wants to eliminate me from the case, for my own sake.

"Just now," he said, "you are sitting very pretty. But one more bit of bad luck and he's ready to jump."

Although he smiled, I have an idea that he is deadly serious; that he knows Greenough is not far away, and that for some unknown reason he expects another bit of bad luck. His face is thin and haggard these days, and from the fact that he sleeps a great deal in the day time, I am inclined to think that he sleeps very little at night.

Between him and Edith, too, I surmise some sort of mysterious understanding. At the same time, there is a noticeable absence of those three-angled conferences in which, some little time ago, we were free to air our various theories.

Willy nilly, I am consigned to innocuous desuetude.

Hayward started yesterday on his vacation.

August 20th.

4:00 A.M. Mr. Bethel was murdered between eleven o'clock and midnight last night. Gordon has escaped. . . .

7:00 A.M. Jane is at last asleep, and I have had some coffee. Perhaps if I record the events of the night it will quiet me. After all, one cannot forget such things; the only possible course is to bring them to the surface, to face them.

But I will not face that room.

Murder. The very word is evil. But no one has ever known how evil until he has seen it. Such things cannot be written; they should not be seen. They should not be.

We have had this murder. We have gone over, inch by inch, the scene of it. We have been spared no shock; the evidence of the struggle is on the walls, the floor, the furniture; we have the very knife with which it was committed. We have even gone further than that. We have followed it outside, along the drive to the garage, and from there by the car to the salt marsh beyond Robinson's Point.

And yet, according to Halliday, until we have gone still further, we have had no murder, according to the law.

Ever since daylight, I have been struggling to see the justice of a law where, when Gordon is found – and Greenough believes he will be found – we cannot convict him unless we also find that bit of old flesh and blood and bone which was once Simon Bethel.

Is it only necessary, to escape justice, that a criminal artfully dispose of his crime?

And by how narrow a margin he did escape it! A matter of minutes. Between my calling Halliday on the telephone and my meeting him at the terrace; perhaps even between that and our entrance into that wrecked room. A matter of minutes.

In one thing only did he make an error, and even that may not have been an error. He may coolly have abandoned his suitcase, packed and hidden in the shrubbery; may have stood there a second or so, considering it, and then decided to let it lie.

The most grievous thing to me is that I should have given him the warning. And the most terrible picture I have is that, when I called Halliday, he stood listening in at the telephone, craftily calculating: "Can I make it? Can I not?" With *that* behind him. . . .

Crafty. As old in crime as crime is old, for all his youth. Out on the bay disposing of his horrible freight, and watching the lanterns as they

319

searched for the boat; seeing them scatter, looking for other boats with which to follow him out onto the water, and then quietly heading back, into the creek again, and escaping through the wood.

Crafty, beyond words.

August 21st.

The excitement is still intense. I have hardly seen Halliday since our trouble; he is working with the police, of which a number have come to assist Greenough. Curious crowds stand outside our gates, which we have been obliged to close and lock. A few of the more adventurous, gaining admission by the lane, are turned back there by guards who are on duty day and night.

Thomas, standing at the gate, has orders to admit only the detectives and duly accredited members of the press.

On the bay we have once more the familiar crowd of searching boats. Off the Point, dragging has been going on, but with no result. Owing to the fact that no guards were placed by the boat, a large portion of it has already been taken away by morbid individuals who will place their trophies, I daresay, on tables or mantel-pieces, and thereafter gloat over them.

Truly, just as the lunatic always insists that

he is sane, so do the sane often demonstrate that they are mad.

And so far, nothing.

Nothing, that is, which leads to Gordon's apprehension. From the time he turned back in the boat and landing, made his escape into the woods above Robinson's Point, he disappeared entirely. Here and there a clue has turned up, to end in disappointment. Greenough believes that he will be found, that he cannot escape the police drag-net, but I am not so sure. . . .

Although almost forty-eight hours have passed Jane has not yet opened up the subject of the telephone, and because of her morbid reserve on such matters, I have not told the police.

Asked how I had happened to be at the telephone and thus receive the alarm, I have replied that the bell rang, that I went to the instrument, and was immediately aware that one of the receivers was down, either at Halliday's or at the main house; that I heard a crash over the wire, followed by a second and nearer one, and after that a silence; that following that I heard, near the receiver, the sobbing breath of exhaustion, and that immediately after that the receiver went up, and I called Halliday frantically; and that, on his replying, I told him my suspicion that something was wrong at the main house, and to meet me there at once.

But there is a discrepancy here which may cause me trouble if they come back to it A telephone such as ours does not ring if one of the receivers is down. And the plain fact is that our telephone did not ring at all that night.

As I have not yet recorded the events of that tragic evening in their sequence, I shall do so now.

Halliday had dined with us, and had been more like himself than for some time past. The news that the house was to be given up had seemed to relieve him, for some strange reason, and I remember he said something which puzzled me at the time.

"After all," he said, "we can't undo what has been done. And it may be the end."

After dinner he and Edith sat on the verandah, and going to lower a shade I saw that she was holding a match while he drew something on a bit of paper. But the match went out almost at once, and I would have thought no more of it, had I not heard Edith say:

"And the cabinet was there?"

"In the corner," he replied.

I am no eaves-dropper, so I drew the shade and turned away.

He left at something after ten, and Edith joined us. She was very quiet, and sat watching me play solitaire while Jane sewed industriously.

At half past ten or thereabouts, Jane suddenly said:

"The telephone is ringing."

Both Edith and I looked up in amazement; the instrument was in the small hall, not ten feet from where I sat; it would have been impossible for it to ring without our hearing it, and we had heard nothing.

"You've been asleep, Jane!" Edith accused her. But I glanced at her, and I remember that she was oddly relaxed in her chair; her face looked white and her eyes were slightly fixed.

"It is ringing," she said, thickly.

And that is how I happened to be at the telephone that night. And how, too, I gave the alarm which enabled the murderer to escape, by calling Halliday.

"Get your revolver and meet me at the main house," I said. "There's something wrong there."

I know that had I not rung the telephone, had I gone for Halliday instead, we would have caught the criminal. But to ring the one house was to ring the other; he may still have been standing there gasping. He had, for all he knew up to that time, the rest of the night in which to finish his deadly work; to dispose of the body, to gather up his suitcase, waiting outside, and get away.

But I called Halliday, and he listened. He

knew then that instead of hours he had only minutes. He must have worked fast, in that ghastly shambles of a room; the car was probably already out, in the lane. He may even have stood there, at the corner of the lane, the engine turning over quietly, and watched Halliday running up toward the house. And perhaps he laughed, that secret laugh of his which had always rather chilled me.

Then – he simply got into the car and drove away. Cool and crafty to the last. No body, no murder. He made for the boat.

He left behind him only two real clues; the knife, which Annie Cochran identifies as one taken from the kitchen, and his packed suitcase. Not intentional, this last. He must have needed clean linen. And certainly that diary of his, in cipher – he would not want that in the hands of the police. But what would the diary matter, after all, if he himself escaped?

August 22nd.

As time goes on the case is complicated with the eagerness of all sorts of people to bring in extraneous circumstances which they consider important.

For instance, Livingstone's butler, the one who bought the knife in Oakville and caused so much excitement by so doing, has been over to get a description of Gordon, preserving an air of mystery which under other circumstances would be vastly entertaining.

Another story concerns a middle-aged man of highly respectable appearance and of a square and heavy build, who was seen walking uncertainly along the main road near the Livingstone place at 1:00 A.M. the night of the murder. A passing car, seeing his state, stopped and asked if he was in trouble.

He replied that he had been struck by a car an hour or so before, and had been lying by the road ever since. His condition bore this out, as he was stained with blood and dirt. He accepted the offer of a lift, and was left at the railroad station at Martin's Ferry to catch the express there for the city.

There have been many similar ones; an innumerable number of people are convinced that they have seen Gordon, and apparently almost any dapper youth of twenty or so, with what Edith calls patent leather hair and an inveterate cigarette habit, is likely at any time to be tapped on the shoulder and taken to a police station. . . .

Of clues of other and lesser sorts there has been almost an embarrassment. Both the library and that portion of the hall near the telephone have furnished finger prints. But as Greenough says:

"Finger prints do not discover criminals; they identify them."

Nevertheless, great pains have been taken to preserve them. On the white marble mantel a very distinct imprint in blood was photographed without difficulty; others, less clear, were dusted with black powder before the camera was used. Detailed pictures were made of the library and hall, before any attempt to put them back to order was permitted, and these prints have been enlarged and carefully studied. One of them with a strange result.

Greenough, handing it to me to-day said:

"This print is defective. You can keep it, if you care to."

But I wonder if it *is* defective. There is what Greenough calls a light streak in the lower corner, but it requires very little imagination to give to this misty outline the semblance of a form, and to the lower portion of it the faint but recognizable appearance of brocade.

I have said nothing. What can I say? . . .

One thing which puzzles the police is the violence of the battle; it seems incredible that Bethel could have made the fight for life which he evidently did. At the same time, they have two problems to solve which repeated searching of the house and wide publicity have not yet answered.

One is the disappearance of the manuscript on which Bethel had worked all summer. Annie Cochran has testified that this manuscript was kept locked in a drawer in the library desk; when Halliday and I entered the house this drawer was standing open and the manuscript was missing. It has not yet been located.

But perhaps the most surprising is the failure of any friend or relative of Simon Bethel to interest himself in the case. Cameron's note to Larkin before Bethel rented the house expressly disclaims any previous knowledge of him.

"Here is a possible tenant for Mr. Porter's house," he wrote, "of which he spoke to me some time ago. I have no acquaintance with Mr. Bethel, save that he called on me a day or so ago, in reference to a statement in a book of mine. I imagine, however, that he would be a quiet and not troublesome tenant."

Halliday brought up this curious situation yesterday, in one of the rare moments he has given us since the murder.

"Has it occurred to you, Skipper," he said, "that it is strange that no one belonging to Mr. Bethel has turned up?"

"I dare say a man can outlive most of his contemporaries and most of his friends."

"He wasn't as old as all that." And he asked, apparently irrelevantly a moment later: "The two evenings you saw him and talked to him, how did he impress you? I mean, his state of mind?"

"The last time, of course, he was frankly frightened. He said as much."

"And before that?"

"He didn't say so, but he was more or less on guard. He had his revolver. Of course, those were rather parlous times."

As a matter of fact, the case is anything but a clear one against Gordon, as it develops. Greenough has been, all along, as convinced of Gordon's guilt as he had previously been of mine. But Benchley is more open to conviction, and a conversation between Halliday and him this morning, on the lawn near the terrace, is still running in my mind.

Halliday had been protesting against Greenough's method of "following a single idea until it went up a blind alley and died there."

"Of course," he said quietly, "you can make a case against Gordon; it's all here. But you'll have something left over that you won't know what to do with. We know that it was Mr. Bethel who hit Gordon and knocked him out some time ago, but who tied him? Where's the boy's own story about seeing a man at the gun room window? Mr. Porter here later on finds that same window open, and sees a man in the lower hall. Who was that? The same hand tied the boy that tied Carroway, and Gordon hadn't even seen this place at that time. What are you going to do with that?"

"Then where's Gordon now?" Benchley asked, practically enough.

"I don't know. Dead, maybe."

Benchley stood thinking.

"I think I get the idea," he said. "The fight, you think, was between Mr. Bethel and this unknown of yours; the boy either saw it and got mixed up in it, or knew he'd be suspected and beat it. Is that it?"

"Well, I would say that a man about to commit such a crime doesn't pack his suitcase, with the idea of escaping with it."

A thought which, I admit, had never occurred to me until that moment.

As a result of this conversation, Benchley has advanced a theory of his own which accounts at least for the failure of any relatives to make inquiry. This is that the old man was in hiding under an assumed name; hiding, in the most secluded spot he could find, from some implacable enemy who had finally caught up with him.

How he reconciles this with the Carroway

murder and the disappearance of Maggie Morrison I do not know, but certain facts seem to bear out this idea. He was, in one sense, a man of mystery. His accounts were paid in cash; the automobile in which he arrived had been bought at second hand a few days before, by the secretary and in the same manner. And all identifying marks had been carefully removed from his clothing.

In addition to all this, there is the puzzling report on the knife itself. Examination under the microscope shows fibers of linen as well as fragments of cellular tissue. But it also reveals minute particles of tobacco leaf, showing it had gone through a pocket.

But Mr. Bethel was not a smoker.

At some one time, then, Bethel clearly secured the knife and wounded his assailant. Not seriously, evidently, since after that he was able to do what he did do, but sufficiently to turn the minds of the police toward the man who claimed to have been struck by an automobile.

This clue, however, has developed nothing. The night was dark, and his rescuers have no description of him, save of a heavy-set figure and a dazed manner of speech. They carried him to Martin's Ferry, but the conductor of the night express remembers carrying no such passenger. . . .

Greenough to-day showed me Gordon's diary, rescued from the suitcase. It has at some time been dropped into water, and certain pages are not legible. If indeed that word may be used where nothing is legible; where each page presents such jumbles of large and small letters as the following sentence, which I have copied as a matter of interest:

"Trn g.K. GTRgg UnMT aot LmGT MotrT."

The record is not a daily one, but apparently was used for jotting down odd thoughts or ideas. It continues, however, at intervals, for the entire period of his stay at Twin Hollows, the last entry having been made on August 17th.

Certain entries are neat and methodical. The one on July 27th, however, after his injury, is by hand, and shows certain erasures and changes. Once or twice in August the record is long, covering more than a page, while the July entries are all brief. On the last page, however, and without comment, he has drawn in, rather carefully, a small circle enclosing a triangle.

Greenough, while attaching a certain interest to it, has not yet sent it to be deciphered by the code experts of his department. As a matter of fact, I suspect him of holding it out, with the idea of being able to claim the reward if he finds Gordon.

Which reward, by the way, now stands at ten thousand dollars.

August 23rd.

Halliday saw a red light in the house the night Bethel was killed. He has just told me.

He ran out, after I telephoned him, and from the foot of the lawn he saw it. It was gone almost at once.

He has asked me to experiment with him to-night, using the lamp from the attic closet. I have given him the keys. Apparently what he wishes to discover is the approximate location of such a light. I have no idea of his purpose. . . .

I understand that the guards who have been watching the house at night have been withdrawn, and that hereafter only such watch will be kept as will suffice to keep away the curious crowds that still throng here in daylight hours.

To-day Annie Cochran and Thomas have been putting the house in order, preparatory to its final closing. I shall never open it again. Thomas has already painted the window boards and put some of them in place. Let us pray that they keep inside what should be inside, and outside what should be out!

August 24th.
The strings of small bells, fastened across the closed and shuttered windows, frequently vibrated as though a hand had been drawn across them."

(From "Eugenia Riggs and Her Phenomena.")

Any coherent record of our last night's experiment is difficult to-day; not only do last night's alarms always seem absurd in to-day's sunshine, but I am not at all certain now that I did not build up, out of my recent reading and what I knew about the house, a bugaboo of my own.

And yet — what a night!

A man is a fool who, preparing to spend a night in a haunted house, where a terrible crime has been recently committed, reads during the early evening the idiotic imaginings which other men have conjured out of their own disordered fancies. Or out of their disordered digestions, according to the newest theory.

Isn't it Wells who has the dyspeptic Mr. Polly sitting on a stile between two thread-bare looking fields, and hating the world in general and his own home in particular, after a meal of pork, suet pudding, treacle, cheese, beer and pickles? And Fraser Harris who attributes "the transcendent nonsense of the post-impressionists" to the absinthe in their blood?

So, last night, I must needs poison my mental digestion in advance; pick up a book which should be suppressed, or sold only to large ladies of a lymphatic type, to read with a box of caramels. And with it fill myself with elementals, hideous masses of matter given temporary life and strange forms; demons, summoned by the diabolical rites of the Black Mass; and ghosts of foul crimes, come to seek revenge on their slayers!

Even before I started the untimely ringing of Clara's alarm clock, upstairs, set my nerves to jangling. And there was a certain psychological preparation for me in the very steps I was obliged to take in order to get out of the house. For a man of my age to put on his pajama coat, and retire into his bed otherwise fully dressed, was an act of deception nerve-racking enough in itself. But when Jane came in after I had retired, tardily remembering a missing button, and demanded the shirt I was still wearing, I broke into a cold sweat.

It was with difficulty that I got her away,

shirtless, and settled down to wait until the house was quiet. . . .

Halliday had opened the main house, and the red lamp was already in the den. Owing to the fact that the windows were boarded from the outside, we had no scruples about lighting it; but although it was better than complete darkness it added very little to the general gaiety. Halliday was quiet and somewhat strained, the house itself hot and airless, and with all outside sounds cut off, depressingly still. I lighted a match and glanced into the library; it was a ghost of a room, the floor bare, the furniture and pictures once more swathed in white.

Only the prisms of the glass chandelier reflected the light and seemed, as it flickered, to be quietly in motion.

Halliday had little to say.

"I would like," he explained, "to reproduce conditions as nearly as they were the night you saw the figure here." He smiled. "I don't suppose you really want to go and stand at the head of that staircase, Skipper, but I'm going to ask you to, just the same"

I looked up the staircase nervously.

"If you are going to reproduce the previous conditions," I protested, "you may recall that I had a revolver at that time!"

"I also seem to remember that you fired it,"

he said, and grinned at me. "It will answer every purpose, and be considerably safer, if you will merely point your finger at me and say 'crash!' "

But no amount of lightness on his part or mine could do more than temporarily lift the gloom; the shadow of tragedy hung over everything at which we looked. Halliday felt it, and suggested that "we get to work and then get out."

The question in his mind, he said, was this: I had said that, a second or so after the shot and the disappearance of the figure, the red light had died out in the den. If, as he believed was possible, this glow came from the lamp upstairs, brought down for some reason, or from a similar lamp, this required that the man I saw had time to go into the den, extinguish the lamp and conceal it, (since it wasn't in evidence later on) get back to the library, and be ready to leave by the broken window before he, Halliday, had turned on the light.

"It's a matter of time," he said. "I was by the terrace when I heard the shot. I figure it took me ten seconds to pick up the chair, run to the window and smash it."

It was nervous work going up the staircase, but I managed it and took up my position. He stood below.

I fired — theoretically — and he did what the figure had done; moved toward the door, still facing me, turned and went into the library. I heard him moving about and the light went out. Then in the darkness he ran into the library again, where he struck a match.

"Twenty seconds," he called.

His voice trailed off; his shadow extended through the den doorway into the hall, and as I watched it, it shows the condition of my nerves that it did not seem to be his shadow at all, but something quite different. For all the world like an old man in a dressing gown. Then the match went out and I heard him coming out into the hall again.

"Did you move a minute ago?" he asked.

"Move!" I said. "I wouldn't move for a million dollars. Strike a light."

"Funny," he said. "I thought I heard something."

He groped his way back to the den, and the red lamp looked actually cheerful after the complete darkness. I heard him go into the library again and apparently stand there and listen, and very shortly after he reappeared and asked me to change places with him.

"See how you can make it, Skipper," he said.

I came down rather more rapidly than I had gone up, and Halliday took my former position. I had never had any particular stomach for the business, and now my one idea was to get it over. I did as Halliday had done, moved to the library door, turned and then, more or less holding my breath, dived into the library and through it to the den. I brought up there, close to the red lamp, caught my foot in the cord and jerked it from the socket. Instantly we were in darkness again, and in absolute silence. Halliday, I believe, was still leaning over the stair-rail, waiting for me to complete the movement, and the sudden plunge into darkness had startled me more than I care to remember.

But I do remember that in a sort of panic I got down on my knees to feel for the connection, and that at that moment, whether due to overstrained nerves or not I cannot say, I distinctly heard a soft movement in the library. Trying to analyze that movement to-day I find it difficult. It was as though the linen coverings in the library had been set in motion, a soft and quiet motion, like that perhaps of a woman with a fan, and above that the faint clink of the prisms on the chandelier, like the ringing of small bells. But whatever had caused it, it was dying away when I noticed it. As if somehow the extinction of the light had taken away its source of power.

(Note: It is to be observed that we secured

this phenomenon later, during the seances. As no explanation of it has ever been given, it remains a portion of that unsolved factor in our equation to which I have referred previously.)

I knelt there, my face covered with a cold sweat, staring in the direction of the library door. I felt that if I looked away, if I were to lower my guard for an instant, something would come through that door.

I was, in effect, holding it back with my eyes!

And Halliday had made no sound. He too, I now know, was listening.

This, as accurately as I can record it, was the situation last night when the next move came. The house was absolutely silent again. Halliday was upstairs, and I was watching the door into the library, when the location of the sounds changed. Protected by my eyes, in front, I was attacked from the rear, so to speak. At the window above and behind me, something was trying to get in. I could hear its hands sliding slimily over the wood of the shutter, keeping on that blind and dreadful groping, until finally some sort of hold was secured and the shutter was shaken.

And with that every last ounce of my self-control left me, and I leaped into the hall as if I had been fired out of a gun.

"Halliday!" I shouted. *"Halliday!"*

339

He came downstairs; rather he leaped down the stairs. He says he found me in a corner, gibbering, and I dare say he did, but I must have told him my story with sufficient clearness, at that, for he left me alone again in that damnable place and ran outside. And as I had no intention whatever of being left alone again for the remainder of my life, I ran also. There was nobody outside the window, but the fresh green paint was the thing that, according to Halliday, saved me from being sent to-day to some sanctuary for the mentally deranged.

It showed unmistakable signs of entirely human investigation. At least a hand with the usual equipment of thumb and fingers has left more than one impression on it. . . .

Later: And now where are we? I am willing, even anxious, to accept Halliday's verdict, that the sounds we both heard in the library were due to an east wind blowing down the chimney, plus the settling and creaking of the old portion of the house.

But we have just returned from an inspection, in broad day, of the marks outside the boarded-up window of the den.

There is a complete imprint of the hand on it, and it shows a broad short thumb and a curved little finger. What is more, there is a complete absence of the usual whorls and ridges of the ordinary hand. One could take this imprint and put it side by side with the one in the bowl of putty. They are identical.

Halliday seems to have seen a great light from somewhere, but to me the situation is as absurd as it is maddening. It is as outrageous as that, out of some forgotten corner of my memory, I should have dug up a triangle within a circle, to find it cropping up soon after as the signature to a crime.

August 25th.

Five days have passed since the murder, and we are apparently as far from its solution as ever.

What work is being done is now centering about the county detective bureau in the city. A deputy constable keeps up a more or less casual surveillance of the property during the day, but is careful to depart before twilight. The dragging of the bay has once more been stopped, and Benchley's idea of an unknown enemy of Bethel's has apparently been abandoned in favor of Gordon as the killer.

At the same time we are not without developments, of a sort.

Although he is reticent on the subject, Halliday seems to feel that the experiment the other night, incomplete as it was, negatives the theory that the man I saw escaped by the broken window in the library.

"Then where did he go?" I asked.

"That's the point," he said. "Where did he go? When we've answered that we'll have answered a number of things."

But he tells me, surprisingly enough, that he has taken up a sort of temporary residence in the house.

"Whoever tried to get in the other night may come back again," he says. And assures me that the place isn't so bad "when one gets used to it."

"I read Kant," he says, as if that explains something.

I have offered to stay with him, but not, I dare say, with any enthusiasm. But he declines with a smile.

"You are too psychic, Skipper!" he says.

But it is perfectly evident that he does not want me.

This morning, going unexpectedly into the boat-house, where this conversation took place, I found him sitting by his table, and spread out before him the bit of linen, the cipher, the broken lens and the top of the ether can which constituted our various exhibits before I was gently eliminated from the case. But he also had a box of figs and a hand mirror before him, and when I entered unexpectedly he was studying himself in the glass.

As he immediately asked me if I cared to go fishing, which I did not, I saw that he was not prepared to make any explanation. . . .

The other development, although it does not solve the crime, or touch on it, came to me through Lear to-day, and throws a new and interesting light on poor old Bethel himself.

Lear did not like his errand; he prefers a presumptuous scepticism to an irrational credulity, and knows no middle ground. Those things which lie beyond his understanding he refers to as "poppycock," a favorite word of his. And to-day he prefaced his business with a small lecture to me, taking me into the drive to deliver it.

"You don't look like a man who has been on a vacation," he began, surveying me. "I know you've had a bad time, but after all, it's no possible responsibility of yours."

"I rented him the house. And I knew I had no business to rent it to anybody."

"Poppycock!" he said, and cleared his throat.

He had fallen into step with me, but at that he stopped and faced me.

"Now see here, Porter," he said, "there's a good bit of talk going around. Some of your friends are saying that you and Jane are laying the blame on some damn fool nonsense about the house itself. That's poor hearing, and it's ridiculous into the bargain. The Morrison girl was not killed in the house."

"I'm not so sure she wasn't. At any rate, *he* was. And I believe the same hand killed them both."

"But a human hand, of course? You're not going to say————"

"Oh, I admit that," I said. "But there are a lot of curious things. If you think the house is normal, spend a night there and see."

"Normal!" he snapped. "Of course the house is normal. It's the people in it who aren't." And warming to his subject: "You and Cameron should be locked up together. And Pettingill," he added.

Which brought him to Cameron, and his errand. . . .

Immediately on Cameron's return from the Adirondacks he had gone to bed with an infected hand, which had been torn by a fishhook, and had been too ill to look at the accumulation of mail. But the day before, although still very weak, he had gone through his letters, and there found one from Mr. Bethel, dated late in July.

In this letter Bethel recited various "abnormal conditions" in the Twin Hollows house, and asked Cameron, at the earliest possible moment, to go out and investigate them.

"And he wants to come?" I asked Lear.

"I tell you he's been sick," Lear said impatiently. "He wants to know about showing it to the police. He doesn't want to be dragged in, if he can help it."

"You've seen it?"

"Yes. There's nothing in it except what I've told you."

"He doesn't describe these abnormal conditions?"

"No. But he said he had made some experiments of his own, and was anxious to have his results verified."

"Experiments? Using a red light?"

"He didn't say," Lear said, with some asperity. "A red light! What in heaven's name has a red light to do with the immortal soul?"

He enlarged on that, savagely. Helena, he said, had been off in a corner saying "om, om" to herself half the summer, and when she dozed off in so doing, would waken to claim that her astral body had been off on some excursion or other.

"I can't appeal to her reason," he said, with a shrug of his thin shoulders, "but I have appealed to her decency. I've asked her if it is fair to intrude on the privacy every human individual is entitled to at times. But it's no good. She keeps a record, and I'm convinced it would jail her."

The only advice I could send Cameron was to use his own judgment concerning the letter. Personally, I do not see what value it has, save to corroborate my own ideas concerning the house. But it has suggested to me the advisability of asking Cameron to come here quietly and look the place over.

I rather think he wants to do so.

August 26th.
All along, I have been impressed by the attitude of at least the summer public to our tragedies; as each one came it brought with it its temporary thrill; for a moment, one might say, the dancing stopped and a bit of drama was enacted on the stage. Then the curtain fell, the band struck up, and the whirl began again, with some inconsiderable of the dancers missing.

Poor Carroway's widow is working at one of the shore hotels, and has bobbed her hair. And a small boy with adenoids delivers our milk and chickens; I caught him this morning chalking up a triangle within a circle on one of the pillars of the gate.

The main house shut and empty, a new assistant keeper at the light-house, and perhaps a closed room and grief at the Morrison farm house, — these are the only apparent scars left, to mark our summer's wounding.

I saw Larkin this morning. He believes that we may be able to sell the property as a hotel site; as this would ensure destroying the house, it seems the best thing.

But one other change I have not recorded.

Watching Halliday as I do, affectionately and not too openly, I can see a very considerable change in him. He is like a man lit from within by some flame, of vengeance perhaps, of resolution certainly. And he is moody at times; his old gaiety is gone. He has put me out of his confidence, not because he does not trust me, but because for some reason he is afraid for me. And the same, I think, is largely true of Edith in the last day or two.

It is as though he said, in effect:

"Keep out. It is dangerous. I am willing to take a chance, but I want to know that the rest of you are safe."

Now and then, however, I gather something. Thus yesterday he said: "You have to remember this; we are not dealing with a criminal, but with an idea."

Again, he has asked me for Uncle Horace's letter, and has been apparently making a study of it.

Only along the lines of what I call the super-normal phenomena of the summer does he show his old openness, and there he is frankly puzzled. My decision not to call in Cameron has, I think, disappointed him. But my reasons are sound. Cameron's coming might result in unpleasant press publicity for us, and more than that, puts me where I do not intend to be placed, among the believers in spiritism.

He accepted that decision to-day, however, without comment. But shortly after he asked Edith for the letter from Evanston, and sat thinking over it for some time.

"Of course, with a little imagination," he said, "you might figure that these people were somehow let in on what happened here last year. But why Evanston?" And after a pause, following a train of thought:

"Of course I suppose, if you grant a spirit world, you have to grant that where time and space do not exist and only vibration counts — whatever that may mean — you could tune in Evanston as well as — well, as easily as you can on the radio."

But he got up soon after, saying that we were all crazy and he himself was the maddest of the lot, and went away.

Livingstone is a curious chap; dapper, fastidious and taciturn. He is almost too much of a gentleman; I have had the feeling, and I think Jane has also, that a part of his reticence is caution, that he is always watchful, subconsciously at least, lest the veneer crack, and something secretly vulgar be exposed.

I am still wondering why he came to see me to-day; he was sitting, gloved and spatted, in our small living room when Clara brought his card to me in the garage and I hurried in. Sitting, too, staring at our ridiculous parlor organ, with an odd look on his face.

"Haven't seen one for years," he said, in his clipped and yet deliberate manner. "Where'd you happen on that one?"

"It was here when we came," I explained.

He gave it another glance before we sat down, and then apparently dismissed it. But not entirely. Now and then he looked toward it, and once I thought I saw a slight smile, as though back in his mind was some equally faint humorous memory. But he came to the point with a certain directness.

"You're a man of sense," he said. "I came because you've got a head on you."

"I used to have," I admitted modestly. "Lately, of course————"

He bent forward.

"Use it," he said. "Don't let this spirit bunk get you. Easiest stuff in the world to fake."

"I don't intend to let it get me."

He brushed that aside, and glanced once more at the organ.

"You take a thing like that," he said, "and start it in the dark. It gets you creepy in no time. They all use it; it used to be organs like that; now it's phonographs. They say it starts the vibrations! Well, I'll tell you what it does; it gets you worked up. Sometimes it covers something the medium wants to do."

"So I imagine," I agreed.

His volubility suddenly left him then, and he seemed rather at a loss.

"Let it alone," he said. "Let well enough alone." After a pause: "There may be something, but let it alone."

And that, so far as I can make out, was the purpose of his visit. He showed a certain relief, as if he had got rid of something momentous to him, and soon after he took an abrupt departure. Being careful to remove his glove, which he had absently put on again, before shaking hands!

Thomas tells me that another attempt was made to get into the house last night. He had left his pruning ladder outside under a tree, and found it upright against Gordon's window this morning. . . .

Later: Halliday corroborates Thomas's story, with further details. He was on the lower floor, reading, when he was disturbed by the crash of a pane of glass above. He ran upstairs, but was evidently heard. There was no one on the ladder when he got there, and a thorough search showed no one in the house.

The window was the one through which we had watched Gordon leave the house by the rope.

August 28th.

It is impossible for me to-night to draw any conclusion from last evening's discovery; I have not my old faith in circumstantial evidence. I can only ask myself if an innocent man hides in his own house. . . .

Jane had one of her bad headaches last night, and at eleven o'clock I took the car and went in to the village pharmacy. It was closed, however, and I was at a loss to know what to do. In the emergency I thought of Hayward's office; like most country doctors he keeps a medicine cabinet and fills many of his own prescriptions. I went there, therefore, and rang the bell.

It took some time and several rings to rouse

the housekeeper, an elderly and taciturn woman, and when she finally opened the door it was to say that the doctor was away, and to attempt to close it again. I prevented this, however, and managed to get past her and into the hall.

"I only want to get some medicine," I explained. "The cabinet is in the back office, isn't it?"

"I'm not allowed to let anybody into the office."

"Nonsense!" I said sharply. "Anyhow, you are not allowing me. I'm going."

She seemed completely at a loss, and I thought too that she was listening. With my hand on the knob of the waiting room, I caught the attentive look on her face, and found myself listening also. It seemed to me that there was somebody moving in the back office, and immediately after I caught the stealthy closing of a door somewhere. With that she appeared to relax.

"You are sure you know what you want?" she asked.

"Quite sure," I said, and went through the waiting room to the consulting office. She followed me and turned on the light, and stood there watching me intently. The room was filled with tobacco smoke, and she saw that I noticed it, for she said:

"My husband was sitting in here. I'd be glad if you don't say anything about it."

I am not suspicious, and the confession satisfied my faint feeling that something was not quite right in the house. I got the tablets from the cabinet, and being nervous about unlabelled bottles went to the desk; there, neatly piled up, were the month's bills for Hayward's professional services, written in his own untidy hand, and one not finished on the pad.

The woman was still watching me, and I managed to write my label, glue it to the bottle, and make my departure without, I think, showing that I had made any discovery whatever.

But nothing can alter my conviction that Hayward is hiding in his own house, and that he was in that back room when I rang the doorbell at something before midnight. Not even Halliday's opinion that, since Hayward is officially at home to-day, he had the right to be "not at home" last night.

"After all," he said, "give the poor devil his due, Skipper. He works hard, and why shouldn't he get back a day earlier than he is expected and steal a few hours to get out his bills? He has to live."

But he seems to me to be a trifle too casual about it. I admit that he puzzles me, these days.

After all, one can find the mysterious where it does not exist. I may not yet know why Halliday considers it necessary to watch the main house at night. But I do know the reason for Livingstone's extraordinary visit.

Mrs. Livingstone, sitting with Jane during her convalescence, read the letter from Evanston, and is eager to form a similar circle, to sit in the house itself. And poor Livingstone is opposing it and is making, for some reason or other, quite a business of it.

"After all, why not?" she urged to-day. "It can be quite secret."

She was supported in this by Edith, and even, half-heartedly, by Jane herself. A change of front which astonishes me. Mrs. Livingstone has apparently some absurd idea that we may receive "a clue, or something," as she vaguely puts it; and on my firm refusal departed, indignantly convinced that I have lost a great opportunity to solve our mystery....

Later: Halliday wants the seance! Nothing has so surprised me in years as his willingness to join the table-tippers. But I suspect in him some purpose not far removed from Mrs. Livingstone's, although just what he hopes to discover baffles me entirely.

"Why not?" he said, when I told him. "After

all, we have to keep an open mind on this thing, and we've had enough already to make something of a case for the other side."

"The other side of what?"

"The other side of the veil," he explained gravely, and then, seeing my face, was obliged to laugh.

" 'There is a pleasure in being mad, which none but madmen know,' " he quoted at me. "I've heard you say that Descartes advises us to seek for truth, freed from all preconceived ideas. Who are we, to stand in the way of truth?"

"And we are to search for it, sitting around a table in the dark?"

"Precisely that, Skipper," he said, with sudden gravity, and has left me to make what I can of it. . . .

Twelve days have now elapsed since the murder here, and the police know no more than they did on the morning of the 20th.

Now and then a car stops outside the gate, but our curious crowds are gone. Save that some nocturnal relic-hunter has chipped a corner off the sun-dial, the place is much as it was before. All this water over the dam, and it has brought us nothing.

September 1st.
I dare say there is no type of investigation in

355

which the grave — no pun here — is so mixed with the gay, as in this particular psychic search on which we are at present engaged. For, let Halliday use it for such purposes as he will, to Jane, Edith and Mrs. Livingstone it is a deadly serious matter.

Their reactions are peculiar. Jane accepts it stoically and without surprise; it is almost as though, from the beginning she has known that it was to happen. But she is nervous; she has eaten almost nothing all day.

Edith shows a peculiar and rather set-faced intensity. Whether she knows that something quite different lies behind it, or only suspects it, I do not know.

Halliday, also, is grave and quiet. He is less interested, however, in the manner of the sitting than in its *dramatis personae*. The list he has made out himself; Hayward, the two Livingstones, Jane, Edith and himself. On my pointing out a slight omission, namely, myself, he told me cheerfully that I belonged among the Scribes and Pharisees.

"The Scribes, anyhow," he said. "You are to sit by the red lamp and make notes. I am particularly anxious to have notes," he added.

On the other hand, Mrs. Livingstone has entered into it with extraordinary zest. She appeared this afternoon, slightly wheezy with the heat, carrying a black curtain of some heavy material and demanding a hammer and assistance before she was fairly out of her car. As it was apparently up to me to furnish both I did so, but anything less conducive to a spiritual state of mind than the preparations which followed at the main house it would be hard to find.

To stand on a ladder in the heat and darkness of the den, and to nail up that curtain across a corner with no more ritual than if I had been hanging a picture; to place inside it a small table and a bell on it, while beside it leaned an old guitar, resurrected from the attic and minus two strings, struck me as poor psychological preparation for confronting the unknown.

But we are curious creatures. The sun was low before we had finished, and as we sat resting from our labors dusk began to creep into the house. And with it came — self-created, of course — a sort of awe of that cabinet I had myself just made; it took on mystery; behind its heavy folds almost anything might happen. It brooded over the room, tall and menacing, with folds that seemed to sway with some unseen life behind them.

I left Mrs. Livingstone placing chairs about a small table and went out into the air!

The arrangements are now complete. Mrs.

Livingstone has brought over a photograph, with a collection of what appear to be most lugubrious records; she also promises Livingstone, alive or dead.

"I left him sulking," she said. "But he will feel better after he's had his dinner."

And to this frivolous measure we start the night's proceedings.

NOTES MADE DURING FIRST SEANCE

Sept. 1st; 11:15 P.M. Present: Jane, Edith, Hayward, the two Livingstones, Halliday and myself. Livingstone and Edith examining house. All outside doors locked and windows boarded. The red lamp on small stand in corner diagonally opposite cabinet and my chair beside it.

11:30 P.M. All is ready. Mrs. Livingstone at end of table, next to cabinet. On her left Jane, Hayward and Mr. Livingstone. On her right, Halliday and Edith. A red silk handkerchief over lamp makes light very faint. I have started the phonograph, according to instructions. I was right about it; it is playing: "Shall We Gather at the River?"

11:45 Small raps on the table, and one strong one, like the blow of a doubled fist.

11:47 The table is moving, twisting about. It

358

ceases and knocks come again.

11:50 The curtain of the cabinet seems to be moving. No one else has apparently noticed it. I have stopped the phonograph.

11:55 The curtain has blown out as far as Mrs. Livingstone's shoulder. All see it. Edith says something has touched her on the right arm. To my inquiry if any one has relaxed his grasp on the hand he is holding, no one has done so.

12:00 The bell inside the cabinet has been knocked from the table, with such violence that it rolls out into the room.

12:10 Nothing since the bell fell. Livingstone has asked if less light is required, and by knocks the reply is "Yes." I have put out lamp.

(The following notes were made in the dark and are not very distinct. I have supplemented them from memory.)

All quiet since the last entry. There is a mouse apparently playing about in the library. Edith says that Jane seems to be in a sort of trance. She is breathing heavily. More raps, apparently on door frame into library. I am cold, but probably nerves.

There is a sense of soft movement in the library; the covers are rustling; the prisms of the chandelier can be heard.

Edith says her chair is being slowly lifted. It has crashed to the floor. A hand has apparently run over the guitar strings. All complain of cold. I am alarmed about Jane.

I notice the herbal odor again; no one else has, apparently.

(Note: At this point, Jane's breathing continuing labored, and my apprehension growing, I insisted on terminating the seance.)

September 2nd.
Jane shows no ill-effect from last night, and indeed appears to have no knowledge of the later phenomena.

"I think I must have fallen asleep," she said this morning. "How silly of me!"

She has no idea of her entranced condition and I have not told her.

She accepts the idea of a second sitting tonight, without enthusiasm, but apparently with the fatalistic idea that what must be must be. She took a little tea and toast this morning. . . .

As to what Halliday had hoped to discover, I am as completely in the dark as ever. On my decision to end the seance, and on turning on the lights as I did without warning, the group was seen to be as it had been at the beginning, except that Mrs. Livingstone's chair appeared to have been pushed back, and was somewhat nearer the cabinet than before.

Hayward, so far as I can tell, had not changed his position. His attitude throughout seemed to me to be one of polite but rather uneasy scepticism. Livingstone, on the other hand, showed strong nervous excitement from first to last, but certainly never left the table.

He is ill to-day, which is not surprising, but I understand the intention is to carry on the experiment without him to-night. . . .

. . . . Regarding the phenomena themselves, what can I do but accept them? Certainly they showed no connection with what Mrs. Livingstone likes to call the spirit world; on the other hand, either they were genuine, or they showed an experience in trickery utterly beyond any member of our small group.

And who would trick us? And why?

Livingstone was right, however, as to the psychological effect of the preliminaries; in spite of myself they influenced me. The music, the low light followed by darkness, the strange and fearful expectancy of something beyond our ken, all added to the history of the house itself and its recent tragedy, had prepared us for anything.

The billowing of the cabinet curtain was particularly terrible. Sceptic as I am, I had the feeling of some dreadful *thing* behind it; something one should not see, and yet somehow might see. ...

Both Crawford and Cameron believe that certain individuals have the ability to project from their bodies rod-like structures of energy, invisible to the naked eye but capable of producing levitations, raps and other phenomena. They believe that these structures are utilized by outside spirits, or "controls." My own conviction is, that if such powers exist, they are not directed from outside, but by the medium's subconscious mind. In that case, of course, it is possible that Jane was the innocent author of last night's entertainment.

Mrs. Livingstone suggests that if we secure anything of interest to-night, I consult Cameron with a view to his joining us later on. ...

NOTES OF SEANCE HELD ON EVENING OF

Sept. 2nd; 1:00 A.M. Largely from memory, since all the later part was held without light, but made immediately following seance. Present: Jane, Edith, Hayward, Halliday, Mrs. Livingstone and myself. Livingstone absent.

I have moved lamp out from corner, and am now near door into hall.

Doors from den and library into hall closed. Door into library open.

11:10 Table moves almost immediately. Edith says is rising from floor. It has risen, but one leg remains on floor.

11:15 All remove hands, and table settles down.

11:20 Loud raps on table. Construed as demand for less light. Handkerchief thrown over lamp. Curtain of cabinet billows into room. Guitar overturned inside cabinet. All quiet now.

No phenomena whatever for about ten minutes. Jane very quiet. Hayward feels her pulse; is fast but strong. Mrs. Livingstone asks if too much light, and rap replies "yes." I have put out the lamp.

(Note: From here on I was able only to jot down a word or two in long hand, the previous night's experiment of making stenographic notes in darkness having shown its practical impossibility. The following record I have since elaborated from memory.)

The bell in cabinet rings violently and is flung across room, striking door into hall.

A small light, bluish-white, about a foot above Jane's head. It shines for a moment and then disappears.

It has flashed again, near the fireplace.

A fine but steady tattoo is being beaten, apparently outside of the door to hall. A tap or two on metal, possibly the fender. Silence.

Jane apparently in trance.

The sounds extend into the library, and there is movement there. The covers seem to be in motion as before. The prisms of chandelier tinkle like small bells. From where I sit I can see a small light over bookcase in library. It is gone.

The herbal odor again.

Jane is groaning and moving in her chair. Mrs. Livingstone and Hayward having trouble holding her hands. She calls: "Here! Here!" sharply.

Hayward says something has touched him on the shoulder. "Something floated by me just now," he says, "on the left. It touched my shoulder."

A crash on the table. I notice the herbal odor once more. Silence again.

Something is in the hall. It is groping its way along. It is at the door beside me. . . .

My notes end here. I had reached the limit of my endurance and, as the switch was beside me, I turned on the lights. As before, Mrs. Livingstone's chair seemed somewhat nearer the cabinet; no other changes in position, except that Halliday had gone out to search hall and lower floor. The bell was on floor near door into hall, and lying on table, "Smyth's Everyday Essays."

To the best of my knowledge this book was in the library at the beginning of the seance.

No signs of disturbance in library or hall, to account for sounds I heard. But an unfortunate situation has arisen, owing to Mrs. Livingstone's failure to lock door from hall to drive. She had pushed the bolt, but as the door was not entirely closed, it had not engaged. We found this door standing open.

This, however, although Hayward seems uneasy, hardly invalidates the extraordinary phenomena secured to-night.

Jane exhausted, and Edith with her.

September 3rd.

I have seen Cameron, and he will come out. He has evidently been seriously ill, but it shows the dominance of the mental over the physical that he brushed aside my apologies and went directly to the matter in hand.

But it is a curious thing to reflect that, a short time ago, it would have been I who was the sceptic and Cameron who would have been ranged on the other side. To-day it was I who was excited. And Cameron who was to be convinced!

"This Edith, of whom you speak," he said, "how old is she?"

"Twenty."

"A nervous type?"

"Yes, and no. Not hysterical, if that's what you mean."

Certain of the phenomena, too, seem to puzzle him. The table levitation, the lights and other manifestations were not unusual, he said, with a strong physical medium present, and this he imagined Jane to be. The book, however, particularly attracted his interest. Over my notes on that he sat thinking for some time.

"You say it crashed onto the table?"

"At the last, yes. But Doctor Hayward, who was nearest the library door, says that after my wife called, 'Here!' he felt something pass his shoulder. Float past, is the way he puts it. He thinks it was the book, and that it dropped onto the table after that."

"About what you heard in the hall; was this hall dark?"

"Yes. There were no lights anywhere in the house."

"You heard footsteps?"

"No. It was like something feeling its way along. You know what I mean." . . .

Toward the end of the conference he leaned

back and studied me through his glasses.

"What started you on this, Porter?" he said.

He did not remind me, although he might well have done so, that my previous attitude, to him and his kind, had been one of a sort of indifferent contempt; that, during his entire time at the university, I had never so much as set foot in his rooms, nor asked him into my house; that on the two or three times only when we had met, I had taken no pains to hide my rejection of him and all that he stood for.

But it was implied in his question, and I dare say I colored. I told him, however, as best I could, and he smiled.

"I rather imagine," he said, "that when we pass over, our interest in this planc of existence is impersonal; we may hope to educate it as to what is beyond. But we hardly carry our desires for revenge with us."

Of all that I had told him, however, the Evanston matter interested him most. Over the letter he sat for a long time, his heavy, almost hairless head sunk forward as he read and reread it.

"Curious," he said. "What do you make out of it?"

"A great deal," I told him, and detailed my discovery of the letter behind the drawer of the desk, and my theory as to old Horace Porter's death. I had brought that letter also, and he studied it as carefully as he had the other.

" 'The enormity of the idea,' " he repeated. "That's a strong phrase. And he threatens to call in the police! Have you any notion as to what this idea may have been?"

"Not the slightest," I said frankly.

"I would like to keep this for a while, if you don't mind," he said at last. "I have a medium here in town — but I forget. You don't believe in such things!"

"I don't know what I believe. But you are welcome to it, of course."

It was only after this matter of the letter that he finally agreed to come out the day after to-morrow.

September 4th.

The words "making trouble," lightly underscored on page 24 of "Smyth's Everyday Essays," are the key to Gordon's cipher. The entire sentence is: "It is often the ingenuous rather than the malicious who go about the world making trouble."

In a few hours, then, we shall have solved our mystery, or at least such portion of it as is locked in the diary. Read with this key we have already translated the sentence I recorded here on the 22nd of August. Although we cannot interpret it without the context, it becomes:

"The G.P. stuff went big last night."

In the same way the scrap of paper found in my garage is now discovered to read, "Smyth, P. 24." Edith's single error lying in the number, which she had remembered as 28.

Halliday suggests that the G.P. above may refer to George Pierce, but makes no attempt to explain the reference. . . .

Halliday's story of his discovery is interesting; certain portions of the two seances he apparently accepts without comment save: "It was the usual stuff," and lets it go at that. Although "usual" is hardly the word I should myself use in that connection. But the book was, as I gather it, not the usual stuff.

"There was something about the way it came, that night of the seance," he says, and makes a gesture. "Mrs. Porter called it, and it came. Like a dog," he says, and watches me to be sure I am not laughing at him.

However that may be, the book and the strange manner of its arrival in our midst had interested him, and he had spent some time over it. Thus, he found where it belonged in the library, and tried to discover some significance in that. But there was none.

"I drew a blank there," he says. "I examined

the wall behind, but there was nothing. You see, it couldn't have been *thrown* in; it wasn't possible. And when Hayward said it touched him, both his hands were being held. In other words, he didn't put it there."

All the time, I gather, he was feeling extremely foolish. He would pause now and then, in order to assure me that he felt "a bit silly." He didn't believe in such things; when there was a natural phenomenon there was a natural law to account for it. Maybe telekinesis, or whatever they called it.

"But there had to be some *reason* for that book," he says. "I just sat down and went through it."

He has taken the key words to the city, and has just telephoned (2 P.M.) that the detective bureau has put a staff to work on it.

"It will be several hours," he said. "It's slow work. But I'll be out with the sheets as soon as they've finished."

September 5th.
Too much exhausted to-day to make any coherent record. The four hours last night in the District Attorney's office have worn me out. I have called off Cameron to-night, for the same reason.

The mystery seems to be increased, rather than solved, by the diary. By such portions, at least, as were read to me. And I do not understand the conditions under which I was questioned, nor the questions themselves. Good God, are they suspecting me again? Halliday is still in town. ...

Later:

Edith has removed my anxiety as to Halliday's return. He has telephoned, and she has just brought me the message.

"He says you are not to worry," she reports. "He is working with them on the case. And you will not be disturbed again."

She looks pale, does Edith, and Jane is not much better. I have told Jane the whole matter; my absence last night had possibly prepared her, but the very confession that I had been subjected to what amounted to the third degree has roused her to a fury of indignation.

"How can they dare such a thing!" she said. "How can they even think it?"

"It's their business to believe a man guilty until he proves his innocence," I reminded her. "And Gordon thought it; you must remember that."

For nothing is more clear to me to-day than that this diary of Gordon's, which Halliday himself carried to the police, has somehow incriminated me.

Halliday is still in town. I can do nothing but wait here, eating my heart out with anxiety, and allowing my imagination to run away with me in a thousand ways.

My women-folk support me according to their kind. Jane serves me sweetbreads for luncheon, and Edith sits by, giving me an occasional almost furtive caress as an evidence of her faith in me.

But Edith is curiously lifeless; that small but burning flame in her which we call optimism, for want of a better word, seems definitely quenched. She is silent and apathetic, and has been so since yesterday.

She seems to resent our having sent in the key to the diary.

"If only you hadn't done that." she said to-day.

"What else could we do? We have to get at the bottom of this thing."

"I don't see that it has got you anywhere. It has only mussed things up."

What she has in her mind I do not know, unless, poor child, she has been building a future on Halliday's solving the crime, and that now that prospect is gone. She tells me that Starr has been on guard at the main house, quietly, for the two nights Halliday has been in town. But if she knows any explanation of his presence she does not give it.

"He's afraid to go inside," she said, scornfully. "He just sits out on the terrace and smokes. If anybody said boo behind him he'd jump into the bay and drown himself."

She has apparently implicit faith in Halliday's ability to keep me from further indignity. But I am not so certain. The sound of a car on the highway sets my pulse to beating like a riveting machine; at the arrival of the Morrison truck a few minutes ago with some belated buttermilk I got up and buttoned my coat.

My place in my little world behind the drain pipe is neither large nor important, but it is difficult for me to imagine it without me.

"Suppose the worst to happen," said Matthew Arnold to the portly jeweler from Cheapside; "suppose even yourself to be the victim; *il n'y a pas d'homme nécessaire* . . . The great mundane movement would still go on, the gravel walks of your villa would still be rolled, dividends would still be paid at the bank, omnibuses would still run, there would be the same old crush at the corner of Fenchurch Street." . . .

This is the sixth. It was on the fourth, then, a few hours after Halliday had gone to the city, that a taxi stopped here, and Greenough got out. There seemed to me to be a trifle more than his usual ponderousness in his manner, and a distinct concentration in the way he looked at me as I came down the staircase. At the same time, he was civility itself, and he stated his errand matter-of-factly. They had a staff working on the diary, and he knew I would like to be present when it was finished.

"It's a long job," he said. "But we've split it into a half dozen parts, and it ought to be ready by eight, or half past."

It was six then, and as our early dinner was almost ready, I asked him to stay. We ate cheerfully enough, took the seven-fifteen express from Oakville, and were in town and at the county building at something before ten. I was surprised but not startled to find Benchley, the Sheriff, there, and three or four other men, including Hemingway, the District Attorney. Hemingway held some typed sheets in his hand when we entered, and was reading them carefully. Halliday was standing by a window staring out into the square, and the first indication I had that anything was wrong was the expression on his face as he turned and saw me.

The second was a polite invitation to Halliday to leave the room, and his manner of receiving it.

"I'm staying," he said flatly. "If there's

any objection to that, I shall advise Mr. Porter to make no statement and to answer no questions, until he can be properly protected."

"Protected?" I asked. "Protected from what?"

"From this strong-arm outfit," said Halliday, and surveyed the room with his jaw thrust forward.

"I am under arrest?"

Hemingway put down the papers and took off his glasses.

"Certainly not," he said. "Your young friend is being slightly dramatic. I know that you want this mystery solved as much as we do; more, since it directly concerns you. This is not a trap, Mr. Porter; we shall ask you some questions, and I hope you will answer them. That is all."

"I reserve the right to interfere in case of any trick," Halliday put in.

"We have framed no trick questions," Hemingway said quietly. "We want the facts, that's all."

He rang a bell, and a secretary came in. My mouth was dry and some one placed a glass of water before me. From that on, for four hours, I answered questions; at the end of that time I walked out, still free although slightly dizzy. . . .

(Note: Halliday has recently secured a copy of the stenographic notes of that night. As they

375

would make a small volume in themselves, I give here only such portions as seem to forward the narrative.)

Q. Your name, please.

A. William Allen Porter.

Q. Age?

A. Forty-six.

Q. Your profession is————?

A. I am a professor of English literature at ———— University.

Q. You own the property at Oakville, known as Twin Hollows?

A. I do. I inherited it something more than a year ago, on the death of my uncle, Horace Porter.

Q. Had you known that this property was to come to you on your Uncle's death?

A. It was always understood between us. He had no other heirs. . . .

Q. Had you any previous acquaintance with Mr. Bethel? I mean, before he took your house?

A. None whatever. I never saw him until he came out to take possession. His secretary inspected the house and negotiations were carried on through my attorney.

Q. In any of your talks with Mr. Bethel, did you gather that he had known Mr. Horace Porter, previous to his death?

A. Never.

Q. When you rented the house, did you retain any keys to it?

A. I have a full set in my possession.

Q. You had access to the house, then?

A. I never used my keys, if that's what you mean.

Q. On the night of the 26th of July, Mr. Bethel's secretary was attacked outside the kitchen door of the house, and managed to ring the bell there before he fell unconscious. Just where were you, Mr. Porter, when that bell rang?

A. The police have my statement as to that. By the sun-dial.

Q. Doctor Hayward was on the road in his car; you were by the sun-dial, close to the house. Yet when he reached you, you had apparently only found this boy. Is that correct?

A. It seems to me that the question there might be, was Hayward on the main road that night, as he says, or nearer to the house than he admits. . . .

Q. You own a boat, I believe?

A. I inherited one with the property. A sloop.

Q. Do you sail the boat yourself?

A. I don't know one end of it from the other. . . .

Q. In your various conversations with Mr.

Bethel, did he ever mention the character of the house? By that, I mean any curious quality in the house itself?

A. He recognized such a quality. Yes.

Q. Did he ever mention a letter written by him to a Mr. Cameron, here in the city? A member of the Society for Physical Research? Relative to the house?

A. Never. But I know of the letter. Cameron sent me word of it a day or so ago.

Q. Are you a believer in spiritualism?

A. I never have been. Recently, however, I————

(Note: Here I caught a warning glance from Halliday and changed what I had intended to say.)

Recently I have been trying to preserve an open mind on the subject.

Q. Why recently?

A. For one thing, Mr. Bethel had found the house queer; so had the secretary. . . .

Q. On the day you asked the secretary to luncheon, the intention was to allow Mr. Bethel to go through his room?

A. Bethel? Certainly not.

Q. I shall read you this entry from Gordon's diary. (reads) "Porter asked me to lunch to-day, so B. could go through my room. They left the knife, but at least they know I have it."

A. That's a lie! I asked him to luncheon so

Halliday could search his room. It was Halliday who found the knife. You can ask him.

Q. We'll let that go, just now, and come to the night you were found in the house, Mr. Porter, by Mr. Halliday.

A. I wasn't found in the house by Mr. Halliday. We had started for it together. The maid, Annie Cochran, had reported a quarrel between Mr. Bethel and Gordon, and that Gordon had gone away. You must remember that we suspected the boy of being the killer. I was anxious, and went for Halliday.

Q. What time did the maid tell you this?

A. About seven thirty, possibly eight o'clock.

Q. And when did you go for Mr. Halliday?

A. It was about eleven, I imagine.

Q. What did you do in the interval?

A. She was nervous, and I took her home. After that we had callers.

Q. Did you see Mr. Bethel, in that interval?

A. No.

Q. Had it occurred to you that Gordon might be going to see the police?

A. I never thought of it. Why should he be going to the police?

Q. Did Mr. Bethel think of it?

A. I've told you; I didn't see him.

Q. On the night of the murder in the house

at Twin Hollows, what led you to your discovery of the crime?

A. My wife heard the telephone ring, and I went to it. All three buildings are on one line, and the receiver at the main house was down. I heard a crash, and heavy breathing near the telephone.

Q. That made you suspicious?

A. I had been expecting trouble between Mr. Bethel and Gordon.

Q. Why did you expect trouble?

A. I knew they had quarreled. Mr. Bethel had told me that it was he who had struck Gordon, mistaking him for a burglar, and that Gordon suspected it.

Q. When did he tell you that?

A. I don't know exactly. About three days before the murder, I think.

Q. Can you remember the burden of that conversation?

A. Very well. He said that he was suspicious of the boy; that he was weak and vicious, and possibly criminal. He knew he was going out at night. On the night of the 26th of July Gordon was out, and he dragged himself downstairs. When he heard him at the kitchen door he struck him. But he maintained that he had not tied him. I believe that, personally. He had one useless hand.

Q. Did you ever have any reason to believe that Mr. Bethel exaggerated his infirmity?

A. Exaggerated it? What do you mean?

Q. You believe he was as helpless as he appeared?

A. I can't imagine a man assuming such a thing. ...

Q. Now, Mr. Porter, you have said that the telephone receiver at the main house was down, and you heard over it enough to alarm you?

A. Yes.

Q. It rang, and you went to it?

A. Yes.

Q. How could it ring, if the other receiver was down?

A. As a matter of fact, I didn't hear it. My wife said it had rung, and to satisfy her I went to it. ...

Q. Did the secretary, Gordon, ever approach you on a matter of money?

A. Money? I don't understand the question.

Q. Did he ever ask you for money? Or intimate that he needed it?

A. Never. He said something once about giving up his position. ...

Q. Where was he, the night you held the conversation with Mr. Bethel, relative to him?

A. Here in the city, I believe.

381

Q. And Mr. Bethel thought he might have gone to the police?

A. That's the second time you have intimated that Gordon had something to tell the police. I can't talk in the dark like this. If anybody wanted to avoid the police, it was this boy. . . .

Q. I am going back to the night Mr. Halliday found you in the house———

A. He didn't *find* me. We had started there together.

Q. You say you saw a figure at the foot of the stairs, and fired at it?

A. I didn't intend to fire.

Q. You didn't recognize this figure?

A. No.

Q. It was not Mr. Bethel?

A. Bethel? No. He was locked in his room. . . .

Q. You say you are not a spiritualist?

A. Certainly not.

Q. You have never made any experiments in spiritualism?

A. I have been present at one or two seances.

Q. When? Recently?

A. We have held two sittings in the main house within the last few days.

Q. When did you first hear of the symbol of

a triangle inside a circle?

A. If you mean in connection with the crimes———

Q. Before that. You told Mr. Greenough, some time ago, that you had heard of it in some other connection.

A. I told him I had happened on it in an old book on Black Magic, and told a group of women about it. It was a purely facetious remark.

Q. Can you account for its use in connection with these crimes?

A. I have no official knowledge that it was used in connection with the crimes. Only with the sheep-killing.

Q. But you know it *was* so used?

A. I know that it was used once when Mr. Greenough did not find it.

Q. Where was that?

A. On a tree near where the Morrison truck was discovered. I have heard it was on Carroway's boat, but I don't know that. I know it was deliberately put on my car, after Mr. Halliday was hurt.

Q. You say, put on the car? Do you mean by that, Mr. Bethel did it?

A. Bethel? How could he? We have thought lately that Gordon was responsible. We found a piece of his cipher near by.

Q. You have felt all along that Gordon was guilty?

A. I won't say that. I would say that the burden of the evidence indicated that he was guilty. Mr. Halliday has had considerable doubt of his guilt.

Q. Have you ever considered that it might be Bethel who killed Gordon?

A. Never. He couldn't have done it.

Q. But if he had had assistance?

A. Are you telling me that Bethel *did* kill Gordon?

Q. I am telling you that somebody killed Gordon, Mr. Porter. His body was washed ashore at Bass Cove this morning.

September 7th.

Halliday has saved me from arrest, by giving to the police the information which he has been gathering on the case all summer. Has made a quiet gesture, which is like him, and given me back to life, liberty, and the pursuit of literature.

He came out late last night, and I understand is still asleep. He has had very little sleep, poor lad, for a long time.

I myself collapsed this morning, and Hayward has put me back to bed. Edith, spreading my coverings neatly before Greenough came up, says I am now so thin that:

"You really make a hollow, William. If it were not for your feet, nobody would know you are there!" . . .

It is impossible to record in detail my conversation this afternoon with Greenough, covering as it did more than an hour. He came in, I thought, slightly uncomfortable and perhaps a little crestfallen, and I motioned him to a chair. He sat down and mopped his face with his handkerchief, and after that stooped and rather deliberately wiped his shoes with it. Then he straightened and looked at me.

"Well, professor," he said, "it's a darned queer world, there's no denying it."

"The world's all right. It's the people in it who mess things up."

"Like fleas on a dog," was his rather abstracted comment. He felt in his pocket, with much the same gesture as on that early visit of his when he had drawn the triangle within the circle on the back of an old envelope. Whether the movement was reminiscent to him, as it was to me, I cannot say. But he glanced at me quickly and then smiled.

"Sort of had me going, you did, there for a while!" he said. "But I was getting pretty close to the facts before this diary came along. Of course, it helped."

He had Gordon's diary in his hand.

"Naturally," he said, fingering the book, "your young friend's information was valuable; I'm not discounting that. The hand-print on the window board, for instance. I'd have found it sooner or later, but it saved time. And the young lady, too. She's done her bit, all right. I've been handicapped by being too well known around here. And Starr's a fool."

He snapped out this last statement, and I gathered that he was still smarting under the knowledge that, without Halliday and Edith, he would still be nowhere. It was, more or less, his defense.

"Of course," he said, "ever since we got hold of this diary of Gordon's, one thing's been pretty clear. Bethel wasn't working alone. According to what I saw of him it wasn't possible. He couldn't even have made a getaway without help. The only question was, who'd helped him."

"So you picked on me?"

"Well," he said wryly, "you'll have to admit that you've seemed to go out of your way all summer to get into trouble! As a matter of fact, *I* didn't pick on you; it was Gordon." He looked at my clock.

"I've only got an hour," he said. "Your niece is sitting on the stairs now, holding a stop-watch on me. I can't read you this thing, but I can tell you what's in it. And believe me, that's plenty." . . .

Briefly, then, the deciphering of the diary had left me in a very bad position. When they had finished it, it was Benchley's idea to arrest me at once. They had the boy's body, a fact they had kept to themselves, and I was within an ace of a charge of murder.

But Halliday had stayed.

"He seemed to feel there was trouble coming," Greenough said. "He hung around and drove us all crazy. He insisted, as he'd brought the key, on his right to read the stuff as it came through; and as it went on, he didn't know exactly what to do.

"Finally, seeing what was in the air, he made a trade with us. He was willing to have you brought in and interrogated, but on condition that if you weren't held he'd come over with something of his own. You get the point, of course. There's a reward involved, and he'd been holding out on us a bit." He waved his hand. "That's natural. We don't hold it against him. But the point is, he made his trade."

Coming to my examination, my answers had apparently impressed Hemingway satisfactorily. On the other hand, added to the diary's constant suspicion of me, was Greenough's own case against me. He passed over that rather airily.

"I wasn't trying to make out a case against you," he said. "As a mater of fact, you couldn't have been the man who attacked Halliday. You weren't here."

"Naturally," I agreed, gravely. "I wasn't here. Of course, if I *had* been here————!"

He glanced at me quickly, but went back to the night of the inquiry.

"The question was, whether to hold you or not. You may remember Hemingway going out, when it was over, and talking to Halliday outside? Well, it was then he made the trade."

Apparently the fact that Gordon had been the victim had not been the surprise to the police that it had been to me. For one thing, the microscope had shown one detail which the detective had not mentioned to me at the time. Caught between the handle of the knife and the blade had been a short piece of hair. The microscope showed this hair not only young, a matter readily determined, and the approximate color of Gordon's; it also showed it liberally coated with pomade. Poor Gordon's glistening, varnished hair!

But Greenough had been inclined at first to

think that there had been two victims, instead of one.

"Dying and passing on," he says, "is not like taking your thumb out of a bowl of soup. It's bound to leave some sort of a hole."

And there had been no hole. If Bethel had died and passed on, no one apparently missed him. As time went on and no queries were received, the thing began to look ominous; as though Bethel himself had been hiding away, under an assumed name.

The idea that Bethel had had an enemy from whom he was hiding, and who had found him, began to intrude itself.

"But," he said, with engaging frankness, "that eliminated you. And you wouldn't be eliminated. You were like some people you've seen, when there's a camera-man about; always getting in front of the machine and into the picture."

" 'And the king will not be able to whip a cat, but I shall be at the tayle of it,' " I quoted. He looked rather bewildered.

Then came the diary, and Gordon brought me in unmistakably, and in a way they had not thought of. Not an enemy, but an accomplice; Bethel hiding there, with my connivance, and the two of us, he the brains presumably and I the hands, working out between us some sinister design which even the boy could not understand.

"Whatever it is," Gordon had written, shortly after the Morrison girl's disappearance, "he's got outside help." And he wonders if I am guilty. But he is not sure of that; he even suspects Bethel, in one entry, of being less helpless than he appeared, and possibly of "working on his own." He abandoned that idea, however, and there was a time when he suspected Thomas; even a time when he thought of bringing his suspicions to me.

But Bethel was beginning to be afraid of him. He thinks Bethel knows he has discovered the boat. He grows alarmed, and buys a knife; he records that "he can take care of himself." But there is bravado in it. Later on, he finds that he is occasionally stealthily locked in at night, for three or four hours, and he buys a rope and hides it in his room. After that matters moved rapidly.

He found the gun room window unlocked on certain nights, and set a watch on it. And on one such night Bethel tried to kill him.

"He tried to kill me last night," he writes on the 27th of July, and goes on to say that Bethel couldn't have tied him, and that "maybe it was Porter." From that time on he suspected me.

And Bethel was watching him. Nothing is so

dramatic in all the diary as the situation un-
consciously revealed between the paralytic and
the boy; each watching the other; the guard up
between them, while the servant is in the room,
and then down again. The boy recklessly mock-
ing, the old man grim and waiting.

And nothing said. The boy goes to the city
and tries to buy a revolver, but there is a new
law in effect, and he fails. He has the knife, and
has to trust to that. He thinks of going to the
police while he is in the city; the reward would
be a big thing. He says: "I could go around the
world on ten thousand." But his case isn't complete; he needs the outside man. He suspects
me, but he "hasn't the goods" on me.

And there are times when he admits the
possibility that I may not be the outside man.
One night he hears the unknown in the house.
There is a reddish glare and he sees a figure
steal into the den. But it "did not look like
Porter." And he is more puzzled than ever, for
Bethel is in his room, asleep, and although the
boy camps on the stairs until daylight, he does
not see the figure again.

"At daylight examined den and library. All
windows closed and locked. It beats me."

It is about this time, too, that he begins to
believe that Bethel is not only watching him,
but that he is expecting trouble from some

other source. He tells Bethel he has seen a figure go into the den at night, and Bethel shows alarm.

"He and the other one have quarreled," he says. "And B.'s afraid of him."

But on the night when he came home, to find Starr, Halliday and myself in the house, his suspicions of me returned in full force. He decides that Bethel and I have had a quarrel, and that one of us has tried to shoot the other! But his knife has been taken; he steals one from the kitchen and carefully sharpens it; but he is not so frightened as he has been. Bethel and I have quarreled, and he "can handle the old man."

But matters were rapidly approaching a climax. Bethel was going to give up the house and let him go. He seems to have dared Bethel to discharge him, and to have more than hinted at what he suspects.

"I can talk of ten thousand," he writes, "or keep quiet for twenty. He can take his choice."

He has the upper hand, now. The other man is no longer in evidence; they have apparently quarreled, and Bethel is left to bear the situation alone. The boy lays various traps, but no one enters the house. "The murder pact" is broken, and the old man sits in his chair and broods.

"Blackmail is an ugly word," he says once.

"Not half so ugly as murder," retorts Gordon, and notes it with satisfaction in his diary.

"Murder" was the last word he wrote there. . . .

But, for all his apparent frankness, Greenough's errand was clearly only to relieve my anxieties concerning myself. He refused all further information.

"We have a suspect, all right," he said. "I don't mind saying that. But we haven't a case yet, and it's touch and go whether we get one. Until we do, we're not talking."

September 8th.

Halliday's attitude is very curious. He is taciturn in the extreme; he avoids any confidential talks with me, and Jane commented on it this morning.

"He worries me," she said, "and he is worrying Edith. If you go out now and look, you'll see him pacing the boat-house verandah, and he has been doing it for the last hour."

I admit that he puzzles me. It was Greenough's errand, so far as I can make out, to relieve my mind as to myself, but to treat Halliday's case, as given to the police, as entirely confidential.

"It's the outside man we are after," he said; "and the outside man we are going to get."

But on my mentioning my right to know who was under suspicion, he only repeated what the detective had said.

"You understand," he said, "there's no case in law yet. Knowing who did a thing, and proving who did it, are different things entirely."

But they would prove it, he was confident. So confident, indeed, that before he left he inquired the make and cost of my car. Evidently he has already mentally banked the reward.

On the other hand, certain things seem to me still to be far from clear.

Halliday, I understand, passed over to the police the following facts:

(a) A copy of the unfinished letter from Horace Porter to some unknown.

(b) A description of the print of a hand, left on the window board.

(c) A small illustration from the book "Eugenia Riggs and her Phenomena," and showing the same hand print.

(d) A sworn statement of the Livingstones' butler, the nature of which I do not know.

(e) An analysis of his own theory of the experiments referred to in the diary.

(f) And a letter to Edith from an anonymous correspondent. (To be referred to later.)

(g) The possibility that the two attempts to enter the main house are due to the fact that, in the haste of the escape, something was left there which is both identifying and incriminating.

But so far as I can discover, he has not told them that, from the time the guards were taken away from the house at night, he was on watch there.

In other words, from shortly after the murder he must have known that something incriminating had been left there, when Bethel and his accomplice, Gordon's "outside man," made their escape the night the secretary was murdered. He may even know what it is, and where. But he has not told Greenough.

Again, there is the fact that a statement by the Livingstones' butler was a portion of the evidence he submitted. Surely they are not endeavoring to incriminate Livingstone!

September 9th.

It is Halliday's idea to hold another seance, using Cameron's coming as the excuse for it. I gather that he believes that, under cover of the seance, another attempt may be made to secure the incriminating evidence left in the house. Not that he says so, but his questions concern-

395

ing the sounds I heard in the hall during the second seance point in that direction.

"This herbal odor you speak of, Skipper," he asked, "was that before you heard the movement outside?"

"Some time before. Yes. But the odor seemed to be *in* the room; the sounds were beyond the door."

"You don't connect them, then?"

"I hadn't thought about it, but I don't believe I do."

"Did you hear any footsteps?"

I had to consider that. "Not footsteps; there was a sort of scraping along the floor."

"And the moment you spoke this noise ceased?"

"Yes."

The whole situation is baffling in the extreme. I cannot ignore the fact that the seances were proposed by Mrs. Livingstone, that it was she who left the hall door unbolted at the second sitting, or that Livingstone himself was absent that second night, presumably ill. At the same time, it was Livingstone who indrectly advised me against the business.

"Let it alone," he warned me. "Let well enough alone."

So far as Halliday is concerned, it is clear that he does not like the idea of another seance, but feels that it is necessary. He assures me the police will be on hand, inside and outside the house, but he does not minimize the fact that there will be a certain risk, and that he dreads taking Jane and Edith into it.

"It's like this," he said to-day, feeling painfully for words. "In a sense, you and I are at the parting of the ways in this thing. We can let it go, and turn loose on the world a cruel and deadly idea which may go on claiming victims indefinitely." He made a small gesture. "Or — we put into the other side of the scale all we have in the world, and then————" He pulled himself up. "There's only possible danger," he said. "Unless things slip, there should be very little."

The same list of those present as before. There is an unconscious emphasis placed by Halliday on Hayward and Livingstone, but perhaps I am over-watchful.

I daresay, thus placed between my duty and my fears, I shall do my duty. I perceive that either Hayward or Livingstone is once more to be allowed access to the house, and under conditions more or less favorable to what is to be done. But which one? . . .

Later: I have done my duty. I have telephoned Cameron, and he will come out to-morrow night.

Halliday has taken every possible precaution as to to-night. As it has been our custom to go over the house before each seance, and as Cameron may do this with unusual thoroughness, it has been decided not to place Greenough and his officers until after the sitting begins. Halliday has therefore to-day connected the bell from that room, which rings in the kitchen, to a temporary extension in the garage, with a buzzer. When the lights are lowered, he will touch the bell, and Greenough is then to smuggle his men in through the kitchen.

While no one can say what changes Cameron may suggest in our previous methods, Halliday imagines he will ask us at first to proceed as usual. In any event, I am to sit as near to the switch as possible, and when Halliday calls for lights, am to be ready to turn them on. . . .

8:30   Everything is ready. But I am concerned about Halliday. Has he some apprehension about his own safety to-night?

He came an hour or so too early to start with the car for Cameron, and borrowing pen and paper, wrote a long communication to Hemingway. What is in it I do not know, but he took it with him, to mail on his way to the station.

(END OF MR. PORTER'S JOURNAL)

CONCLUSION

CHAPTER I

The Journal takes us up to the evening of September 10th, 1922. It was to the fourth and last tragedy of that summer, which filled the next day's papers, that little Pettingill referred, in the conversation recorded in the introduction of this Journal.

It was with this tragedy that, as Pettingill said aggrievedly, the story "quit" on them. And quit it did. We felt then that the best thing to do, under the circumstances, was to let it rest. Once more, *de mortuis nil nisi bonum.*

There was nothing to be gained by giving the story to the public, and much to be lost. At that time, it is to be remembered, a wave of spiritualism, or rather spiritism, was spreading over the country; it was still filled, too, with postwar psychopaths. The very nature of the experiment which had been tried was of the sort to seize on the neurotic imagination, and set it a-flame. It was not considered advisable to allow it publicity.

Now, of course, things are different. The search goes on, and perhaps some day, not by this method but by some legitimate and scientific one, survival may be proved. I do not know; I do not greatly care. After all, I am a Christian, and my faith is built on a life after death. But I accept that; I do not require proof of it. . . .

Picture us, then, that evening of September 10th, when the Journal ends, waiting for we knew not what; Jane picking up her tapestry and putting it down again; Edith powdering her nose with hands that shook in spite of her best efforts; Halliday at the railroad station with the car to meet Cameron; and off in the woodland, where the red lamp of the lighthouse flashed its danger signal every ten seconds from the end of Robinson's Point, Greenough and a half dozen officers.

Picture us, too, when we had all gathered; Cameron, with his hand still bandaged, presented to the *dramatis personae* of the play and eyeing each one in turn shrewdly; Mrs. Livingstone garrulous and uneasy; and Livingstone a sort of waxy white and with a nervous trembling I had never observed before. Of us all, only Halliday seemed natural. And

Hayward, natural because he was never at ease.

What Cameron made of it I do not know. Very probably he saw in us only a group of sensation-seekers, excited by some small contact with a world beyond our knowledge, and if he felt surprise at all, it was that I had joined the ranks.

He himself did not appear to take the matter seriously. He made it plain that he had come in this manner at my request; that his own methods would be entirely different. When Edith, I think it was, asked him if he made any preparation for such affairs, he laughed and shook his head.

"Except that I sometimes take a cup of coffee to keep me awake!" he said.

On the way up the drive I walked with Livingstone. Why, I hardly know, except that he seemed to drift toward me. He never spoke but once, and it seemed to me that he was surveying the shrubbery and trees, like a man who suspected a trap. Once — he was on my left — I was aware that he had put his hand to his hip pocket, and I was so startled that I stumbled and almost fell. I knew, as confidently as I have ever known anything, that he had a revolver there.

"Careful, man," he said.

Those were his only words during our slow

progress toward the main house, and so tense were his nerves that they sounded like a curse.

Cameron and Edith were leading, and I could hear her talking, carrying on valiantly, although as it turned out she knew better than any of us, except Halliday, the terrible possibilities ahead. Hayward walked alone and behind us, his rubber soled shoes making no sound on the drive. It made me uneasy, somehow; that silent progress of his; it was stealthy and disconcerting. And I think Livingstone felt it so too, for he stopped once and turned around.

Yet, at the time, as between the two men, my suspicion that evening certainly pointed to Livingstone. Not to go into the cruelty of my ignorance, a cruelty which I now understand but then bitterly resented, I had had both men under close observation during the time we waited for Cameron. And it had seemed to me that Livingstone was the more uneasy of the two. Another thing which I regarded as highly significant was his asking for water just before we left the Lodge, and holding the glass with a trembling hand.

And, as it happens, it was that very glass of water which crystallized my suspicions. The glass and the hand which held it. For the hand was a small and wide one, with a short thumb and a bent little finger!

From that time on, my mind was focused on Livingstone. It milled about, seeking some explanation. I could see Livingstone in the case plainly enough; I could see him, pursuing with old Bethel the "sinister design" to which Gordon had referred, but to which I had no key. I could see him, with his knowledge of the country, using that knowledge in furtherance of that idea which my Uncle Horace had termed a menace to society in general. With the swiftness with which thought creates visions, I could even see him hailing poor Maggie Morrison in the storm, and her stopping her truck when she recognized him.

But I could not see him in connection with Eugenia Riggs and her bowl of putty. Strange that I did not; that it required Jane's smelling salts for me to find that connection. A small green glass bottle, in Edith's room, used as a temporary paper weight on her desk.

As I say, my suspicions were of Livingstone, during that strange walk up the drive. But I had by no means eliminated Hayward.

He was there, behind me, walking with a curious stealth, and with an uneasiness that somehow, without words, communicated itself to me.

All emotions are waves, I daresay. I caught

the contagion of the fear from him; desperate, deadly fear.

And once in the house, my suspicions of him increased rather than diminished. For one thing, he offered to take Cameron through the house, and on Halliday's ignoring that, and going off with Cameron himself, was distinctly surly. He remained in the hall at the foot of the stairs, apparently listening to their progress and gnawing at his fingers.

Watching him from the den, I saw him make a move to go up the stairs, but he caught my eye and abandoned the idea.

It was then that Jane felt faint, and I went back to the Lodge for her smelling salts. . . .

The letter, undoubtedly the letter which Halliday had shown to the police, was lying open on Edith's desk, under the green bottle, and as I lifted the salts it blew to the floor. I glanced at it as I picked it up.

CHAPTER II

In recording the events leading up to the amazing *denouement* that night — the details of the seance — I am under certain difficulties.

Thus, I kept no notes. For the first time I found myself a part of the circle, sitting between Livingstone and Jane, and with Cameron near the lamp, prepared to make the notes of what should occur.

"Of course," he said, as we took our places, "we are not observing the usual precautions of what I would call a test seance. All we are attempting to do is to reproduce, as nearly as possible, the conditions existing at the other two sittings. And ———" he glanced at me and smiled "———if Mr. Porter's admission to the circle proves to be disturbing, we can eliminate him."

He asked us to remain quiet, no matter what happened, and to be certain that no hand was freed without an immediate statement to that effect.

"Not that I expect fraud, of course," he added. "But it is customary, under the circumstances."

I am quite certain that nobody, except myself, saw Halliday touch the bell as the light was reduced to the faint glow of the red lamp.

It was not surprising, I daresay, that beyond certain movements of the table and fine raps on its surface, we got nothing at first! in fact, that we got anything at all was probably due solely to Jane's ignorance of the underlying situation. Livingstone, next to me, was so nervous that his hands twitched on the table; across, Halliday was beside Hayward, and as my eyes grew accustomed to the semi-darkness, I could see him, forbidden recourse to his fingers, jerking his head savagely.

And, for the life of me, I could not see where all this was leading us. A breaking of the circle was, by Cameron's order, immediately to be announced. Even in complete darkness, when that came — as I felt it would — what was it that Halliday expected to happen?

But the table continued to move. It began to slide along the carpet; my grasp on Livingstone's hand was relaxed, and indeed, later, as it began to rock violently, it was all I could do to retain contact with the table at all. I began to see possibilities in this, but when it had quieted the circle remained as before.

Very soon after that came the signal for darkness, and Cameron extinguished the lamp. Soon Edith, near the cabinet, said the curtain had come out into the room, and was touching her. The next moment, as before, the bell fell from the stand inside the cabinet, and the guitar strings were lightly touched.

Without warning Cameron turned on the lamp; the curtain subsided and all sounds ceased. He was apparently satisfied, and after a few moments of experiment with the lamp on, resulting only in a creaking and knocking on the table, again extinguished it. On a repetition of the blowing out of the curtain, however, he left his chair for the first time, and with a pocket flash examined the cabinet thoroughly, even the wall coming in for close inspection.

When he had finished with that, however, I sensed a change in him. I believe now that he suspected fraud, but I am not certain. He said rather sharply that he was there in good faith and not to provide an evening's amusement, and that he hoped any suspicious movement would be reported.

"This is not a game," he said shortly.

Jane was very quiet, and now I heard again the heavy breathing which I knew preceded the trance condition, or that auto-hypnotism which we know as trance.

"Who is that?" Cameron asked in a low tone.

"Mrs. Porter," Halliday said. "Quiet, everybody!"

The room was completely dark, and save for Jane's heavy breathing, entirely quiet. Strangely enough, for the moment I forgot our purpose there; forgot Greenough and his men, scattered through the house; I had a premonition, if I may call it that, that we were on the verge of some tremendous psychic experience. I cannot explain it; I do not know now what unseen forces were gathered there together. I even admit that probably I too, like Jane, had hypnotized myself.

And then two things were happening, and at the same time.

There was something moving in the library, a soft foot-fall with, it seemed to me, an irregularity. For all the world like the dragging of a partially useless foot, and – Livingstone was quietly releasing his grip on my hand.

I made a clutch at him, and he whispered savagely:

"Let go, you fool."

The next moment he had drawn his revolver, and was stealthily getting to his feet.

The dragging foot moved out into the hall. Livingstone, revolver in hand, was standing beside me, and there was a quiet movement across the table. Cameron was apparently listening also; he made no comment, however, and in the darkness and the silence the footsteps went into the hall, and there ceased.

I had no idea of the passage of time; ten seconds or an hour Livingstone may have stood beside me. Ten seconds or an hour, and then Greenough's voice at the top of the staircase:

"All right. Careful below."

Livingstone moved then. He made a wild dash for the red lamp and turned it on. Hayward was not to be seen, and Halliday,

408

revolver in hand, was starting for the cabinet.

"More light," he called. "Light! Quick!"

I had a confused impression of Halliday, jerking the curtains of the cabinet aside; of somebody else there with him, both on guard, as it were, at the wall; of some sort of rapid movement upstairs; of the door from the den into the hall being open where it had been closed before, and of a crash somewhere not far away, as of a falling body, followed by a sort of dreadful pause.

And all this is in the time it took me to get around the chairs and to the wall switch near the door. And it was then, in the shocked silence which followed the sound of that fall, in the instant between my finding the switch and turning it on, that I will swear that I saw once more by the glow of the red lamp the figure at the foot of the stairs, looking up.

Saw it and recognized it. Watched it turn toward me with fixed and staring eyes, felt the cold wind which suddenly eddied about me, and frantically turning on the light, saw it fade like smoke into the empty air. . . .

Behind the curtains of the cabinet somebody was working at the wall. Edith, very pale, was supporting Jane, who still remained in her strange auto-hypnotic condition. Livingstone's arm was about his wife.

And this was the picture when Greenough came running triumphantly down the stairs, the reward apparently in his pocket, and saw us there. He paid no attention to the rest of us, but stared at Livingstone with eyes which could not believe what they saw.

"Good God!" he said. "Then who is in there?"

He pointed to the wall behind the cabinet.

CHAPTER III

The steps by which Halliday solved the murder at the main house, and with it the mystery which had preceded it, constitute an interesting story in themselves. So certain was he that, by the time we were ready for the third seance, his material was already in the hands of the District Attorney. And it was not the material he had given to Greenough.

For the solution of a portion of the mystery, then, one must go back to the main house, and consider the older part of it. It is well known that many houses of that period were provided with hidden passages, by which the owners hoped to escape the Excise. Such an attempt, many years ago, had cost George Pierce his life.

But the passage leading from the old kitchen,

now the den, to a closet in the room above it, had been blocked up for many years. The builder was dead; by all the laws of chance time might have gone on and the passage remained undiscovered.

In 1899, however, Eugenia Riggs bought the property, and in making repairs the old passage was discovered. Although she denies using it for fraudulent purposes, neither Halliday nor I doubt that she did so. She points to the plastered wall as her defense, but Halliday assures me that a portion of the base-board, hinged to swing out, but locked from within, would have allowed easy access to the cabinet.

But Halliday had at the beginning no knowledge of this passage, with its ladder to the upper floor. He reached it by pure deduction.

"It had to be there," he says modestly. "And it was." . . .

Up to the time young Gordon was attacked at the kitchen door, however, Halliday was frankly at sea. That is, he had certain suspicions, but that was all. He had discovered, for instance, that the cipher found in my garage was written on the same sort of bond paper as that used by Gordon, by the simple expedient of having Annie Cochran get him a sheet of it, on some excuse or other.

But his actual case began, I believe, with that

attack on Gordon. At least he began at that time definitely to associate the criminal with the house.

"There was something fishy about it," is the way he puts it.

And with Bethel's story to me, forced by his fear that the boy knew it was he who had attacked him, the belief that it was "fishy" gained ground.

"Gordon was knocked out," he says. "And that ought to have been enough. But it was not. He was tied, too, tied while he was still unconscious. Somebody wasn't taking a chance that he'd get back into the house very soon."

It was that "play for time," as he terms it, that made him suspicious.

All this time, of course, he was ignorant of any underlying motive; he makes it clear that he simply began, first to associate the crimes with the house, and then with Bethel. He kept going back to his copy of the unfinished letter, but:

"It didn't help much," he says quietly. "Only, there was murder indicated in it. And we were having murder."

He had three clues, two of them certain, one doubtful. The certain ones were the linen from the oar-lock of the boat, torn from a sheet belonging to the main house, and the small portion of the cipher. The one he was not certain about was the lens from an eyeglass, outside the culvert.

He began to watch the house; he "didn't get" Gordon in the situation at all; there was no situation there, really; nothing, that is, that he could lay his hand on. But on the night I called him and he started toward Robinson's Point, as he came back toward the house he saw the figure of a man, certainly not Gordon, enter the house by the gun room window. When he got there the window was closed and locked.

He was puzzled. He looked around for me, but I was not in sight. Still searching for me, he made a round of the house, and so was on the terrace when I fired the shot. From that time on he saw Bethel somehow connected with the mystery, but only as the brains.

"There was some devil's work afoot," he said. "But always I came up against that paralysis of his. He had to have outside help."

On the night in question, then, he was certain that this accomplice was still in the house through all that followed; through Hayward's arrival and Starr's. He was so certain by that time of Gordon's innocence that he very nearly took him into his confidence the next day. But he was afraid of the boy; he was not dependable; Halliday had an idea that "he was playing his own game."

But if this man was in the house that night, where was he?

He grew suspicious of the den, after that, and he found out through Starr the name of the builder who had put in the panelling in the den, for Uncle Horace. It was a long story, but in the end he learned something.

Tearing the old base-board prior to putting up the panels, the building had happened on the old passage to the room overhead, and he had called Horace Porter's attention to it. It seems to have appealed to the poor old chap; it belonged, somehow, to the room, with the antique stuff he was putting into it. He built in a sliding panel; it was not a particularly skillful piece of work, but it answered. And he kept his secret, at least from me.

I doubt if he ever used it, until Prohibition came in. Then, no drinker himself, he put there a small and choice supply of liquors, some of which we found later on. And one bottle of which placed Halliday in peril of his life, a day or so after the night I had fired the shot into the hall.

He had borrowed Annie Cochran's key to the kitchen door, and after midnight entered the house and went to the den. Although he is reticent about this portion of it, I gather that the house was not all it should be that night.

"You know the sort of thing," he says.

But, pressed as to that, he admits that he was hearing small and inexplicable sounds from the library. Chairs seemed to move, and once he was certain that the curtain in the doorway behind him blew out into the room. When he looked back over his shoulder, however, it was hanging as before.

He had no trouble in finding the panel, and as carefully as he could he stepped inside. But he had touched one of the bottles and it fell over.

"It didn't make much noise," he says, "but it was enough. He was awake, and paralysis or no paralysis, I hadn't time to move before he was in the closet overhead, and opening the trap in the floor."

He had not had time to move, and even if he had, there were the infernal bottles all around him. So he stood without breathing, waiting for he knew not what.

"Things looked pretty poor," he says. "I didn't know when he'd strike a match and see me. And it was good-night if he did!"

But Bethel had no match, evidently. He stood listening intently, and in the darkness below Halliday held his breath and waited. Then Bethel moved. He left the trap door above open and went for a light, and Halliday crawled out and closed the panel quietly.

From that time on, however, he knew Bethel was no more helpless than he was. He abandoned the idea of an accomplice, and concentrated on the man himself. . . .

Annie Cochran was working with him; that is, she did what he asked her, although she seems not to have known at any time the direction in which he was working. Her own mind was already made up; she believed Gordon to be guilty. She made no protest, however, when he asked her to break Mr. Bethel's spectacles one early morning, and give him the fragments. But she did it, pretending afterwards that she had thrown the pieces into the stove.

Bethel was watchful and suspicious by that time, and she had a bad time of it, but what is important here is that Halliday took the fragments into the city, and established beyond a doubt that they and the piece of a lens found near the culvert were made from the same prescription.

And he had no more than made his discovery, when Gordon, attempting at last the blackmail which he had been threatening, was put out of the way as quickly and ruthlessly as had been poor Peter Carroway.

"Twenty-four hours," Halliday says bitterly, "and we would have saved him."

416

But twenty-four hours later Bethel had made good his escape, and everything was apparently over.

But from that time Bethel as Bethel, ceased to exist for Halliday. . . .

He was not working alone, however. Very early, he had realized that he needed assistance, real assistance. Annie Cochran's help was always of the below-stairs order. And he found the help he wanted after the night Gordon was attacked, in Hayward. As a matter of fact, it was Hayward who went to him.

"He was worried about you, Skipper," Halliday says, with a grin. "He considered it quite possible that the attempt to wrangle English literature into too many brain corrals might have driven you slightly mad."

And breaks off to wonder, "by Jove," if that's where the English get their collegiate term of wrangler!

On the night, then, when Gordon was hurt, the doctor was impulsively on his way to Halliday and the boat-house.

"He came within an inch of having you locked up that night," says Halliday.

Later on, he did go to Halliday, and Halliday then and there enlisted him in his service. He was not shrewd but he was willing and earnest, and from that time on he was useful. He had started, presumably, on his vacation but actually on a very different errand, when the murder at the main house occurred, and Halliday recalled him by wire.

But when he returned, it was, at Halliday's request, to hide in the Livingstone house. It was from there that he came, at night, to assist Halliday in guarding the main house. And to provide, by the way, that sworn statement of the Livingstones' butler, that after the murder they had concealed some one in the house, which threw Greenough so completely off the track.

One perceives, of course, that the Livingstones had been brought into the case. Dragged in, is the way Halliday puts it. But after the first conference between the doctor and himself they were in it, willy nilly.

"Who," Halliday asked Hayward, referring to his copy of my Uncle Horace's letter, "were likely to have access to Horace Porter at night?"

"No one, so far as I know. The Livingstones, possibly."

"Then the man who came in while he was writing this letter might have been Livingstone?"

"He was ill that night. I was with him."

"Then Livingstone's out," said Halliday, and turned in a new direction.

"Some theory, some wickedness, was put up to him. And it horrified and alarmed him. A man doesn't present such a theory without leading up to it. Let's try this: what subject was most interesting Horace Porter during the last years, or months, of his life?"

"Spiritism, I imagine. I know he was working on it."

"Alone? A man doesn't work that sort of thing alone, as a rule."

"I'll ask Mrs. Livingstone, if you like. She may know."

And ask the Livingstones he did, with the result that Halliday got his first real clue, and elaborated the daring theory which culminated in that fatal fall from the ladder, in the secret passage on the tragic night of the 10th of September. . . .

All this time, of course, it remained only a theory. Hayward scouted it at first, but came to it later on; the Livingstones offered a more difficult problem.

"They didn't want to be involved," Halliday says. "But after Edith's letter came I more or less had them. And of course after he'd tried to get into the house, and left the print of his hand on the window board, they had to come in. They'd denied any knowledge of the passage before that. But he knew it as well as I did, or better, and that there was a chance old Bethel knew it too, and had used it."

This letter of Edith's, to which I have already referred, runs as follows:

"Dear Madam:

"I have read your article with great interest, and would like to suggest that a good medium might be very useful under the circumstances.

"You have one of the best in the country in your vicinity. She has retired, and is now living under another name somewhere in the vicinity of Oakville. I understand her husband has made considerable money, but she may be willing to help in spite of that.

"When I knew her she was known as Eugenia Riggs, but this was her maiden name, which she had retained. Her husband's name is Livingstone; I do not know his initials.

"She has abandoned the profession in which she made so great a success, but I understand is still keenly interested."

The letter is not signed. . . .

Halliday did not require that knowledge; he had suspected it before. But it gave him a lever.

One attempt had already been made by Bethel to get back into the house. Time was getting short; before long we would have to go back to the city, and although we knew by that time who and what Bethel was, he could prove nothing. To go was to abandon the case.

He could not secure the arrest of a man because his lens prescription was the same as the murderer's. Or on the strength of an unsigned book manuscript left behind the wall of the den. He could not prove that Maggie Morrison had died in the process of the experiment Gordon had puzzled over, because the mud on the truck wheels corresponded with the red iron-clay of the lane into the main house. He could not prove his own interpretation of the abbreviations S. and G.T. so liberally scattered through the diary. And he could not prove that it was Bethel who, looking for the broken lens in or near the culvert, had found my fountain pen there. A fact which Gordon had noted in the Journal as follows: "I have them now, sure. W.P. was here last night and left his fountain pen."

But he could, through the Livingstones, take a chance on proving all these things. And, against Livingstone's protests and fears, prove it he did.

"As a matter of fact," he says, "they were in a

bad position themselves, and they knew it. They had to come over again!" . . .

Things were, indeed, rather parlous for the Livingstones. The butler's story had turned the suspicions of the police toward them. And on the night of my threatened arrest Halliday deliberately used them to avert that catastrophe.

"As a matter of fact," he says cheerfully, "I gave the police a very pretty case against them. It was all there, according to Greenough. Even to the hand-print!"

But he held them off. He had done what he wanted, turned the police along the true one. And in this he says, and I believe, that his purpose was not mercenary.

"The situation was peculiar," he says. "The slightest slip, the faintest suspicion, and he was off."

And he goes back again to the subtlety and wariness of the criminal himself; so watchful, so wary, that throughout it had even been necessary to keep me in ignorance.

"You had to carry on, Skipper," he says. "In a way, the whole thing hung on you. Even then, you nearly wrecked us once."

Which he, he tells me the night of the second seance, when the criminal actually fell into the trap and entered the house. Livingstone was on guard upstairs that night, and everything would have ended then probably.

"But you spilled the beans!" he accuses me.

From the first the seances were devised for a purpose, and I gather that some of the phenomena were deliberately faked, in pursuit of that purpose. On the other hand, Mrs. Livingstone has always been firm in her statement that "things happened" which she cannot explain. The sounds in the library, the lights and the arrival of the book on the table are among them.

But, trickery or genuine psychic manifestations, in the end they served their purpose. I called the third seance, and the mystery was solved. . . .

It is not surprising that my memory of those last few moments is a clouded one; I was, of all those present except the police, the only one in complete ignorance of the meaning of what was going on about me. Edith knew, and was bravely taking her risk with the others; even my dear Jane knew a little; no wonder she required her smelling salts.

Actually, out of the confusion, only two pictures remain in my mind:

One was of Greenough staring at Livingstone, and then jerking aside the curtains of the cabinet, where Halliday and Hayward had

opened the panel and after turning on the red
globe hanging there, were stooping over a body
at the bottom of the ladder.

The other is of that figure at the foot of the
stairs.

I know now that it could not have been there;
that it was lying, dead of a broken neck, at the
foot of the ladder. I have heard all the theories,
but I cannot reconcile them with the fact. How
could I have imagined it? I did not know then
who was inside the wall.

I am not a spiritist, but once in every man's
life comes to him the one experience which he
can explain by no law of nature as he under-
stands them.

To every man his ghost, and to me, mine.

In the dim light of the red lamp, dead though
he was behind the panel, I will swear that I saw
Cameron, *alias* Simon Bethel, standing at the
foot of the stairs and looking up.

Chapter IV

Who are we to judge him? If a man sincerely
believes that there is no death, the taking of life
to prove it must seem a trivial thing.

He may feel, and from his book manuscript
hastily hidden behind the wall of the den we

gather he did feel, that the security of the individual counted as nothing against the proof of survival to the human race.

But that he was entirely sane, in those last months, none of us can believe. Cruelty is a symptom of the borderland between sanity and madness; so too is the weakening of what we call the Herd instinct. It is well known at the University that for the year previous to his death he had been distinctly anti-social.

Certainly, too, he fulfilled the axiom that insanity is the exaggeration of one particular mental activity. And that he combined this single exaggeration with a high grade of intelligence only proves the close relation between madness and genius: Kant, unable to work unless gazing at a ruined tower; Hawthorne, cutting up his bits of paper; Wagner's periodical violences.

The very audacity of his disguise, the consistency with which he lived the part he was playing, points to what I believe is called dissociation; toward the last there seems to have been a genuine duality of personality: during the day old Simon Bethel, dragging his helpless foot and without effort holding his withered hand to its spastic contraction; at night, the active Cameron, making his exits on his nocturnal adventures by the gun room window; wandering afoot incredible distances; watching the door of Gordon's room and locking him in; learning from me of Halliday's interest in the case, and trying to burn him out; very early realizing the embarrassment of my own presence at the Lodge, and warning me away by that letter from Salem, Ohio.

It seems clear that he had not expected me at the Lodge; Larkin apparently told Gordon, but Gordon neglected to inform him. Just what he felt, what terror and anger, when I greeted him at the house on his arrival will never be known. I remember now how he watched me, peering up at me through his disguising spectacles, with the beef cube in his hand, and waiting. Waiting.

But the disguise held. My own very slight acquaintance with him, my near-sightedness, my total lack of suspicion, all were in his favor. And of the perfection of the disguise itself, it is enough to say that Gordon apparently never suspected it. He did suspect the paralysis.

"He moved his arm to-day," he wrote once, in the diary. "He knows I saw it, and he has watched me ever since."

"It takes very little to change an appearance beyond casual recognition," Halliday tells me. "The idea is to take a few important points and substitute their opposites. Take a man with

426

partial paralysis; one side of his face drops, you see. Well, he can't imitate that, but he can put a fig in the other cheek and raise it. Put hair on a bald-headed man, and watch the change. And there are other things; eyebrows now————"

Only once did I come anywhere near the truth, and then it slipped past me, and I did not catch it. That was on the night he sent for me, after he had struck Gordon down. He was frightened that night, we know now. Gordon was suspicious; might even have gone to the police.

And that night he tested his disguise and me.

I have recorded the revolt I felt after his attack on the Christian faith. And that I had the feeling of having heard almost the same thing, eons ago. I *had* heard the same thing, from Cameron, on the first occasion of my meeting him. . . .

Much of the explanation of that tragic summer becomes mere surmise, naturally. There is no surmise, however, necessary as regards Cameron's coming to the third seance, at my invitation. So far as he knew, we still believed that Simon Bethel was dead. That our circle, so innocent in appearance, so naive, was a cleverly devised trap seems not to have occurred to him. My frankness, the product of my ignorance, would probably have reassured a man less

427

driven by necessity than he was.

But even had he suspected something, I believe he would have come. His other attempts, to enter the house and secure the manuscript, had failed. And any day some bit of mischance, a mouse behind a panel, a casual repair, and this book of his, with its characteristic phrasing, its references to his earlier works, would be in the hands of the police.

With what secret eagerness he accepted my invitation we can only guess. Halliday, carefully plotting, had already discounted his acceptance in advance.

"I knew he would come, of course," he says. "He wanted to get in. We offered him not only that, but darkness to cover any move he wanted to make. It had to work out."

And here he explains the necessity of having the criminal caught *flagrante delictu*. It had to be shown, he says, not only that Cameron had written the manuscript, but that it was he who had hidden it where it lay.

"The case against him stood or fell by that," he says. . . .

But aside from this, much of the explanation of that tragic summer becomes pure guesswork. We have, however, elaborated the following as fulfilling our requirements as to the situation:

We know for instance that on old Horace

Porter's developing interest in spiritism, Mrs. Livingstone referred him to Cameron. But we do not know why that interest developed.

Is it too much, I wonder, to say that the house itself led him to it? In this I know I am on dangerous ground, and it becomes still more dangerous if one grants that Mrs. Livingstone's gift of a red lamp led him to experimenting with it.

We do know, however, that after he had had this lamp for three months or so, he got in touch with Cameron, and it seems probable that such experiments as were made there at night with this lamp roused Cameron to fever heat.

Mrs. Livingstone believes there was a pact between them, the usual one of the first to "pass over" to come back if possible. We do not know that, but it seems plausible. Neither Halliday nor I believe, however, as she does, that Cameron killed the older man, in a fit of rage over the rejection of his proposal to carry their investigations to the criminal point.

What seems more probable is that Cameron had very early recognized the advantages of the house for the psychic and scientific experiments he had in mind, and that he finally submitted the idea to old Horace. With what growing horror and indignation they were received we know from his letter.

They turned a possible ally into an angry and dangerous enemy; the rejection of the proposition, with the threat which accompanied it, left Cameron stripped before the world as an enemy to society. He went home and brooded over it.

"But he couldn't let it rest at that," Halliday says. "He went back. And the old man was at his desk. There was danger in Cameron that night, and the poor old chap was frightened. We'll say he crumpled his letter up in his hand, and Cameron didn't see it. Maybe there was an argument, and Cameron knocked him down. But he got up again, and he managed to drop the letter into an open drawer; after that, his heart failed, and he fell for good."

We acquit him of that. Of the others—? . . .

We are, with regard to the underlying motive, the so-called experiments, again obliged to resort to surmise. We know, for instance, of Cameron's early experiments in weighing the body before and immediately after death. He has himself recorded them. But in the manuscript of his book he distinctly states his belief that the vital principle, whatever that may be, is weakened by long illness, and his belief that those who pass over suddenly out of full health, are more able to manifest themselves.

He quotes numerous instances of murdered men, whom tradition believes to have returned for motives of vengeance. But he himself believes that this ability to return is due to the strength of the unweakened vital principle. The *whole* spirit, he calls it. And although his manuscript in itself does not deal with any discoveries he may have made during the summer, there are accompanying it certain pages of figures which seem to prove that he made more than one experiment along those lines during his occupancy of the house.

What waifs and strays he picked up on those night journeys of his we do not know; poor wanderers, probably, with no place in the world from which they could be missed.

At the same time, Halliday feels that the experiments were not necessarily to be with life and death; he suggests that they were to lie, rather, in deep narcosis, pushed to the danger point, and that it was under this narcosis that Maggie Morrison, for one, succumbed.

Among Cameron's papers, later on, we found a curious document entitled, "The reality of the Soul through a study of the effects of Chloroform and Curari on the Animal Economy," with this note in Cameron's hand:

"The soul and the body are separated by the agency of anaesthesia. The soul is not a breath, but an entity."

Of the nature of the further tests made we have no idea. Halliday believes that, shown the space behind the wall by Horace Porter, he later utilized it to conceal such apparatus as he used in his experiments.

"It seemed to be full of stuff," he says, "the night I found it."

But later on, as the chase narrowed, he got rid of it bit by bit at night, probably throwing it into the bay. This is borne out by the fact that, late that following autumn, going back to Twin Hollows to look over the property with a real estate dealer, I found washed up on the beach the battered fragments of a camera.

Only a portion of the lens remained in the frame, but this lens had been of quartz. As nearly as I can discover, the theory of quartz used in such a manner is to photograph the ultra-violet. In other words, I daresay, to make visible that strange world which may lie beyond the spectrum and our normal vision.

Did he obtain anything? We shall never know.

But sometimes I wonder. Suppose a man to have done what he had done to prove the immortality of the soul; to have taken lives and have risked his own, to give to the world the survival after death it so pathetically craves.

And he fails; there is nothing. His own conviction has not weakened, but his proofs are not there.

Then, in the twinkling of an eye, he himself breaks through the veil. With that idea dominant, he passes over to the other side, perhaps to the long sleep, perhaps not. But in that instant between waking and sleeping, to prove his point! To make good his contention! To justify his course!

I wonder.

And I wonder, too, if at that moment of realization the supreme irony of the situation could have occurred to him? That the wounded hand, the one injury poor Gordon had managed to inflict on him, was the factor which had shot him, head-foremost, into eternity? . . .

Was Cameron our sheep-killer? We believe so, with certain reservations. We know he was at Bass Cove, under an assumed name, at the time, probably looking over the ground.

At the same time, it seems unlikely that he killed the first lot of Nylie's sheep; that we believe was an act of revenge on the part of a man Nylie had recently discharged.

But that the idea seized on his imagination seems probable. He was planning that mad campaign of his, and it fell in well with what was to come. It prepared the neighborhood, in a sense, but it set them looking for a maniac with a religious mania. And it was an effective alibi for him, occurring before his arrival at the house.

Jane has always believed that he added the symbol in chalk deliberately to incriminate me. I do not. He added it, after Helena Lear had told him of it, as he added the stone altar, a madman's conception of a madman's act.

Carroway's murder was incidental to that preparation of his, but in view of all we know, we can reconstruct it fairly well.

Thus we have the boy, tiring of carrying his rifle, putting it away in the darkness and possibly dozing. We have the appearance of the killer, and Carroway unable to locate his rifle quickly, following him to the waterfront and reaching it too late.

Underneath our float the killer should have found his knife, but as we know, Halliday had taken it away. They were two unarmed men, then, who met that night on the quiet surface of the bay. And one of them, although nobody knew it, was not sane.

Unarmed only in one sense, however, for Cameron had an oar. And used it.

When it was over, he apparently rowed back quietly to the creek beyond Robinson's Point, left his boat there, and walked to Bass Cove.

The proprietor of the small hotel there seems never to have known that he was out at night.

"He was a very quiet gentleman," he says, "and always went to bed early." ...

One thing which had puzzled us, in the Morrison case, was that the girl had stopped her truck, at a time when the nerves of the countryside were on edge. It seems probable, therefore, that on some nights, at least, it was not the square and muscular Cameron who went forth, but an old and crippled man.

Shown to her by the lightning flashes that night, age and infirmity by the roadside and a storm going, what wonder that she stopped? The only marvel is that, this bait having proven successful, it does not appear to have been used again ...

And now, postpone it as I may, I have come to that portion of our summer to which I have early referred as the X in our equation. We have solved our problem. We may say quite properly, *Quod erat demonstrandum*. But there remains still the unsolved factor.

Much that impressed me strongly at the time has lost its impression now. It is a curious fact that a man may see a ghost — and many believe that they have done so — without any lasting belief in so-called survival after death. And so it is with me.

On editing my Journal, however, I find myself confronting the same questions which confronted me during that terrible summer.

Have I a body, or is my body all there is of me? In other words, am I an intelligence served by certain physical organs? Or am I certain physical organs, actuated by an intelligence as temporary as they?

Frankly, I do not know.

But any careful analysis of the extra-normal phenomena of the summer seems to show, every so often, some other-world intelligence, struggling to get through to us. As though—

We have never had, as I have said, any explanation of the coming of the book during the second seance, nor of the sounds from the library. While much of the physical phenomena of the first two seances was deliberately engineered by Mrs. Livingstone, in pursuance of Halliday's plan to get Cameron into the house, these two things remain without explanation.

The same thing is true of my finding of the letter, of the light-house apparition, of the sitting at Evanston, and of Jane's clairvoyant visions. None of which, by the way, she has had since. And yet all of which had their part, large or small, in our solving and understanding of the crimes.

Peter Geiss, and the figure in the fore-rigging of the sloop, my own vision of Cameron at the foot of the stairs, when he lay dead behind the panel, what am I to say of these?

Am I to accept them as I do Jane's "vision without eyes" as no more extraordinary than the feats of somnambulists, who go through their curious nightly progress with closed eyelids?

Am I to accept them, refute them, or evade them?...

There are, however, certain incidents which, puzzling as they were at the time, lend themselves to very simple explanation. Among these are the cough I heard more than once, and Hadly's story of the materialization in the Oakville cemetery.

Throughout Gordon's diary, here and there, were the letters S. and G.T. There was also, in one place, a sentence which translated, became "The G. P. stuff went great last night."

Halliday believes that Gordon was what we know as a medium, and that it was in that capacity primarily that Cameron took him to the country. The S. he therefore translates as "sitting," and the G.T. as "genuine trance." After the G.T. there almost invariably follows the rather pathetic entry: "Feel rotten to-day," or "all in."

Hadly's ghost, then, in all probability was the secretary, securing data for the "sittings" which he so carefully differentiates from the nights when he went into genuine trance. Being honest with himself, poor boy, and honest nowhere else. And the same was no doubt true as to the dry cough which he practised on me, the night I was in the garage, almost to my undoing.

It was during those "sittings" too, almost certainly, that under pretended control from beyond he began to ferret out, with the cunning of his kind, the story underneath; to bring back Horace Porter, and watch the reaction; to mention the boat he had discovered, and see the man across from him, in the dim red light, twitch and tremble.

To play him, to fool him, and at the last to threaten and blackmail him. And, in the end, to die.

But there remain these things I cannot explain. One of the most curious is the herbal odor; that this was not a purely subjective impression is shown by the fact that both Hayward and Edith noticed it during the second seance. The scent of flowers is, I believe, not unusual during certain psychic experiments; Warren speaks of the impression of tube roses being waved before him in the dark by some ghostly hand.

Of this, as of the other inexplicable phenomena, I can only say that at the time I did not doubt them; living them again, as I prepare this manuscript, I accept them once more. But I do not explain them.

"You wish," said Cicero, "to have the explanation of these things? Very well...I might tell you that the magnet is a body which attracts iron and attaches itself to it; but because I could not give you the explanation of it, would you deny it?" ...

In closing this record, I cannot do better than copy the following extract from my Journal, made the following June.

June 1st, 1923.

Our little Edith was married to-day. Heigh-ho. And again, heigh-ho.

I have done the proper thing; led her up the aisle to Halliday (and would as lief have knocked him down as not) stepped back out of the picture and her life, and feeling for my handkerchief, like the besotted old fool I am, pulled out a washcloth instead.

Fortunate, perhaps, as I was on the verge of loud and broken sobs!

How we begrudge the happiness of others when it is at our expense! How I hated Halliday when, once in the house, he put his arms around her and held her close. How I resented that calm air of possession with which he took his place in the line beside her, and shook hands smilingly with the hysterical crowd that kissed and blessed them, on the way to the dining room and food.

And yet — how happy they are, and how safe she is.

"My *wife*," he said. "Forever and ever. Amen."

Old glass and new glass; china, silver and linen; the Lears' candle-sticks; every corner of the house filled with guests and gifts — and Jock. And for the two of them nothing and nobody; just a space filled with shadows which smiled and passed; themselves the only reality.

And perhaps they are. Love at least is real; the one reality perhaps. "Love, thou art absolute; sole Lord of life and death."

So they have gone, and to-night Jane and I are alone. Safe and quiet — and alone, alas, behind the drain pipe.

Heigh-ho!

THE END